Rosemary Rowe is the maiden name of author Rosemary Aitken, who was born in Cornwall during the Second World War. She is a highly qualified academic, and has written more than a dozen bestselling textbooks on English Language and communication. She has written fiction for many years under her married name.

She is the mother of two adult children and has two grandchildren living in New Zealand, where she herself lived for twenty years. She now lives in Gloucestershire with her cat, and owns a small holiday cottage by the sea in Cornwall.

Rosemary Rowe's first crime novel, THE GERMANICUS MOSAIC, which introduced Libertus, is also available from Headline.

'The story is agreeably written, gets on briskly with its plot, and ends with a highly satisfactory double-take solution'   Gerald Kaufman, *Scotsman*

'Rowe has the clever idea of making her detective-figure a mosaicist, and, therefore an expert in puzzles and patterns. Into the bargain he is a freed Celtic slave, and thus an outsider to the brutalities of the conquerors, and a character with whom the reader can sympathise'

Independent

'A considerable achievement'   *The Times*

Also by Rosemary Rowe

The Germanicus Mosaic

A Pattern of
Blood

Rosemary Rowe

HEADLINE

First published in 2000
by HEADLINE BOOK PUBLISHING

First published in paperback in 2000
by HEADLINE BOOK PUBLISHING

10 9 8 7 6 5 4 3 2

ISBN 0 7472 6102 4

Printed and bound in Great Britain by
Clays Ltd, St Ives plc

HEADLINE BOOK PUBLISHING
A division of the Hodder Headline Group
338 Euston Road
London NW1 3BH
www.headline.co.uk
www.hodderheadline.com

For my son

Author's Foreword

A Pattern of Blood is set in the closing weeks of AD 186. Most of Britain was then 'Britannia', the northernmost outpost of the hugely successful Roman Empire: occupied by Roman legions, subject to Roman law and taxes, criss-crossed by Roman military roads and presided over by a provincial governor answerable directly to Rome. Celtic tribal traditions, languages and settlements remained, especially in the countryside, but after two centuries of imperial rule, most townspeople had adopted Roman habits. Latin was the language of the educated, and Roman citizenship – with its commercial, legal and social status – the ambition of all. Citizenship was not at this time auto-matic for all free men born in the Empire, but a privilege to be earned (by those not lucky enough to be born to it), generally by service to the army or the Emperor, although slaves of important citizens, such as Libertus, could be bequeathed the coveted status, along with their freedom, on the death of their masters. Local magistrates and town councillors, such as Quintus, were traditionally rewarded with citizenship and rank, especially if they offered loyal support to Rome.

Loyalty was indeed an issue. Internal tribal warfare had ceased, and the province had settled into an uneasy peace, apart from a few skirmishes on the northern and western borders. Nevertheless, there was unrest, especially and most dangerously in the army. Emperor Commodus was already unpopular and, following an earlier assassination attempt, was becoming increasingly unbalanced. Disaffection was growing, and some of the soldiery tried to persuade the provincial governor of Britain, Pertinax, to claim the imperial purple. He refused, and after being badly wounded in the ensuing mêlée, denounced the conspirators to Commodus. The political tension hinted at in the novel is a historical one, and would have been understood in every important town.

Corinium (Cirencester) was one such town. It was a *civitas*, a market town, and a centre of local government for the surrounding areas, presided over by a sort of town and district council. (In this it was different from neighbouring Glevum (Gloucester) which was a *colonia*, a very high-status settlement founded for ex-legionaries, and a sort of city state in its own right.) High office in the council, once a route to power and status, had become a ruinously expensive honour, since a large financial contribution was a prerequisite for election, and once in office, councillors were expected to make generous and repeated donations to the upkeep and beautification of the town. Despite this, senior office such as that of *decurion* was fiercely sought after because of the influence it afforded.

A decurion was by definition a wealthy man, one who might afford a private physician, for instance. Greek-trained doctors were a fashionable accessory at this period, following the example of the former Emperor, Marcus Aurelius, who attached the famous Galen to his household. Some doctors were highly skilled and the delicate operations that they sometimes performed seem remarkable to modern eyes – almost as remarkable as some of the other treatments which are also recorded.

Women, of course, could not be elected to civic office, nor could any young man under twenty-five. In fact, a man of any age was regarded as a minor for legal purposes, as long as the *paterfamilias* was alive while women were regarded as legal children, under the protection of some male 'guardian' all their lives. Despite this, they sometimes had considerable financial freedom in practice. They were able to inherit and own property, and some very wealthy and influential women existed. Marriages were often arranged, but were seldom legally binding – either party could dissolve a union simply by leaving it and declaring it over – and, unless she was proved to have been unfaithful, a wife's dowry reverted to her upon divorce.

All this, of course, related to wealthy Roman citizens. Most ordinary people lacked that distinction: some were freedmen or freeborn, scratching a precarious living from a trade or farm: thousands more were slaves, merely chattels of their masters, with no more status than any other domestic animal. Some slaves led pitiful lives, although others were highly regarded by their owners: indeed, a well-fed slave in a kindly household might have a more enviable life than many a free man struggling to eke out an existence in a squalid hut.

There were many routes into slavery. A man might be born to it, forced into it by capture or crime, driven to it by destitution, and some gamblers even staked their freedom on the fall of a dice. A few servants, such as Mutuus, were bondsmen, rather than slaves. Their labour, rather than their persons, belonged to their masters. Bondage was a state of temporary servitude, often enforced, but sometimes voluntarily entered into to clear a debt or an obligation, and did not permanently deprive a man of his legal status, as slavery did. 'Noxal surrender' into bondage – where a paterfamilias would give someone's labour in settlement of a debt – was unusual by this period, but not entirely unknown.

The Romano-British background in this book has been derived from a wide variety of (sometimes contradictory) written and pictorial sources. However, although I have done my best to create an accurate picture, this remains a work of fiction, and there is no claim to total academic authenticity. Commodus, Pertinax and Galen (and the latter's public exhibitions of dissection) are historically attested, as is the existence and (basic) geography of Corinium and Glevum. All other places and characters in the story are the product of my imagination.

Relata refero. Ne Iupiter quidem omnibus placet. I only tell you what I heard. Jove himself can't please everybody.

ROMAN BRITAIN

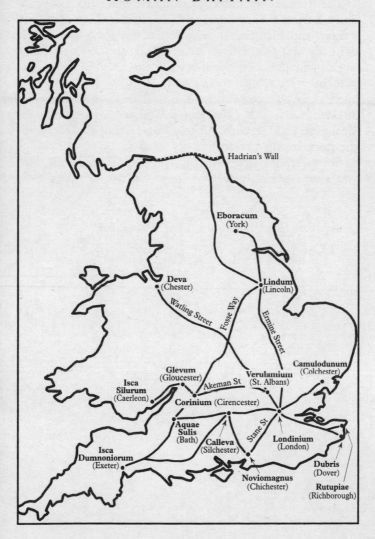

Prologue

I was in Corinium, as it happens, the night Quintus was attacked. Of course, I had no idea then who he was, or how significant that stabbing would turn out to be. At the time I was simply glad to be safely inside the town walls, and away from the dangers of the open road at night.

I had come to the town looking for my wife – or at least for news of her. It was a pleasure I had been promising myself for months, ever since I had heard that a slave woman called Gwellia had been offered for sale at the market there some time before. Naturally, I couldn't be sure that it was my Gwellia, nor even that if I found her I would recognise her: after all, it was twenty years since we were seized, separated and sold into slavery. But ever since I had gained my own freedom (and with it the coveted status of Roman citizen), I had never ceased to look for her. I was almost fifty now, an old man, and she was ten years younger. I wondered ruefully if she would recognise this weather-beaten, grey-haired creature as the athletic young Celtic nobleman she had once married.

All the same, I had come. Delay after delay had thwarted me until now, but I had done it in the end, though only by leaving my mosaic workshop on the outskirts of Glevum to the mercies of my slaveboy-cum-assistant, Junio, and braving the twenty miles or so to Corinium on my own.

A damp and weary business it had been too. It was raining, and I had been obliged to trudge almost the whole

1

way on the miry edges, since the military road is exactly that – a military road, giving priority to army traffic. I kept a knife at my belt, as most people did in case of having the opportunity to eat, and I had one hand on that as I struggled along, keeping a keen eye open for brigands and wolves. Even the military road is wild and lonely in places, and the stout staff which travellers carry is not merely for support. Without Junio, too, I felt peculiarly vulnerable. Fortunately, just as I was about to seek a bed at an unwholesome inn, a friendly farmer offered me a ride for the last few miles in his bone-juddering cart, though even then I had arrived after sunset and spent an uncomfortable half-hour being questioned at the hands of the town watch.

Now, therefore, I wanted nothing more than to find a cheap, cleanish place to sleep and a bowl of something warm from one of the *thermopolia* – the takeaway hot-drink and soup stalls. Some of them seemed to be still open, their shopfronts open to the street and warm steam mingling with the smoke of oil lamps and charcoal stoves in their shadowy red interiors.

I had no lantern or taper, and my hand tightened nervously around my staff – the streets of a strange town are no place to be wandering alone at night. This was not Glevum, that respectable colonia of retired legionaries, with a handy Roman garrison still in residence: this was a *civitas*, a market town, notorious for its vagrants and pickpockets, and the law was evidently less strictly enforced. In Glevum at this hour, the streets would be thronged with creaking carts and lighted wagons – it is forbidden to bring civilian wheeled transport inside the city walls by day. Here the paved streets, though rutted by wheels and stained with recent dung, were eerily empty.

I felt a little shiver of anxiety. It was getting very dark. Only the glimmer of candles behind the shutters of the town houses, the glow of the *thermopolia* and a single blazing torch glimpsed down a side alley gave any light to the streets. Silent too, merely the muffled creak of a distant wagon, the snuffling of stabled horses, faint murmurs and music from the houses and the ringing of running footsteps somewhere nearby, as sandalled feet struck the flagstone paving. I wrapped my cloak closer about myself and quickened my pace.

Suddenly, I heard a noise. I stopped, listening. There was a sort of humming buzz, which resolved itself swiftly into voices. Voices and footsteps, and they were coming towards me. A crowd, by the sound of it, far away down the main street to my left; a mass of men, clattering down the street together, all shouting and singing at once.

'The blues, the blues, the blues are champions.' A pair of youths, arms around each other's shoulders, lurched around the corner into the light of a thermopolium. They had been drinking, by the look of them: one still carried a small amphora and his toga was stained with wine. They stared at me a moment, and vanished into the fast-food stall. There had been chariot racing, obviously, and no doubt the young men had staked on the blue team and were about to spend their winnings. Doubtless the owners of the food stall had stayed open on that very account.

More racegoers were coming into view now with their attendant lantern-bearers. Citizens, mostly – some of them high officials judging by the purple stripes on their togas and the deference with which less favoured individuals stepped aside to let them pass. I closed my free hand around my purse. There are usually pickpockets in a crowd, however brutal the Roman penalty for theft, and chariot crowds are in any case famously belligerent. This was not a good place to be a stranger. I stepped back into a shadowy alcove, to avoid unwelcome attention. My foot touched something soft, and a rat scuttled into the rubbish. My heart missed a beat.

Then a hand from behind me plucked at my cloak.

I could not have cried out if I had wished to – my tongue was cleaving to my mouth. I whirled around, staff at the ready.

There was a woman beside me, almost invisible in the darkness under a huge dark evil-smelling cloak, which covered her from head to foot. She was hidden in the shadows, but I could just make out a white, raddled face, warty and sunken. The eyes were wild and feverish, but the gnarled hand on my cloak fringe was firm enough.

'Spare me a quadrans, mister, and I will tell your fate.'

I looked at her with distaste. I am not much drawn to fortune-tellers, in any case, and this one looked more like a prophetess from ancient republican Rome than any modern soothsayer I had ever met. Most female diviners these days are respectable, retired Vestal virgins, or proper priestesses at a shrine – a little wild-haired and fanatical sometimes, but generally respectable, sleek and well-fed after a lifetime in the temples. This one looked as if she was halfway to the other world already; she was dirty, smelly and half-starved, and the warts did nothing to enhance her appearance. Not, altogether, a convincing visionary: if she could really foresee the future, I thought, she might have foreseen some way of avoiding her malodorous state.

However, it is never sensible to cross a woman who claims to have magical powers. I freed my cloak and fumbled for a brass coin.

She tested it with her toothless gums and favoured me with a smile. Then she looked up at the moon, dimly visible through the clouds. She seemed about to say something, but at that moment another little group of racegoers passed the end of the street with an evidently rich man among them. Richer than ever now, probably, since he was wearing a blue favour pinned to his cloak.

The woman looked from me to him, and shook her head. 'I can tell you nothing now,' she hissed. 'Come to see me again and I will give you your answer.' She slunk away, and I saw her accost one of the group.

I laughed inwardly at the transparent trick, and turned my attention to the takeaway stall. The owner was a hairy brute of a man who was looking at me speculatively. I was just passing over my few coins in exchange for a bowl of questionable broth with hoof parts floating in it, when there was a shout from outside.

'Stop! Stop, thief! Stop that man!'

I dashed into the street, spilling most of my broth – which may have been a mercy. It was hard to see in the darkness, but there appeared to be a disturbance down a narrow alley opposite, between two towering walls. A small tunic-clad figure was lying in the road some way along it, probably a torch-bearer, since there was a blazing torch lying beside him. In its light I could see the wealthy man with the ribband now slumped against the wall. A man was leaning over him, and in the flicker of the torch I saw the glint of a dagger. Another ruffian with a club loitered menacingly in the shadows.

'Stop them!' The man I had just seen accosted by the soothsayer had wrested himself away and was running up the street towards his friend, but it was too late. The figure with the dagger stooped, cut free his victim's purse and the two robbers disappeared like arrows up the empty alleyway into the night. The pursuer was an older man, and there was no chance of catching the thieves. None of the onlookers, I noticed, had lifted a finger to help.

A small crowd was gathering at the entrance to the

alleyway. I joined them, craning my neck to see the little drama unfold. The man had given up his chase now, and had gone back to his companion and was kneeling beside him, lifting his head, holding a hand to his heart. He turned to the watchers, and, still panting from his exertions, gasped out, 'A litter. Fetch a litter. Quickly, while there is still time.' He picked up the torch and set it against the wall, where it maximised the illumination.

He was a good-looking man, now that the light struck him. Tall and striking, although his head was bald. His face – intelligent and mobile in the half-dark – was remarkable for the intense concentration with which he was taking something from the pouch at his own belt. Herbs, I realised a moment later as he placed them in his mouth and began to chew them. The man was carrying a kit of medicinal herbs and bandages, like a soldier going to battle. Sure enough, a moment later he was parting the folds of the bloodstained toga and applying the improvised poultice to his friend's wound.

'Stand aside, there.' One of the *aediles*, the market police, appeared behind me, jostling through the crowd and making way for the litter which had now appeared. I stepped aside smartly. The last thing I wanted was an interview with the aediles, on suspicion of being a stranger at the scene of a crime. The authorities have very effective ways of dealing with witnesses they are dubious of, so effective that people often confess to things they couldn't possibly have done in the first place. I had no wish to have my memory tested.

I wasn't wearing my toga either, and that made me an immediate offender, should anyone arrest me. Strictly, as a male Roman citizen, I am required to wear a toga in public at all times, but like many of my humbler fellow citizens, I usually ignore the instruction. They are expensive to clean and awkward to put on, and I have never learned to wear one with grace. It may be different in Rome, but no one in the Insula Britannica is going to stop a mosaic-maker with a handcart and ask him why he isn't more formally dressed. I had thought about wearing it on the morrow, in fact, to give myself more status when I wanted information, but had decided against it. My toga needed cleaning, and besides, wearing a toga on a trip like this would be to invite the attention of pickpockets and a higher price at every hostelry.

Now, though, I was sincerely regretting the decision. A toga would have ensured, at least, that I wasn't manhandled by the aediles. I slipped back into the thermopolium. The crowd was in any case beginning to drift away.

'Still alive, is he?' I realised that the stallholder had been standing at my elbow.

I nodded. 'It seems so. Otherwise he would not have applied the poultice. Badly wounded, though. Lucky his friend was there, and so well equipped.'

The man spat into the corner, expertly missing the food vats. 'Well, he would be. That's his doctor, that is. Best medicus in Corinium. All right for some, being able to afford a private physician.'

'Just as well he could,' I said. 'Who is he, anyway, the man who was attacked?'

The stallkeeper gaped at me. 'You don't know? That's Quintus Ulpius Decianus. He is one of the councillors here, a *decurion*. Richest man in Corinium, or one of them.'

'I see.' I did see. If Quintus Ulpius was a decurion, he would be worth robbing. A decurion is one of the highest officials in municipal administration, and the chief requirements for election to the office are the possession of a sizeable property and payment of a large fee into the official coffers. And, presumably, he had just won something on the chariot races.

'Stranger here, are you?' The stallholder spat again, less accurately this time. Two racegoers had come into the shop, wearing favours for the green team, and they were looking at me menacingly. I remembered that their team had lost, and I smiled nervously.

'Here on business for a day or two,' I said.

'Only, I thought you might be looking for a bed,' the stallholder said. 'My brother keeps an inn.'

I was so relieved, I let myself be persuaded. It cost too much, of course, five *as* coins for a shared bed, and five more for a blanket, but at least it took me away from the hostile crowds and the eagle eye of the aediles.

My visit to the town was not much more successful in other ways. I devoted two days to my enterprise, lost four days' earnings and gained nothing more than the name of a possible slave trader and a rash of flea bites from sharing my bed at the inn with an unsavoury fellow traveller. Of course, it did not prevent me from planning assiduously to come again as soon as I could afford it. If I could find that slave trader, he might be able to remember who had bought Gwellia. But in the meantime, I was not sorry to go home.

Someone might have remembered seeing me at the scene: that could still mean being dragged before the authorities.

At least, I thought, as I began the weary walk back to Glevum in the drizzle, by the time I next got to Corinium this whole affair would have been forgotten. And, fortunately, the stabbing of a decurion was none of my affair.

Which only shows how wrong a man can be.

Chapter One

Even when the invitation came, many days later, I did not foresee trouble. In fact, I was inclined to be foolishly flattered. Junio, my servant-cum-assistant, came out from my ramshackle workroom to fetch a piece of marble, and found me standing among the stone heaps at the entrance to the shop, staring thoughtfully down the crowded, muddy street.

It was not difficult to see what I was looking at. Here, among the butcher's stalls, rickety workshops, bedraggled donkeys and second-hand clothes sellers, that smart, gold-bordered tunic and scarlet cloak stood out like a centurion in a slave market.

'A messenger?' Junio rubbed a dusty hand through his tousled curls. 'I thought I heard voices. Good news, then, master?'

I realised that I was smirking inanely, and I adopted a more dignified expression. 'An invitation from my patron, Marcus. I am to dine with him tomorrow, at his new villa. Alone.' I tried to keep the self-satisfaction from my voice.

Junio whistled. 'A private dinner with the regional governor's personal representative, eh? I wonder what he wants.'

I frowned. He was right. Junio was only a boy still, but he understood the world. He was perhaps fifteen or sixteen years old, I could not be sure. When I found him, half-starved and shivering in a slave market eight years ago, they didn't know his age. He was simply a tearful, terrified child and I had tossed the slaver a few coins and taken him home. And now here he was, taller than I am, and showing more sense than I had done. Taking infernal liberties, too, by telling me so.

I put on my sternest face. 'You are impertinent. Kindly do not speak of Marcus Aurelius Septimus so.'

'Oh, come, master,' Junio persisted, selecting his piece of marble from the heap. 'How long has His Excellence been your patron? Two years? Three? When has he ever sought you out, unless he wanted something? And it must be something important. I know how highly he values your intelligence, but he wouldn't invite a simple tradesman to dinner just for the pleasure of his company. Not even you.'

I glowered at him. He was right, again. Wealthy and influential Romans like Marcus do not usually invite mere pavement-makers to dine with them privately in their country villas. Obviously Marcus wanted something. And it was clearly something significant. Generally, if Marcus wanted me to do something, he simply sent for me and ordered me to do it.

'I imagine,' I said loftily, 'that it concerns the librarium mosaic at his new country house. It needs repairing, and I assume that he is about to offer me the commission. After all, I was responsible for his getting the villa in the first place.'

'And for seeing that he needed a new pavement to go into it,' Junio reminded me cheerfully. 'Perhaps you are right. No doubt he thinks you owe him another. After all, it was you who ordered the new floor to be dug up.'

'Only in order to solve a murder!'

Junio grinned. 'True. Though you know what His

Excellence is like. He probably thinks a dinner invitation is better than payment.'

He had a point there, too. The problem in dealing with Marcus is that he affects to regard me – at least for payment purposes – as a valued artist and thinker, to whom mere money would be an insult. In fact, such insults would be very welcome, if only to buy food and candles and to pay the rent, all of which are getting more expensive by the year. There are mutterings everywhere that the Emperor himself will have to 'do something' soon, though I doubt, myself, that the boorish, addle-pated Commodus will ever bestir his imperial self sufficiently to introduce a double denarius or to restrict the price of wheat. In the meantime, a poor tradesman has to count every *sestertius*. I was not, however, about to admit that to Junio.

'Marcus knows everyone of importance in the whole of Glevum,' I said, with some justice. 'He has already put a number of valuable contracts my way. If his pavement is admired, I shall have wealthy clients clamouring at my door.'

'That would be a sight, indeed!' Junio agreed. I could see his eyes dancing at the mental picture of those 'wealthy clients' coming to my shop in person. My workshop is outside the colonia walls, down on the marshy lands beside the river where the rents are cheap, away from the fine Roman paving and lofty buildings of Glevum proper, with its forum, fountains and fine open spaces. Rich citizens rarely come here. I could imagine them, pot-bellied and self-important, wrinkling their fastidious noses at the mingling smells from the tannery and tallow-maker's, and trying vainly not to trail their togas in the mire. Despite my anxiety, I found myself suppressing a smile.

Junio was thinking of togas too. 'I suppose you will be wanting to wear your formal dress for the occasion?'

I groaned aloud. I had not worn it to Corinium, but this dinner with Marcus was a different matter. 'I'll have to wear it, I suppose. Poor unbleached woollen thing that it is.'

Marcus himself would undoubtedly be sporting a dazzling white linen affair imported from Rome, with a broad stripe of deep imperial purple round the edge – a reminder, if anyone doubted it, that he is of patrician blood. Marcus's family name is Aurelius, and though that is a very common name, he is widely whispered to be related to the Emperor. He has never confirmed this rumour, but he hasn't denied it, either. Personally, I don't question the truth of it – at least, not when Marcus is listening.

'You will want your toga cleaned, then, master.'

I had forgotten that. My toga still had an unofficial stripe of its own – a rim of grime around the bottom from the last time I'd worn it, visiting an important customer up a narrow lane in muddy weather. Junio had wanted to take it to the fuller's earlier, but I had demurred because we had got so behind in the shop.

I looked at Junio in dismay. 'What am I to do? There isn't time to send it to the fuller's and have it bleached before tomorrow night.'

Junio shook his head, grinning. 'Well, this is a chance to try that famous Celtic "washing mixture" you brought back from Corinium. We'll see if it's as good as you claim.'

I hadn't brought it from Corinium, in fact. I'd got it from a Dubonnai farm I knew, which I had visited on the way home to arrange to buy their distinctive red stone for tiles. I was made welcome, as usual, in the cheerful smokiness of the roundhouse, and I struck a bargain for the tiles over a pitcher of honeyed mead with the owner, sitting around the central fire, attended by dogs and chickens, toothless women and bold-eyed girls. The Dubonnai (or 'Dobunni' as the Romans call them) had been making soap, and hearing that I remembered it from my youth, with typical Celtic generosity they insisted that I take some home in a pottery jar. It was not identical to ours – I was seized into slavery from the south-west of the island – but it was very similar.

Junio was intrigued when I showed him. He had never heard of soap. He was half-Celt himself, but had been raised by Roman owners who preferred more civilised cleaning methods.

I waxed eloquent about it, extolling its virtues and reminiscing about my own roundhouse and how my young wife and my grandmother used to save goose grease to soften their hands, or to boil up with lye from the wood ashes into a washing mixture. I remembered it vividly – a strong, sticky substance vigorously applied by my grand-mother to clothes, cooking implements and even, occasionally, to people.

Junio had been fascinated. He usually was when I started talking about my younger days. He had been born in servitude, and couldn't remember his own family. Or he affected to be fascinated – perhaps he was only humouring his master.

Whatever the truth, I was not hugely enthusiastic about having this untried substance used inexpertly upon my only toga, but there was little else to do, and after my paeans of praise for it, I could hardly back down now. So we set to work with the soap.

It was smelly and caustic and irritated the skin, but it was fairly effective, rubbed into the hems, though we used a whole amphora of fresh drinking water to rinse them off. How Gwellia and my grandmother would have laughed at our efforts! I remembered my wife standing knee-deep in the river, skirt looped up to her waist, rinsing her small-clothes in the running stream. How beautiful she had been, with her plaited hair and laughing eyes, her bronzed thighs glistening with wet. But it did not do to think of that. I dragged my attention back to the toga.

I wore it next evening to Marcus's villa. It was not altogether dry, since there was too much stone dust in the back workshop to dry the thing off properly in front of the cooking fire, and we had been reduced to stretching it out to air in front of the window space upstairs.

Marcus had sent a cart for us, because the villa was some miles from Glevum, so we rode like rich men. I had been to the house before, when it was owned by a retired centurion, but I was struck again by how imposing it looked in the twilight, with the lanterns at the gatehouse, the surrounding farm and the villa itself glimmering with candles, a long, low building with lofty rooms. Of course, it had been built to impress. The visitor was intended to marvel at its opulence and realise that no expense had been spared. I realised.

I felt more than usually at a disadvantage, though, as I was shown into the echoing marble atrium to wait, in a toga that was still slightly moist at the edges and which gave off a warm, steamy smell in the heat of the braziers and the underfloor hypocaust heating. If I had known what was in store for me, I would have felt more doubtful still.

The slave at the inner door looked at my damp hems with disdain, but a toga is still a toga. He announced me with a flourish – all three Roman names, as befitted a citizen. 'Longinus Flavius Libertus has arrived, master.' He gave me that look again. 'The mosaic-maker.' That was to put me in my place. Important citizens do not have trades, they live on the income from their lands and 'managed' businesses. He didn't mention Junio, of course, who was following me to take my cloak, any more than he would have mentioned a pet dog if I had happened to bring one with me.

'Libertus, my old friend! Welcome, welcome.' Marcus came bustling to greet me, his toga even more pristine and elegant than I had feared. Its dazzling whiteness was set off to perfection by the glint of the heavy gold brooch on his slim shoulder and the equally heavy seal ring on his outstretched hand. They could parade him around the forum, I thought, as an advertisement for the fuller's – except for that imperial border. In fact, with his short-cropped fair hair, hooded eyes, patrician nose and fine features, he looked every inch an Aurelian. He was still a young man, but he had an effortless air of command. Perhaps the rumours about his ancestry were true.

All this effort at elegance was making me increasingly uneasy. What did he want with me? It was in any case an awkward moment. Normally, I would have made a formal obeisance, on my knees, but I was supposed to be his dinner guest. I compromised by bowing deeply over his hand and bending my knees slightly. 'Excellence! I am honoured by your gracious invitation.'

It seemed to do the trick. Marcus smiled. 'Nonsense! I wished to reward you, old friend, for your help.' He made the slightest of gestures and two slaves came running, with a folding chair for him and a stool for me. Dates, figs and honeyed fruit, I noticed, were already set out for us on a magnificent inlaid table nearby, together with two cups and a jug of something which I took to be cooled wine. He waved a hand at them. 'A little something to while away the time before dinner? A mere trifle.'

My heart sank further. I am not in a general way a lover of dried dates and figs – like many Roman appetisers they are too sweet for my taste – but since every item on that table, from the food and wine to the fine goblets with 'Don't be thirsty' worked into the glass, had been especially imported from somewhere else, one didn't have to be a tax collector to work out that this entertainment of Marcus's was a very expensive 'trifle' indeed.

Junio – who had relieved me of my mantle and was now being led away to wait for me in the slave quarters, as the custom was – caught my eye and gave me an expressive look. Whatever my host wanted, his face said, it wasn't a bread-and-apples matter.

I couldn't ask Marcus what it was, of course. That would have been a breach of etiquette. Instead, I was obliged to perch on the stool and eat with a determined appearance of enjoyment and gratitude, while Marcus gossiped about his twin passions, pleasure and politics, and boasted about the exploits of his contacts in the army.

At last, however, he worked around to it, although by such a circuitous route that even then I didn't see it coming.

'My cousin, now,' he said, 'been made a *doublarius* already, and on the governor's staff. Twice the pay – and at his age, too. He'll go far. He was the one who sent me the wine. You like it?'

I made an inspired guess. 'Rhenish?' Wine is not my preferred drink, and my judgement is limited to an estimation of how much it looks like weak blood and how much it tastes like strong vinegar. However, I knew that Rhenish wine was much esteemed this year, and, since Marcus clearly expected me to say something, it seemed like a sensible guess. Even if I was wrong, I reasoned, I had paid him a compliment.

Marcus gave a nod of approval. 'Not quite, not quite. But a good guess. Even better than Rhenish, in fact. It's

Falernian. From the vineyards south of Rome. Best wine in the world. That young scoundrel knows a good vintage when he samples it. They looted a cellar, apparently belonging to that rebellious legion in the north-west. You heard about that?' He signalled to the slave, and I found myself contemplating another glassful of whatever it was. All I knew, I thought glumly, was that it wasn't ale.

I shook my head. I had heard vague rumours, of course, but there are always rumours in Glevum, often incredible and usually contradictory. This legion or that has won a skirmish, or lost it. The governor is dead, is married, is coming to Glevum, has been visited by Jupiter himself in the shape of a butterfly. Even the truth tends to be so modified when passed on by word of mouth from traveller to traveller that I had come to pay little attention to rumour. If there was any serious trouble one would learn of it soon enough.

But obviously there had been truth in this. Marcus was still smiling, toying with his goblet, but there was no smile in his voice. 'Oh, yes, quite a serious affair. Set on the governor and murdered his bodyguard. Left him for dead, I hear.'

I hadn't heard that story. I put down my glass and gulped – not at the wine. 'Left the governor for dead? You mean Pertinax? Your friend? The Governor of Britain?' My mind was racing, trying to organise my thoughts as well as I could through the filter of Falernian wine. My patron derived his authority from the governor directly. If Pertinax fell, then Marcus fell with him, and any political assassin might strike at Marcus too. 'That governor?'

Marcus regarded me with that affectionate intensity people reserve for the seriously stupid. 'That governor.'

'Oh.' There seemed to be nothing else to say. Suddenly everything, the invitation, the wine, the exotic fruits – the whole expensive and uncalled-for occasion – seemed depressingly ominous. Marcus had used me before now to get to the bottom of various unpleasant incidents, such as the death of an ex-centurion or the theft of a quantity of gold, which seemed to him to threaten the dignity of Rome. He valued my discretion, he said. Now, I realised, he was about to ask me to be discreet again, but on a grander scale. I didn't like it. I didn't like it a bit. Meddling in that kind of murky politics is a certain short cut to an early grave – often by interestingly agonising routes.

I was considering the feasibility of pleading some unavoidable appointment – my own funeral, perhaps – when Marcus went on. 'Of course, Pertinax has already ordered the punishment of the guilty legion. It will be severe, naturally. Part of the reason he was sent here was to instil discipline into the ranks.'

I breathed out again. If Pertinax had identified his attackers, perhaps my discretion would not be needed after all.

I had exhaled too soon. Marcus bit delicately into a particularly bilious-looking fig. 'But something else has arisen from this. Something nearer home.'

I almost choked on my non-Rhenish wine.

Marcus regarded me benevolently. 'Do I remember hearing that you visited Corinium about the last full moon? Something to do with trying to trace that wife of yours?'

I nodded, my mouth suddenly dry.

'You didn't, by any chance, hear anything about a stabbing? An acquaintance of mine, a fellow named Quintus Ulpius Decianus. He is one of the councillors there, a decurion. I have received word to say that he was attacked walking home from watching a chariot race. His slave was killed and he was wounded.'

I gulped. I am obliged by custom to attend upon my

patron regularly. I had informed him of my visit to Corinium, but – apart from telling Junio – I had kept carefully discreet about the robbery. Now, it seemed, I was about to pay for that discretion.

'Street robbers, wasn't it?' I enquired.

Marcus shook his head. 'That seemed likely, at first. But there is something else. A friend had attended him to the races, and saw the end of the attack. Only the end, because he stopped to speak to a soothsayer. It was dark, of course, and he didn't see the attackers properly, but as he came around the corner he saw someone standing over Quintus with a dagger. He shouted and gave chase, but he is not as young as he was, and by that time it was too late. Quintus was lying wounded on the chariot grooves, and his lantern-bearer was dead. One might have suspected the friend of staging the robbery, except that he saved Quintus's life.'

'I know,' I said. 'I happened to see some of it myself.' Marcus looked about to expostulate, so I added quickly, 'It was just as well the friend was there. He is a doctor, I believe? Without his care the man might have died of his wounds. He seemed to be carrying an army medical pack.'

Marcus nodded. 'He always does, apparently. He is a retired army surgeon. Quintus is recovering well, though he can remember little of the attack. But the surgeon – Sollers, his name is – seems to think that their real aim was not robbery. Their first action was to attack Quintus, he says. It wasn't until Sollers shouted that the thief cut the purse free, and ran. He has warned Quintus to be on his guard.'

I nodded. 'I was impressed with him. He deserves his name, obviously.' 'Sollers' is a cognomen meaning 'clever' or 'capable'. A man doesn't earn a name like that for nothing. 'What has this to do with Pertinax? You think this was somehow political? Or aimed at Quintus personally?'

It was possible. There were, after all, other rich men among the racegoers, but only Quintus had been attacked. Perhaps it had been pre-arranged. I was liking this less and less. 'Did Quintus Ulpius have particular enemies?' I suggested hopefully. 'Some individual that he punished or did not recommend for preferment?'

That would not have surprised me either. Decurions, especially in wealthy cities like Corinium, are not the most popular of citizens. True, they are voted into office, but since decurions are responsible for allocating contracts for public works and also for collecting taxes, they are often viewed with jaundiced eyes, especially by those who did not secure the contracts or who had to pay the tax. And, of course, by those who have not managed to become decurions.

'Well,' Marcus said, 'there is some problem over his wife. She was a wealthy woman, apparently, and she left her former husband to marry Quintus. You know what these heiresses are like.'

I did indeed. A woman who leaves her husband, or is divorced from a free marriage, is entitled to take her dowry with her. The Empire is full of attractive *vaduae* who ally themselves to one influential man after another. 'Then that is the likely explanation,' I said. 'This Quintus would not be the first victim of marital revenge.'

Marcus drained his winecup before he spoke. 'Perhaps,' he said, 'but I fear the worst. Quintus is a known supporter of the governor's. He has supported him openly in the forum, and sent him personal gifts. He has also entertained me royally.'

Of course! It had not occurred to me to wonder how Marcus came to number a Corinium decurion among his acquaintance. No doubt he had been in receipt of some 'personal gifts' himself.

'His friendship with the governor was well known?'

'He has many *clientes* on that account,' Marcus said.

I nodded. Every powerful man has his band of followers who visit him daily to pay court and bring gifts, hoping for patronage, or letters of recommendation to the mighty.

'Two days ago, for the first time since the attack, he was well enough to entertain them. But after the visitors had left, something was found in the colonnade. A wax writing tablet. And on it was scratched in crude letters "Remember Pertinax". Quintus thought it was a threat – related to the attack on the governor. He sent me a message yesterday, sealed and delivered by special courier. He fears another attack. That is where you come in, Libertus.'

I gaped at him. 'You want me to go to Corinium and prevent it? To find out what happened?' If this was a political intrigue at the highest level, I thought, I might as well stab myself in the back with my dagger now, and save someone else the trouble. I began to burble. 'But Excellence, I've already been there trying to trace Gwellia. I was at the scene. I shall attract suspicion if I wander about asking questions. I shall be arrested, or people will take me for a government spy.' Which, of course, is exactly what I would be. It was not a comfortable thought.

Marcus was not to be swayed. This was dangerous for him too, both politically and personally. He smiled. 'Oh, I don't want you to ask questions. At least, not openly. Quintus is undertaking some extensions to the public baths. I want you to design a pavement for him. It will give you a reason to be there, and you can keep your ears and eyes open.'

This was not a request, of course, although it was couched as one. It was a command, and a command from Marcus had all the force of a governor's edict. If he asked you to go, you went – if you knew what was good for you.

Whatever the dangers might be.

He smiled. 'The pavement should be a valuable commission, and I knew you would welcome the chance to continue your search for . . . Gwellia, is it?' Marcus himself had left a woman in Rome, but he surrounded himself with pretty women, and always regarded my loyalty to my former wife as an amusing aberration.

I made one last effort. 'I have customers . . .' I said feebly.

'Refer them to me. And don't worry about the travel. I shall take you to Corinium myself. Quintus will arrange accommodation.' He clapped his hands. 'Now, enough of business: the slaves shall bring us some water for our hands, we'll send for our napkins and spoons and go in to dine. I presume you have your own knife with you?'

I nodded, but my heart was not in it.

It was a pity, really. Marcus had arranged a simple but robust menu of my favourite Roman foods. Sea bream with lovage, then baked veal with leeks and aniseed, all rounded off with almond cakes with honey and pepper. Even the dreaded pickled fish sauce was served separately as a dip, in deference to my taste. I appreciated the gesture but somehow, with this visit to Corinium hanging over me, I had lost my appetite.

'Well, at least I get a chance to go back to Corinium,' I said, when, much later – after musicians and a comic recitation at which I remembered to laugh heartily – we bounced wearily home again. I smiled at Junio ruefully.

He grinned back, understanding perfectly. 'So now we know what Marcus wanted.'

Chapter Two

We went to Corinium the next day. Marcus had requisitioned a closed imperial carriage with a following cart for luggage and two mounted cavalrymen as escort, so the journey took only a few hours. One glimpse of the official insignia and the two outriders, and all other users of the military highway made way for us, as if by magic. It could hardly have been more different from my last visit to the town. This time, by comparison, the journey was luxury – not just for my ageing bones, but even for Junio, lurching along behind in the luggage cart with the other possessions. It was barely noon before the earth ramparts and wooden stockades of the town came into view, with their imposing newly built stone gatehouses and the slate roof of the basilica glittering beyond.

No surly questions at swordpoint on our arrival, either. The guards at the gate straightened smartly at our approach, lifting their arms in salute, and we whisked under the portico and into the town without so much as a challenge.

Corinium is a fine place by daylight. A man can buy anything here if he has the money for it: the little booths around the market place display oil, wine, leather, bone, glass, pottery, perfumes, herbs and statues from all over the Empire, while the many *macella* of the market house itself teem with the sounds and smells of livestock and the raucous calls of butchers, offering fresh-killed meat of every variety. The laws about wheeled transport were openly flouted, and as we swept down the road towards the forum we sent a dozen handcarts scurrying from our path, loaded with everything from turnips and roasted birds to firewood and fleeces. I wondered how many of these traders would exchange their freedom of movement for the dreadful hubbub and congestion of Glevum at night, despite the automatic Roman citizenship a colonia confers on those who live within its walls.

There was at least one inn, I knew, and there were doubtless others, but Quintus Ulpius, it seemed, had insisted on entertaining the whole party in his own house. That argued a residence of a certain size, but as we rattled up to his imposing outer wall and bowled through the gates, I realised that this was a town house grander than anything I had ever seen in Glevum – or anywhere else, for that matter. The dwelling did not open directly onto the street, as most such houses do, but was set back amid a screen of trees, behind a formal garden with statues and arbours, and a colonnaded walkway skirting the outer wall. It was more like a country villa than a town residence. There was even an elaborate water basin, where an overweight Neptune straddled a disconsolate dolphin in a cascade, fed, as I discovered later, from a private water supply piped in from a nearby stream.

Behind the leafy screen of branches I could glimpse the house itself, a fine stone building in the Roman style, with an extra wing on either side. I had an impression of graceful verandas, lofty rooms, and a fountain glimpsed through the open door suggested a further courtyard beyond. At the door, a veritable army of blue-tunicked slaves stood ready to rush out and help us to descend. Being a decurion has manifest advantages.

In more ways than one, I discovered. A pair of house

slaves showed us down a paved passageway to the atrium. There was no open central pool, as they reputedly have in sunnier climates, but the effect had been echoed by an amusing blue mosaic depicting sea horses and dolphins. I had just time to admire this, a beautiful inlaid table and the fine painted walls, before a woman came to meet us. She was a small, shapely woman in a Roman stola, with bright, dark eyes and a little smile that made the heart skip. This, presumably, was the heiress wife that Marcus had spoken of.

Her first words confirmed it. 'I am Julia, Quintus's wife,' she said simply. She had a way of lowering her eyes which I found quite charming. 'My husband had hoped to greet you himself, but he is still weak from his wound, and has tired himself meeting clientes. He begs that you will refresh yourself, and he will see you as soon as he is rested.'

If jealousy over his wife *had* been the motive for that attack, I thought, it would be understandable. This was an enchanting woman. She was no longer young – perhaps as much as twenty-five years old – but she was still undeniably attractive: not classically beautiful and statuesque in the pale Roman style, but dark, curvaceous and fine-featured. There was no doubt about her wealth: her soft amethyst-coloured *stola* or over-tunic, was of the finest quality, worn over a long shift of deep lilac wool. She wore a plaited girdle of purple silk, and her neck and wrists were heavy with gold. Her hair had been prinked and curled in the latest fashion, her eyebrows were plucked, and as she moved she gave off a faint aura of some exotic perfume which, even to my untutored senses, smelled extremely expensive. And yet she conducted herself with simplicity, and the brightness of those downcast eyes was due, I realised, not merely to the painted kohl line edging them, but also to tears. She seemed deeply moved by her husband's plight.

Marcus was looking at her appreciatively. No wonder Ulpius had made enemies, I thought. Taking one thing with another, the decurion was an enviable man.

He had arranged a gracious reception. Junio visibly fretted at not being allowed to attend me personally, as our baggage was bestowed, garlands distributed and our feet and hands washed, but that could not be helped. We were visitors in this house, and he was taken off to the attic to play dice and eat bread and cheese with Marcus's serving boy, while we were shown to couches into the elaborate dining room and a tray of fruit and watered wine was set before us. Two attractive young slave boys, so alike they might have been brothers, hastened to attend us. In this household, even a snack was offered with a flourish.

'I am sorry,' Marcus said, when the rituals of hospitality had been observed, 'that Quintus is so ill. I came especially in response to his letter. I have brought the pavement-maker that I told him of, too, to discuss designs for the caldarium. Libertus is also skilled at solving mysteries. He will discover who attacked your husband, if anyone can.'

Julia turned to me, and I felt the force of that beguiling smile. 'Then you are thrice welcome, citizen. I would offer a thousand *sestertii* to learn who stabbed my husband. And this caldarium means so much to Quintus. He will want the finest pavements. You knew, of course, that he was proposing to endow the new hot room in the public bathhouse to mark his year in senior office? It will win him support with the populace, he says – the poorer electors appreciate a warm place to go in the winter – and probably an honorary edict from the administrative council.'

And, I realised, make him a favoured candidate for even higher office. No wonder the man attracted clientes. This generous 'gift to the town' might even, in the end, prove personally profitable to the donor. A project of this size would be worth thousands of denarii, and the man dispensing money on that scale could be sure of generous 'donations' from dozens of wealthy hopefuls. Someone, for example, would have to supply the building stone, someone's ships would bring the marble from Italy, someone's potteries and forests provide the water channels and gutters. There must also, I thought wryly, be several humble but ambitious mosaic-makers even now devoting precious time and possessions to wooing Ulpius, or even promising to alter their wills in his favour, in an attempt to win this contract for the caldarium pavement. They were wasting their time, poor souls, if they but knew it. That commission was already mine. The decurion had ambitions, in his turn, and could not afford to ignore a recommendation from someone as important as Marcus.

Basking in this knowledge, I smiled at Julia. 'You know a great deal about the project.' I meant it as a compliment. Not many women understood the practicalities of power.

She favoured me with that smile again, glancing up under her eyelashes as though we were conspirators. 'He does sometimes discuss these things with me, and not just with his council of friends. After all, he has the usufruct of my dowry.'

Of course, since theirs was a 'free marriage', her husband could legally invest the income from her lands and fortune, provided he didn't deplete it. No wonder he discussed his projects with her. No wonder, either, that her former spouse bitterly resented that she had chosen to leave him. Previously, he would have had the rights to that dowry.

Marcus was visibly unhappy with all this vulgar talk of money, and anxious to begin the real business which had brought us here. He said, suddenly, 'Is Quintus able to receive us now?'

She flashed him an apologetic smile. 'I will go and see. But please, gentlemen, I beg of you, if he receives you, do not overtire him. He is still frail. Sollers says the wound is deep and might yet become infected. Last night, in fact, my husband seemed to have a slight fever. Sollers was worried; he watched all night with him, but this morning Quintus declared that he felt better and insisted on receiving his clientes again.' She dimpled. 'He is an obstinate man. And he wants to see you, I know. But you will remember, won't you, that he is still weak?'

'Of course,' Marcus said, and she was gone, through the inner door into the courtyard. He turned to me. 'A charming woman.'

I hid my smile. 'Devoted, too. See how she went to check on his condition for herself, and did not merely send a slave.'

I meant it as a warning, but Marcus merely chuckled. 'If you knew Quintus, that would not surprise you. She is right to call him obstinate. If Quintus decides upon a thing, he is hard to shake. He wants to see us. Therefore a slave would have been ordered to fetch us, whatever the state of his master's health.' He picked up the remaining slices of pear and popped them one by one into his mouth.

I watched him in silence. If Ulpius is as immovable as that, I thought, he might make an intractable enemy in political matters. And he supported Pertinax, so he would be no friend to those with more flexible allegiances. That could win him implacable enemies – and powerful ones. It was an uncomfortable thought, and it was some moments before I plucked up the courage to share it with Marcus.

My patron thought about it for a moment. 'You think that was the motive for this attack?'

'It had occurred to me. When Pertinax was lying close to death, there must have been local councillors in Corinium who were ready to change their support to someone more likely to survive and reward them for their allegiance. Probably they said so in private. In that case, Quintus knows who they were. And that is no light matter. Sedition against the governor is a capital offence.'

Marcus looked at me gloomily. He was about to say something when there was a noise in the adjoining room. The screen was flung back and a young man strode in from the atrium. The slaves attending us stepped back, startled, to let him pass.

He was a tall, thin young man with a narrow face, close-set eyes and a petulant expression. He looked dishevelled: his hair was tousled and curly, there was the faint down of a beard on his unshaven chin, and though his rings were costly, his toga was stained with wine and his hems were even more frowzy than my own. The effect was to make him look childish, although there was no childhood *bulla* around his neck, and he was obviously a man.

'Where is the woman?'

'The woman?' Marcus sounded even more startled than I was at this peremptory greeting. 'What do you mean, citizen?' He had risen to his feet, bridling, and his voice was ominous.

I winced. I have seen men flogged for showing less disrespect, but the young man seemed oblivious.

'What do I mean? Why, Julia. The woman. My father's new wife.' He caught my frantic glance, and seemed, at last, to see that there was some impropriety in his behaviour. He added, 'I'm Maximilian, by the way. Quintus's son. I've just come from my father – I've upset him as usual. He wants to see her.'

'She has this minute gone to him,' Marcus said, in the same icy tone.

Maximilian shook his head. 'Well, I did not see her, and I have just left his bedside. I shall have to look for her. If she doesn't turn up at once, it'll be my fault. Everything is my fault, since she came to this house.' He turned to the slaves at the door. 'Well, what are you waiting for? Go and find your mistress and tell her my father wants her. Now!'

The two slaves looked at each other and scuttled off, while Maximilian leaned over casually and helped himself to the remaining fruit which had been set for us. Son of a decurion he might be, I thought, but he had appalling manners. And no sense of self-preservation. It was bad enough showing disrespect to his father, calling him by his familiar name, Quintus, instead of using his *nomen* properly, but now he was being equally disrespectful to Marcus, though the wide purple stripe on Marcus's toga should have warned the boy that this was no ordinary guest. I glanced at my patron. He was looking increasingly dangerous. At any moment, I thought, there would be serious trouble.

'This is Marcus Aurelius Septimus,' I said, 'my patron. We await an audience with your father.'

'Marcus? My father's guest?' The boy paled. 'Forgive me, Excellence. I took you for the two clientes my father still has waiting – otherwise I should never have presumed . . .'

'I see.' Marcus was laconic. 'Do you usually treat your father's friends like this?'

'These two are scarcely friends,' the boy said heatedly. 'They are not even strictly clientes. They told the secretary they were here on business. They sought audience with my father, but only because they have grievances against him. They should never have been admitted through the gates at all, with Quintus so ill, but they claimed friendship with me, apparently. My father thinks it is all my fault, of course, though I have scarcely set eyes on either of them. But he insisted that he would see them once they were here – he wouldn't have it said that he shirked his duty to callers.'

'But he hasn't seen them?' Marcus said.

'Not yet. Sollers kept them from him – he thought Quintus should be rested before receiving them – though of course that wasn't right either. "Skulking round the property, spying on his goods", my father says. That's why I thought you were the two in question – it would be just like Julia to order refreshment for them. She has a talent for spending my father's money.'

She had brought a large dowry with her, I remembered, so perhaps she felt it was her own money. Though of course a man like Quintus would have extensive estates and interests of his own. 'And you fear for your inheritance?' I asked. He was not a prepossessing young man, but I could follow that grievance, at least.

He shot me a look. 'And with reason! Julia and that Sollers of hers have poisoned my father's mind against me. He's threatening to disinherit me, and leave it all to them. He says I'm lazy, but what am I to do? I have no businesses. And I can hardly invest. He refuses to increase my allowance, now, even enough to pay my rent and wine bills.'

I nodded. It was a common enough story. In Roman law, of course, a man, even a grown man, is under tutelage until his father dies, dependent on him for every penny and unable to enter any legal contract without his permission. It is not a recipe for family happiness. I think we Celts manage these things better.

'And as for that woman,' Maximilian went on, 'he's becoming a laughing stock. He is completely blind where

31

Julia's concerned. And she's turned him against me. She has made him turn me out to live in a measly flat, and then when I come to visit him because he's ill, what does he do? Flies into a temper, sends me away and asks for Julia. And all I did was ask for a few denarii.' He stopped. 'I'd better make sure they've found her. If she doesn't go to him, it will be my fault again.'

He went to the courtyard door. But before he could put a hand to the latch, the door burst open and one of the two slaves came panting in. He flung himself at Maximilian's feet.

'Master! Master, come quickly. It is Quintus Ulpius, your father. He has been attacked again. We found him slumped on the floor, blood pouring from a wound in his back. He had been crawling to the doorway. We raised his head, and he managed to whisper to us. He asked us to fetch Sollers, but I cannot find him. So I have come to you . . . Oh, young master, come quickly. I fear your father is dead.'

Chapter Three

There was a stunned silence, and then Maximilian spoke.

'Dead? My father? He can't be! Let me see!' He threw us an agonised look, then, thrusting the slave aside with his foot, rushed out past us into the rear courtyard.

Marcus and I exchanged glances – it is rather an awkward social situation, finding yourself the guest of a man who has been unexpectedly murdered – but in the end there was nothing to do but follow. Out we went, skirting the herb gardens and flower beds, and when the boy disappeared in through another door we simply went in after him.

The room we entered was a large one, and formed the corner between the main block and one of the front wings of the house. It was not, as I expected, a master bedroom, but a kind of additional reception room, obviously designed as a place where the master of the house could meet his clientes without the inconvenience of having them trespass on his private apartments. It was lavishly decorated, with real blue-green glass in the windows, a painted frieze on the plasterwork and a fine tiled pavement on the floor. It boasted no less than three doors, not only the one by which we had just entered, but two interior folding doors: one to the side, which evidently led to the rest of the house, and another door straight ahead, through which we could see a long, thin ante-room, presumably for appellants to wait in, since there were stone benches around the wall and a sturdy central table for cumbersome gifts. By contrast, a carved and gilded couch was set in the centre of the main room, piled with embroidered pillows and blankets, with an elegant low table beside it. A lighted brazier of beaten metal stood to one side, and an exquisite but uncomfortable-looking stool to the other. There was another, similar stool against the wall. The effect was more like an emperor's court than the home of a private citizen.

It was, however, a private home, and the citizen was there to prove it. His presence was a primitive outrage in this most civilised of rooms. He was lying, stretched out, face down upon the floor, like a kind of bizarre mosaic. Part of his toga had been pulled aside, revealing his shoulder and under-tunic. I could glimpse the bindings around the ribs, where the earlier wound had been dressed, there was a reddened bruise on the back of the exposed arm and the hilt of a dagger was still visible, driven in under the shoulder blade. A dreadful seeping stain was making an additional red-brown stripe on his curial robe, before running down to mingle with the black, brown and white of the dancing deities depicted in the tiles.

Maximilian had stopped short just inside the doorway, staring, and was gnawing the middle joint of his finger. The impression he gave was not so much of grief as of consternation, like a pupil waiting for his *paedagogus* knowing he has failed to construe his text. He did not look in our direction.

Marcus nodded to me, and I stole forward, bent down and tentatively raised the head. It felt absurdly heavy, as if each grizzled iron-grey curl was made of iron indeed. The head was half-turned towards me, and as I raised it I could see the face. The jaw had dropped open: there was blood-flecked foam on the lips, and a pair of fishlike eyes stared at me, lifeless. The effect was grotesque, a kind of macabre astonishment, as if death had taken an unwarrantable liberty by arriving so unexpectedly. I lowered the head hastily.

'He's dead, isn't he? The slaves were right.' That was Maximilian, his voice sharp and childish.

I got to my feet. 'It seems so.'

'They'll blame me. You watch! Julia and Sollers. They'll say it was my fault he was unattended. Just because I sent the slaves away from the door. I didn't want them listening in. But you're my witnesses. I only came to ask him for money . . .'

'We are your witnesses that you were here,' I pointed out gently. 'We cannot testify to what you said. We have only your word for that.'

'Anyway,' Marcus said slowly, 'you won't need to ask him for money now, will you, Maximilian? You will be free to make your own decisions. I think you said he was intending to disinherit you. Presumably that means he hadn't done so yet – and now, of course, he never will.'

Maximilian brightened. 'That's true, isn't it? So his fortune will come to me. Or at least most of it. You're right. I'm no longer under tutelage. No more measly *peculium* – he never gave me enough to live on. Well, much good it has done him! Now I can spend money on what I like.' He sounded delighted. I wondered if he realised that Marcus had just made out a very good case for suspecting him of murder. Parricide by disaffected sons who hope to gain financial independence must be one of the most frequent crimes in the Empire.

Maximilian, however, seemed oblivious. 'I wonder how much money there is?'

The spectacle of this arrogant and idle young man greedily assessing the wealth of the father who lay dead at his feet was, to say the least, singularly unattractive. I knew

Marcus, and when I saw him crisping his fingers, I knew that he, too, longed to land a satisfying punch on that peevish, spoiled face.

My patron said sharply, 'We shan't know that until the will is publicly read in the forum. There may be heavy expenses.' The tone of his voice suggested that, under the circumstances, he hoped the inheritance would be severely depleted. 'No doubt your father has left instructions for memorial games, or even a building to be erected in his honour, and, of course, there may be co-heirs. Someone may even enter a *querela* against the testament, on the grounds that your father intended to revoke it.'

Maximilian smirked. 'It would need seven witnesses to prove that. Besides, Julia wouldn't take it to trial. If a will is found to be invalid, most of the money tends to end up in the hands of the treasury, and then she wouldn't get any either.'

'Then let's hope for your sake that it isn't invalid already. I presume he has made a new will since he remarried? Otherwise she can claim under the praetor's edict.'

There was a pause while Maximilian took this in. Then he said, rather petulantly, 'I don't know. I suppose so. But I'm his next of kin.' His face fell. 'I suppose that also means I'll be responsible for all these contracts he's entered into. The gods alone know how many denarii that will run to. And I'll have to succeed him as decurion, and that will be more expense. Always supposing that that woman hasn't spent it all, anyway. Oh, Mercury! Nothing is ever as simple as it seems.'

He was interrupted by a voice from the door behind us. 'Maximilian, I see, is demonstrating his usual filial piety. I hear that his father has been stabbed again. Maximilian's grief is truly heart-rending, don't you find?' He came forward as he spoke.

36

I recognised him at once. He was a tallish, grey-haired man, slightly balding and running a little to fat, but with that unforgettable mobile, intelligent face, and the shrewdest pair of eyes I have ever seen. He was not wearing a toga today – not even a plain white one like mine – though as an ex-army surgeon he was obviously entitled to one. Instead he wore a long amber robe like an outsized tunic, tied at the waist. Even so, he had an air of such professional competence about him that even Marcus stepped back and allowed him to speak. 'I am Hermogenes Valerius Sollers, citizens. The slaves told me I was needed.' He stopped, staring at the body where it lay. 'Great Hermes! What is he doing on the floor?'

'He has been stabbed,' Marcus said, rather unnecessarily, since the fact was only too evident. 'He was crawling to the door when the servants found him.'

A look of genuine horror crossed Sollers's face. 'Crawling to the door! Then he was alive after he was stabbed! Poor man, how he must have suffered. Did he have time . . . did he manage to tell them who had done this to him?'

Marcus shook his head. 'It seems not.'

Sollers said, 'But if he had strength enough to crawl, perhaps there is still hope. Excuse me, citizens. I must examine him.' He brushed past us and went to kneel beside Quintus. 'My poor old friend, what has happened here?' Deftly, he began to run his hands over the body, lifting back the tunic to examine the wound.

I watched him as he worked, the clever hands probing the wound, and I was struck once again by his skill. Greek-trained, I guessed, as many doctors were. It was not a difficult deduction, given that he swore by Hermes and spoke slightly accented, although excellent, Latin, but I was pleased with myself for making it. His name, of course, pointed in the same direction, but that was less reliable evidence, since he had probably adopted that when he achieved Roman citizenship.

Wherever he had trained, he was good. The examination could not have been more gentle and painstaking if the body under his hands had been that of his own brother. I could see why Quintus valued him as a companion. Many wealthy men boast of keeping a private physician in their homes, not only to oversee the family's health, but also to dazzle dinner guests with learned discussions of philosophy and science. Unlike many of his fellow doctors, I thought, Sollers would acquit himself with equal distinction in either role.

We watched him in silence now, as he continued his grim work. At last he got to his feet.

'We are too late, citizens. He is dead.' He examined his own bloodstained hands with dismay. I noticed that some of Quintus's blood had stained his sleeve. 'This is a tragic welcome to this house. But I am impolite, citizens. And Maximilian, too. What can we say? In the name of my poor dead friend, I greet you. You are Marcus Aurelius Septimus, of course, and you, citizen, must be the pavement-maker. I have heard of you.' He turned to Marcus. 'Should I, do you think, remove that dagger, Excellence? We must send for the slaves to arrange Quintus's body for the funeral, and it is not seemly to leave him with that weapon in him.'

Marcus seemed momentarily startled at being appealed to in this way. Like the rest of us, he had instinctively deferred to Sollers up to now. However, it did not take him long to recollect himself. He rearranged his toga, casually, but so that the aristocratic stripe was more in evidence, and said, briskly, 'Yes. Do that please. Then we will have them wash this floor, and after that perhaps his wife would like to see him.'

Sollers smiled. 'At once, Excellence.' He bent down

again, and with a violence that made me avert my eyes, seized the dagger hilt and jerked it free. When I looked again, he was holding the dripping blade. There was an unreal and macabre theatricality about the scene, as if we were all condemned slaves at the playhouse, forced to play our parts to the death in a bloodthirsty tragedy. I have seen men killed before, of course, and Marcus is a frequent visitor to the amphitheatre, but even he paled.

'I am sorry, citizens.' Sollers seemed to feel that some explanatory comment was necessary. 'The weapon had been driven in with some force. As you see, the blade has chipped on a bone.' He held it out for our inspection. There were fresh bloodstains on his robe, I noticed.

It occurred to me that the killer must have carried similar tell-tale splashes. In fact, when I came to think of it, there was surprisingly little blood. A stabbing can be a horribly messy affair. I said as much to Sollers.

He looked at me in surprise. 'You are astute, citizen. Yes, there is often much more blood. But the assailant was lucky. I bled Ulpius myself, not an hour ago, to reduce the fever and help him to rest. If he was stabbed shortly after, he would not bleed so fiercely. There would be no spurting. And leaving the blade in the wound would help to staunch it too. The murderer may have escaped with no more than bloodied hands.'

I turned to Marcus, but he was inspecting the weapon, without removing it from Sollers's hand. It was a vicious dagger, with a short, sharp metal blade and an elaborately carved hilt in some kind of dark wood. It was very unusual.

'This belonged to Quintus?' he asked. It seemed a likely explanation. Murderers do not commonly leave behind weapons of such striking individuality.

Sollers surprised me. 'No, I do not think so. Most likely it belonged to one of the clientes.' He shrugged. 'It is my fault, gentlemen. After that attack . . .' he shot a look at Maximilian, who looked bewildered, 'I took the precaution of removing all personal weapons and knives from anyone wishing to visit him.'

I nodded. It was unusual, but not unheard of. It is not unknown for people to be asked to leave their blades with a servant. Some dicing dens demand it, for example, and personal visitors to the Emperor are rumoured to be routinely searched at the door for weapons and poisons.

'You don't know who owns it?' Marcus asked.

'Not for certain. I remember having seen it – it is rather a remarkable object – but I could not swear to the owner.'

'Well, I could. If anybody deigned to ask me!' That was Maximilian, more petulant than ever. 'But no. Here I am, heir presumptive to my father's estate – so this is my house you are standing in, or it will be very soon – and what happens? Everyone ignores me. Everyone always ignores me, at least while that buffoon is around.' He gestured savagely at Sollers.

It was an extraordinary outburst. 'Buffoon' was the last word I should use to describe Sollers. If anything, it seemed more appropriate to Maximilian himself.

Marcus seemed to think so too. 'You say you recognise this knife?'

'Is it yours?' Sollers sounded genuinely surprised.

Maximilian flushed. 'You'd like that, wouldn't you? I dare say you'd like to prove that I murdered my father. That would be a nice neat solution for everyone. I came in here, sent the slaves away and stabbed him in the back. Well, I didn't. And it isn't my knife either. But I know whose knife it is, and so would you if you had your eyes half open. It belongs to that fool, Flavius. I've seen him with it a dozen times. And now, if you'll excuse me, I'm going to the bathhouse. I need to perform the ritual wash and to change my toga. After all, this was *my* father. I shall be wanted to close his eyes, put the coin in his mouth and begin the lament. And *I* shall lead the procession, after the musicians, and make the funeral oration, too. You can tell that woman as much, from me.' He turned away from Sollers and spoke to Marcus and myself, finding a sudden dignity. 'Citizens, welcome to my father's house. My house, as it now is. Though this man still thinks he runs it, as you see.'

He turned on his heel and left the room.

There was a stunned silence.

'He is upset,' Sollers said. 'It has been a shock. To all of us. It is bad enough that there was one attack on Quintus Ulpius's life – but another! And to think that I unsuspectingly seem to have arranged to provide a weapon.'

'Where did you put the knives?' Marcus asked.

'I did not put them anywhere. I asked the clientes to leave them on the table in the ante-room. They were in full view; anyone might have seen them. I explained that Ulpius was . . . well, understandably upset . . . after the attack, and asked them to leave their blades outside as a courtesy.' He seemed embarrassed.

I guessed that he had represented Quintus to the waiting clientes as a man obsessed, half crazed with fever and fear. Perhaps he had been. After all, he had sent that letter to Marcus, saying that he feared another attack. And with justification, it seemed.

'So,' I said, 'there was more than one blade on the table?'

'One or two at a time, no more. The callers collected them as they left.' Sollers smiled ruefully. 'I did not imagine there was any danger. The weapons were on public view. Ulpius insisted on seeing his clients privately, one by one, but his secretary was present throughout, sitting on that stool by the wall, and there were always slaves at the door. The clientes simply called into the ante-room as they left, to pick up their knives and summon the next appellant. I even looked in on Ulpius myself from time to time, to make sure he was not overtiring himself. He was never alone – until Maximilian came.'

'I see.' I did see, but there was an obvious question I needed to ask. 'Who is Flavius?'

Sollers looked grave. 'You do not know? I had thought you had heard the gossip. Flavius is a substantial landowner near the town. He has a large estate, and many interests: wool, dyeing, pottery even. He is a rich man, though not as rich as he was.'

'And he had come to see Quintus Ulpius about a contract?'

Sollers shook his head. 'In a manner of speaking. He came to see Ulpius about Julia. He was her previous husband.'

Marcus took a sharp breath. 'He was here? And he left his knife?'

'More than that,' I said, suddenly understanding. 'He's here now. Maximilian told us that there were still two visitors waiting to be seen.'

'Great Hermes!' Sollers said. 'I had forgotten that. I sent them away so that Ulpius could rest, before Maximilian came. Presumably they are still waiting, somewhere on the estate. They will not know of Ulpius's death.'

Unless they were there when it happened, I thought. After all, it was Flavius's dagger. And he did have a motive – one which I could understand.

'We must have him found at once,' Marcus said. 'And the other client, whoever that is. Maximilian said they both had grudges against Quintus.'

'Maximilian sees grudges everywhere,' Sollers said. 'But

you are right – the poor fellows must be found, and told the tragic news.'

'Not merely told,' Marcus said. 'I want them sent to me. There has been a murder here. Send word to the gatehouse that no one may leave the house or enter it.'

Sollers looked startled. 'But surely, Excellence . . .?'

Marcus silenced him with a look. 'There is no room for argument. This is a question for the governor – and I am his representative. Quintus was not merely a citizen, he was a senior magistrate, loyal to Pertinax. I shall oversee this questioning myself. Libertus will help me. Have the slaves prepare a room for us, and perhaps something to eat. The killer must be in the house. There is no time to lose.'

Sollers inclined his head. 'Of course, Excellence. I was merely about to observe that Maximilian may have left already, since you have given him permission to go to the bathhouse. But I will convey your orders, naturally.'

Marcus looked sheepish. 'There is no bathhouse on the property?' It was a reasonable assumption, in fact; most men of such conspicuous wealth prefer to conduct their ablutions in private.

Sollers smiled gravely. 'Ulpius has long intended to build one, but the price of office is high, as you know. Besides, I think he enjoyed the bathhouse. When he was well he used it as a kind of unofficial office for meeting his friends and business acquaintances. But now, perhaps, with your permission, Excellence, the slaves could also be instructed to clean this room and prepare the body for burial? I should like to see my friend afforded some dignity.'

Marcus flushed. Sollers was right again. There was perhaps something unseemly in conducting this conversation with a dead man at our feet. 'Of course.'

'And, if you have no objection, Excellence, when I have

conveyed your instructions, perhaps I could go to Julia? She will have learned of this by now, and she will be distressed.'

'Of course,' Marcus said again, and we went, all three, out into the courtyard. Sollers set off towards the slaves' quarters at the rear.

But almost before he had disappeared, a party of slaves arrived from the kitchen and filed into the room we had just left, ready with water bowls, cloths, linen wraps and anointing oils.

Someone, obviously, had given orders already.

Chapter Four

Marcus and I exchanged looks and went back to the atrium. A table had been set there, with two stools and a jug of wine.

'Maximilian seems to be taking his new role as head of the household seriously,' Marcus said wryly. 'He appears to have thought of everything. Except a slave. It appears we shall have to pour our own wine!'

'I'll see if I can find someone,' I said. 'And I'll look for this Flavius and his friend while I'm about it. They cannot be far away.'

Marcus nodded, and I left him to wait in comfort, while I set off in search of a servant to pour the wine. Strictly speaking, I should have sent a slave to find the missing clientes too, since I was a guest in the house, but I welcomed the chance to look around a little.

I had some idea, now, of the layout of the residence. The whole building was shaped like a giant H, the principal rooms across the centre, with attics above, and two wings projecting forwards and back on either side. I had been to the rear of the house. There, I knew, were the bedrooms and other private apartments ranged along each side of the central courtyard garden; while beyond the herb gardens, arbours and central water basin, the top of the H was almost closed off by a separate block which obviously contained the kitchens and the servants' quarters, and a two-seater latrine over the drain. Presumably the rest of the household offices – the rubbish heap, oil stores, orchard, poultry yard and stables – lay beyond, the whole enclosed behind the massive wall which ran around the entire property.

I did not go that way. Quintus's waiting room and reception salon formed one of the forward wings of the H, so instead of going into the rear courtyard, where the slave quarters were, I went out into the front court, and looked to my right, where the front entrance to the ante-room lay.

The door to the ante-room was open, and through it I could glimpse the table and a portion of the bench. Nothing more: the room was too long, and in any case the inner door would screen any view of the reception room beyond, where the funeral preparations must by now be under way. But I had seen what I wanted. Anyone coming from the reception room could have come out this way and rinsed his hands in the central fountain. Or he might have done so in the rear courtyard. In either case, he ran a considerable risk of being observed.

I looked around for possible witnesses, but there was no one in sight. As I watched, however, a page in a turquoise tunic emerged onto the farther veranda, one of those handsome young boys that every wealthy Romanised household seems to keep as a pet.

I summoned him with a gesture. 'Slaves in this household are like donkey-hire men at a market. Lots of them around, but you can never find one when you need one. Where is everybody?'

He was obviously terrified, but he had been trained in flirtation, and batted his eyelids at me. 'Your pardon, citizen. We are in confusion. No one is at their usual station. I, for instance, apart from carrying messages for the family or for guests, usually attend exclusively on Quintus Ulpius.' He smiled at me ingratiatingly, but I said nothing and he babbled on, as if explanations might win my favour. 'But since we heard of my master's death, everyone is giving different orders.'

'Such as?'

He counted them off on his fingers. 'Two slaves were sent into the town for anointing oils. Citizen Maximilian demanded another four to go with him to the bathhouses, and two others were needed to attend my master.' He was running out of fingers, and he spread his hands in a hopeless gesture. 'Then Julia Honoria sent down orders, wanting messages carried all over the place – to funeral musicians, stonemasons, orators, anointers, and even to the market to order food for the funeral feast. She even has the garden slaves cutting greenery and herbs. In the end there were only three of us left in the slaves' waiting room. Then Sollers came in and ordered us to come and get the study ready for His Excellence. Me, Rollo! I did my best, but I am no cleaning slave. In the end the other two said I was in the way, and sent me outside. So here I am. Can I serve you in any way, citizen?'

Not in the way he presumably served Quintus, I thought. I have no taste for pretty young pages. Nor as a witness, either. According to the testimony I had just heard he was in the slaves' room until after the murder. I toyed for a moment with the idea of sending him to look for the missing men, but one glance at his exquisite turquoise tunic and embroidered slippers was enough to dissuade me. His function was merely to look decorative. He would be more concerned with keeping his expensive shoes clean than in doing anything useful. As the slaves cleaning the study obviously recognised.

And there was Junio, banished to the attic, I thought with irritation. But it wasn't this lad's fault. I tipped him a couple of copper *asses*, which brought a smile back to his face, then I sent him off to pour the wine for Marcus, and set out to find the missing clientes myself.

It did not take me long. They were sitting together halfway down one of the colonnades in the front courtyard, in a little leafy arched arbour with a stone seat. The place was screened from the rest of the garden by a semicircular area of thick hedge and a portly and charmless statue of Minerva – so secluded that I might have walked straight past it, had I not heard the murmur of voices.

'It is absolutely typical of the man,' one of them was saying. 'Absolutely typical. Keeps me waiting until last, and then has me sent away to kick my heels in the garden while he is "resting". I suppose I shall count myself lucky if he consents to see me before dark.'

I grinned to myself. The rituals of visiting a patron are less formally observed here than they are in Rome. Marcus, for example, does not require me to attend him every morning and night, as many patrons expect their followers to do in the imperial city. But supplicants are usually received in strict order of social precedence. Keeping important visitors waiting is a deliberate insult.

'It is the same for me.' The other voice was older, high-pitched and querulous. 'He's kept me waiting as well. And in this cold wind, too. As least you've been able to walk around and enjoy the garden. With my aching joints and swollen knees it is all I can do to hobble to the nearest seat and sit on it.'

'Enjoy the garden! Enjoy it! When it's planted with exotic shrubs purchased with my wife's dowry? You wait till I see Quintus. I'll plant *him* – three feet deep, with a coin in his mouth to pay the ferryman. I'll even donate the money myself.'

There was a pause, and then a nervous cackle of laughter. 'Don't worry! I'll help you pay it, three times over. And if you're going to plant him, I'll give you some fertiliser – from my cesspit. It's no more than he deserves.'

Eavesdropping is not very dignified, but it is often fascinating. And, in the circumstances, illuminating. I inched a little closer to the hedge.

'Don't worry,' the same voice went on. 'I hate him as much as you do. You heard how he treated me? Standing up in the amphitheatre and denouncing me to the council, persuading them not to re-elect me to office. Me, Paulus Avidius Lupus, after I have served this town as decurion for eleven years.'

Flavius – the younger man had to be Flavius – sounded unimpressed. 'I heard that he had opposed your selection as magistrate. I also heard that you had done the same to him.'

'That was years ago, when he first sought election to the ordo. Anyway, it isn't at all the same thing. My father was born a Roman citizen. His wasn't, he was merely a free man with "Latin rights" and a lot of money from doing deals with the army. That's what I pointed out to the voters. Of course, that's all been forgotten. Quintus has joined the equites since then – with his money he can afford to buy his way to a knighthood. And he's been a *curia* member for years. But he's never forgotten it. Never. He has used his power and influence to ruin my family – there is not a tax or imperial obligation that does not fall on me twice over, and he loses no opportunity to support my creditors in the courts.'

Flavius began to say something, but Lupus was not to be silenced.

'He stopped my re-election, yet he is still demanding that I make a retiring contribution to the curial purse. For urgent civic repairs. You heard what happened? I imagine all Corinium knows by now. Some idiot sited the whole forum on poor ground: the Jupiter column is cracking and half the basilica is sinking into a ditch. Quintus is demanding huge contributions from everyone on the council. It will cost me thousands. He's setting out to ruin me. My only hope was to be re-elected magistrate. That way I could at least sell a few contracts, or attract goodwill gifts from wealthy followers. I managed to get myself nominated. That cost me a fortune. And then he put a stop to it. Rest assured, young man, any enemy of Quintus's is a friend of mine.'

Flavius gave a mirthless laugh. 'In that case, you are the friend of half Corinium. Unfortunately, the other half adores him. The man who brings Quintus down will need a broad back. Or exceptionally good fortune.'

'Exactly what I was thinking,' Lupus said. 'Do you know . . .' He dropped his voice, and I could catch only snatches of the rest '. . . insisted on stealing him . . . Would have cost me half my estate to pay the fine . . . Thousands of sesterces . . .'

I might have gone on listening for longer, but at that moment a servant in a smart ochre tunic came bustling out of the far wing of the house, and stopped on the veranda to stare at me. I made a feeble pretence that I was merely bending over in order to re-fasten my sandal. The slave gave me a disdainful look – real gentlemen do not go around tying their own sandal straps with one ear in the hedge – and disappeared back into the building. I should have to be more careful, I thought, or my spying activities would be common gossip among the servants. Chastened, I went around to confront the speakers openly.

They were not a prepossessing pair. Flavius, the younger man, was perhaps thirty-five years old, but already thickset and paunchy. He might have been handsome, once, but he had gone to seed, and now managed somehow to combine dark features with a high colour, so that he appeared at once swarthy and florid. The idea of such a man being married to the beautiful Julia seemed an outrage to natural justice.

The other was older, probably even older than I was: stooping and scrawny, with wiry limbs and grey, thinning hair which he had vainly attempted to hide under an absurd and very obvious hairpiece. His skin had the yellowish-white tinge which is often associated with the infirm, and he clutched his right arm stiffly to his bosom as though it pained him, but the alacrity with which he leaped to his feet when I appeared suggested a certain sprightliness. Clearly the aching knees he had complained of were not troubling him now.

'And who in the name of Mithras are you?' Flavius demanded furiously. 'Bursting in unannounced upon your betters in this way?'

'Forgive me, citizens,' I said, trying to look humble. Purple-edged togas demand deference. Even the younger man was a narrow-striper, and the badly draped robe of the other carried the broad stripe of senior office – though, incidentally, how I was supposed to deduce this through a thicket it was hard to see. 'I am Libertus, a pavement-maker. I have come from Glevum with my patron, the governor's representative, to see about laying a mosaic. We are guests in this house.'

The mention of Marcus won me a little more respect. Flavius, who had been scowling at me aggressively, glanced nervously at Lupus and took a step backwards. 'You were looking for us?'

'I was, citizens. I bring serious news. Did you know that Quintus Ulpius had been stabbed?'

It was not, taken all in all, the most intelligent of questions. If Junio had been there he would undoubtedly have reminded me of the fact. But the results were startling.

Flavius reacted angrily. 'Of course I know. That is why I am obliged to dance attendance on him here, like a tradesman begging for payment. Of course he was stabbed. But if you are looking for sympathy, or a subscription, you have come to the wrong people. If I could find the man who stabbed him, I would clap him warmly on the back. And I dare say Lupus here feels the same. He was just telling me his grievances.'

If he was looking for warm support, he was disappointed. Lupus's pale skin grew even paler, and when he spoke his voice seemed scarcely under his control. 'Flavius, my friend,' he plucked at his own toga folds with his stiffly held hand, 'be careful what you say. Words spoken in jest are quickly misconstrued.' He turned to me. 'I had grievances against Quintus, yes, but I did not stab him. I have been sitting here on this bench all the time. Flavius will tell you.'

Flavius looked from Lupus to me and back again. 'What? You mean Quintus has been stabbed – again?'

Lupus looked shaken, but he said steadily, 'Well . . . I imagine so. This good citizen would hardly come to tell us something which the whole town has known for a month. This is some new attack. Is that not so, citizen? That is what you mean?' His eyes, deep-set and too close together, gazed at me anxiously.

'That is exactly what I mean,' I said. 'Ulpius was recovering from his first wound, but he has been stabbed again, in the last hour. And this time fatally.'

It was Flavius's turn to pale. 'Quintus is dead?' He shook his head. 'Well, that solves my problem, then. And yours too, Lupus. And since I do not imagine that his family will expect me among the mourners, I shall return home.

Excuse me, gentlemen.' He made to walk past me out of the arbour.

I forestalled him, choosing my words carefully. 'I am afraid not, citizen. I think my patron will wish to question you. When Ulpius was found there was a dagger in his back. A very unusual dagger, with a carved black wood handle. They say it is yours.'

He looked at me for a moment, the colour in his cheeks darkening. Then he snorted. 'Mine! Well, what of that? It was on the table in the ante-room for all to see. It does not mean I killed him. What sort of assassin would leave an identifying knife in his victim?'

Perhaps the sort of assassin, I thought, who expected us to reason in that way. But I did not say so. 'Perhaps a man who had no choice,' I said. 'Withdrawing the knife from the wound was difficult. It is possible the killer intended to remove it, but could not stop to do so. There was so little time in which to commit the crime – unexpected delay would be fatal.'

Flavius licked his lips. 'So you think . . .?'

'I do not think anything, citizen. Except that owning the murder weapon does not absolve you from the crime. Marcus will wish to question everyone. You too, I'm afraid, Lupus.'

Lupus looked too terrified to protest, but Flavius was still scowling. For a moment he was silent. He seemed to be thinking furiously. Then he did speak, and when he did so his words were unexpected.

'I want to speak to Julia,' he said.

Chapter Five

Flavius got his chance to see Julia more quickly than he imagined. When we reached the house she was already in the atrium. She had changed into a simple dark brown Grecian coat, presumably out of respect for the dead, and was looking pale and shaken. Indeed, she was leaning heavily on Sollers for support, to Marcus's obvious irritation. The news of her husband's death had been a visible blow to her. She looked, if possible, more beautiful in grief.

I tore my eyes away from her and turned to Marcus. 'I bring you the citizens Flavius and Lupus, Excellence. I found them waiting in the colonnade.' I said nothing about hearing their conversation. That was information I preferred to keep to myself, at least for the present.

Lupus greeted Marcus with all the deference due to his rank, and Flavius muttered his way through the appropriate formula. His attention, though, was elsewhere. Throughout the whole of the formalities his eyes never left his former wife.

'Julia!' he said, as soon as it was decently possible to do so. Marcus, who was already frowning, compressed his lips. 'Julia, I must talk to you.'

At that she relinquished Sollers's arm – to the satisfaction of every other man present – and drew herself up proudly. She had stripped herself of her finery – presumably in deference to the news – and wore a simple jet necklet. She looked pale, but magnificent. 'Flavius. I heard that you were here. I have nothing to say to you. Our marriage is over. And you can have nothing to say to me – at least nothing that cannot be said here, in public.'

It was courageous. Now that Julia had no husband as protector, she had few legal rights. Flavius was a wealthy man and he would make a powerful enemy.

At the moment, however, he merely looked despairing. 'But Julia! You know what I want to say to you.'

'I know,' Julia said, 'I have heard it all before and I do not want to hear it again. There was no sorcery which made me leave you. I left because I did not want to stay. And do not send me gifts and messages. I will not accept them – do you understand? You are wasting your time. I shall simply throw them away, as I did the others.' I looked at her with growing admiration. A lady to be reckoned with, obviously.

'Julia! I came here to plead with you . . .'

'You lie!' the woman said. 'You knew I would not speak to you. You came here to "plead" with my husband, as you call it. My poor sick, wounded husband. To threaten him, or try to bribe him, perhaps? And then he is found with your knife in his body. What am I to think of that, Flavius?'

He interrupted her. 'I did not stab Quintus, I swear it. By all the gods.'

She withered him with a glance. 'Perhaps you did not strike the fatal blow yourself – perhaps you are too much of a coward for that – but I know you, Flavius. I know what you are capable of.'

'Julia . . .'

She ignored him. 'I do not know, Flavius, what you hoped to gain by this. Did you think that with my husband dead I would turn back to you? If not from love, then at least from fear? Never, Flavius. Do you hear me? Not even if he leaves you guardianship of me under his will. I shall kill myself first. And if this death is proved against you I shall have my revenge, never fear. Citizen you may be, but if you did this, I swear I will see you thrown to the beasts.'

That was even possible, in fact – the murder of a decurion would call for the most savage rigours of the law. But even if wealth and status saved Flavius from being tied bleeding to a stake in the arena, to be set on by wolves or dogs, the other legal remedies were unpleasant enough. Flavius paled.

'I swear I did not murder Ulpius. Before Jupiter, Greatest and Best, I didn't even see him. I came to seek an audience, but he treated me like a common trader. I was sent away to wait. It was humiliating, but I had to see him. I was in the front court all the time after that. Lupus was there. Ask him.'

But they hadn't been together all that time, I thought. I knew that, if the others didn't. I looked at the elderly decurion, in his absurd wig.

Lupus licked his lips. 'Well,' he said, 'I am an old man. I can't walk about like Flavius can, I just went to the arbour and sat down.' He looked at Flavius nervously. 'But he was in the garden, certainly. He couldn't have got into that room to stab Ulpius without my seeing him. And I couldn't have done it, either. He would have seen me. We can vouch for each other in that, can't we, Flavius?'

If Lupus had been paid money in the public theatre to represent the part of a shifty and untrustworthy conspirator, he could not have done it better. Everything about him – his faltering tones, the way he fidgeted from foot to foot and the way he refused to meet our gaze – contrived to make him seem about as reliable as a second-hand donkey dealer at a fair.

'Well, we shall hear your story in a moment,' Marcus

said, in a voice which suggested that he shared my opinion of donkey dealers. 'I shall want to question everyone. Libertus will assist – he witnessed the original attack, and he may have additional questions.' He turned to Lupus and Flavius. 'I am sorry to make you wait again, citizens. Perhaps you should send a message to your homes. This may take a little time. I presume you could give them a bed here, if necessary?' he added, to Julia.

She looked at Sollers uncertainly. He nodded, and she said, 'I am sure we can contrive something. There are couches in the *triclinium*.'

'Great Minerva! I can't stay here,' Flavius expostulated angrily. 'I am expected tonight at the dinner of an important client. Besides, I have appointments, business, affairs . . .'

Marcus looked at him coolly. 'Of course, if you prefer a more formal detention, I am sure that it can be arranged. A night in the town gaol, perhaps?'

Flavius subsided, still muttering.

'Then if there is no objection . . .' Marcus began, but he was interrupted by a loud disturbance in the front court. There was a great deal of banging, followed by cursing and raised voices, and we all stopped, silent in amazement.

A moment later Maximilian stormed into the room, accompanied by two slaves. He wore a clean toga, this time edged with the black stripe of mourning that tradition demanded. Following a recent custom there were ashes rubbed onto his forehead, but otherwise he was hardly the traditional picture of grief. On the contrary, he was clearly furious.

He wasted no time on civilities. 'What is going on here? I am to be master of this house, yet I come home to start mourning my father, and find myself locked out of it like a criminal, and have to threaten the gatekeeper before he will consent to let me in. On whose authority were the gates locked?'

Marcus was looking dangerous. 'On mine.'

'Oh!' Maximilian looked nonplussed. 'I see. Then I must defer and apologise, naturally. But it is humiliating, having to hammer on your own gates for admittance. And who are these . . . gentlemen?' He gestured contemptuously towards Lupus and Flavius.

'We have seen you,' Lupus put in eagerly, 'at the chariot races. You remember?'

'Oh, I think he knows you well enough,' Sollers said. 'He identified Flavius as the owner of that knife only a moment ago.'

Maximilan flushed angrily. Interesting, I thought. The youth was a convincing actor, but a poor liar. Had he really forgotten what he had said to us? Perhaps these two men were genuinely friends of his.

Marcus, however, had no time for such speculations. He looked at Maximilian stonily. 'They were visiting your father. I asked them to remain. Just as I asked the gate-keeper to lock the gates. I presume you too would wish to prevent the murderer's escape? Even if that left you embarrassed in the street?'

That was a threat, and Maximilian knew it. Failure to take satisfactory steps to find a benefactor's killer is sufficient legal grounds for having a legacy overturned. He said sullenly, 'I apologise, Excellence. I bow to your decision. My house is at your command. Obviously.'

Marcus ignored the hidden barb in the last remark, but I knew that he had noted it, and that it would not be forgotten. Sooner or later, Maximilian would pay for that, and for his earlier rudeness. Marcus took his position very seriously. For the moment, though, he contented himself with a tight smile. 'In that case, perhaps we could make a start?'

'Of course.' Maximilian gave a brief nod to one of his attendants, who scurried away instantly. 'And with your permission, I shall begin preparations for the lament.' His voice was carefully polite, but his manner was still defiant. By proposing to begin the lamentation he made it deliberately difficult for Marcus to send for him for questioning: one cannot interrupt a mourner's wailing without showing serious disrespect to the dead. I saw Marcus's jaw tighten. I did not care for Maximilian, but I was tempted to utter a warning. This was a dangerous game.

It was Sollers who spoke. 'Permit me a suggestion, Excellence. My friend has, of course, left instructions for his funeral. He revised them shortly after he was stabbed in the street. I witnessed them myself, and no doubt Mutuus knows where to find them. Ulpius wished, I know, to have a burial – in order that Julia might be interred with him – and had already purchased a stone coffin and a tombstone, and named the professional mourners and arrangers that he wished to have. Since there is all this to organise, could you graciously break with tradition and deal with some of the menials first, and let them return to work? The gatekeepers, perhaps, so that we can admit the anointing women and funeral arrangers when they come; and the personal slaves who were on duty in this part of the house at the time? While you are doing that, perhaps I could, with your permission, make a start with my own duties. If poor Ulpius is to be cleansed for burial, his wounds must be decently dressed and covered.'

Marcus looked at me, and I nodded. It was exactly what I should have chosen myself. Maximilian, however, shot Sollers a poisonous look. 'I shall be needed for the ritual too. I am the heir here. It may be your job to tend his wounds, but it is my place to close his eyes and burn the herbs and light the candles around the body.'

'Of course,' Sollers said smoothly. 'Perhaps you should be spoken to immediately after the servants – that will give you time to take a little sustenance before the lament begins.' I realised as soon as he had spoken that this was exactly what he had always intended. 'Perhaps the other citizens could also go to the triclinium?' Sollers went on. 'I have already spoken to the cooks, and they are preparing a light meal.'

It was neatly done: in one deft and deferential move Sollers had promoted himself over Maximilian as the organiser of the household. I glanced at Marcus, wondering how he would react – it should have been his place to decide on the order of interrogation – but he was nodding approvingly.

Sollers's suggestions also overcame a difficult social dilemma for all of us. By custom a household does not offer formal meals while officially in mourning, except for the funeral banquet – presumably lest the spirit of the departed might feel neglected or peckish and return in spectral form to join the feast. On the other hand, there were important guests in the house who must be offered hospitality. By suggesting refreshment before the lament, Sollers solved the problem delicately.

Not everyone, however, was so pleased. 'You spoke to the cooks? In my father's house?' Maximilian cried, heatedly. 'I seem to have no position here at all.'

This outburst restored my patron to positive good humour. 'Very well,' he said, ignoring Maximilian. 'Sollers, please see that it is arranged. Libertus and I will take refreshment in the study, and we will deal with people in the order you suggest.'

It was soon arranged. Marcus and I were shown into the room, which had been prepared for us with oil lamps and a brazier and even a water-clock to enable us to keep track of time. A couch and table had been provided for Marcus, and after we had partaken of a 'snack' (a tray of cold roast meats with fish pickle, and a selection of bread and cheeses which would have been a fine meal in my house), we were ready to begin.

Marcus and I had worked together before. What he liked was to have people brought before him one by one. He did most of the questioning, sitting in state on a chair, while I squatted on my stool beside him and threw in an additional query now and then.

It was a system which worked well in many ways. Marcus had authority and status. Even members of the curia could be exiled at a word from the governor's agent, and he could open the doors of the gaol or bring the torturer running. People who would have dismissed me with a supercilious stare were inclined to grovel helpfully to Marcus.

However, terror can tie as many tongues as it loosens. I have often found that a little unguarded gossip is more help in an enquiry than hours of carefully constructed testimony – and no one is truly unguarded in the presence of an imperial agent. Besides, Marcus is inclined to lose patience with a line of questioning if he cannot see the immediate relevance of it, so I didn't expect this joint questioning session to produce any immediate answers.

Even so, I was surprised by how little we learned.

Sollers was right to suggest starting with the gatekeepers. Their testimony was crucial because, from their little rooms beside the front and back gates they could see everyone who came in and out of the house.

The keeper of the main gate was whiter than goat's cheese with terror, but his story was quite clear. Yes, there had been a small crowd of clientes calling at the house early this morning. Yes, he recognised most of them. Two of them were strangers, but they claimed to have been invited by Maximilian, and they were admitted. Then our party arrived, and then Maximilian in a litter, but by this time most of the visitors had left again. When the message came to close the gates there were, by the keeper's calculation, apart from ourselves, only the two strangers within the walls, an 'elderly councillor with a wig, and a red-faced narrow-striper who had left a fancy carriage waiting in the street'. Lupus and Flavius, evidently.

Marcus pressed him fiercely, but he was adamant. No one else had come to the house, and no one else had left it. The walls around the property were high, and no one could have scaled them without ladders and grapple irons. Whoever stabbed Quintus had not escaped that way.

The slave guarding the back gate had a similar story to tell. Various slaves had come and gone, sent into the town for oils and provisions, but there had been no strangers admitted. Visitors did not often come to that gate, which was reserved for animals and for access to the small farm at the rear of the property, where fresh food for the table was reared.

The slave who kept this gate was older, plumper and more confident. 'We get an occasional tradesman or peddler, but there were none this morning, only a scruffy urchin asking for alms, and another wanting Maximilian. I sent them both packing. No one else. Though I am expecting a delivery of charcoal for the kitchens, and the funeral musicians and anointers will be at the front gates in a minute. And, of course, the slaves will be back with their various purchases. Are we to let them in?'

We gave them permission, and let them go.

'Well,' Marcus said, taking another sip of wine, 'what does that tell us?'

'Only what we knew before,' I said. 'Whoever stabbed Ulpius is still on the property. There is no question of some stranger with a grievance coming in on an off chance and murdering him, unless whoever it is is still hiding here somewhere.'

'But you think that is improbable?'

'With respect, Excellence, I think it is almost impossible,' I said. 'Any assassin would bring his weapon with him. He could not rely on finding one to hand. And how could he know that Ulpius would be unattended? Usually the man is surrounded by slaves and secretaries.'

Marcus thought about that for a moment, and then rewarded me with a smile. 'Well done, Libertus. Now we are making progress. I had come to the same conclusion myself. The facts seem to argue that the murder was committed by somebody already inside the house.'

'There is only one problem, Excellence,' I told him gloomily.

He looked at me quizzically. 'And that is?'

'Exactly the same objections seem to apply to them.'

Chapter Six

Sollers had rounded up for us all the slaves who were anywhere near Quintus's reception room at the time of the murder. There were at least a dozen of them, and when I first glimpsed them, lined up outside the door of the study, my heart sank at how long the questioning was going to take. A closer inspection, however, made me simply goggle. If it were not for the ochre-tunicked figures of the secretary and the chief slave – who stood out from the others like two Vestal virgins at an orgy – I might have suspected that I had drunk too much watered wine and was seeing everything double. We brought the chief slave in to question him, and soon discovered why.

The poor man was half gibbering with fright lest the death of his master might be attributed to a slave's negligence, which of course would ultimately be his personal responsibility. He was more impassioned than the forum orators in his desire to explain to us how no possible blame could attach to any servant under his control.

Ulpius, it seemed, not only possessed an enormous number of slaves, drawn from all over the Empire, but – whether to impress the populace or because he felt it befitted his position – generally deployed them in pairs, except for those with specialist functions like the secretary and the exquisite page I had seen earlier. Many of the 'pairs' were even matched as closely as possible for height and appearance – hence, presumably, the physical similarity of the two boys who had attended us on our arrival. This piece of conspicuous extravagance must have cost a fortune, and, apart from amusing Quintus, was evidently designed to dazzle visitors with an exhibition of wealth.

It had certainly dazzled Marcus: I shouldn't be surprised to find matched pairs of serving lads at his own banquets in future. Quintus's servants, though, were probably less enthusiastic about the arrangement. Slaves have little enough privacy in any household, but short of being manacled together, these poor creatures could scarcely have had less. The pairs ate together, worked together, washed together, waited together and even shared the same sleeping space in the slaves' quarters. If I had been treated so when I was a slave, I should have found life ten times harder to bear, especially since a man could not even choose the companion who was linked to him with these invisible chains.

However, it did have one advantage now, from our point of view. The system meant that each half of a 'pair' had at least one witness to his movements for the entire day: indeed, I thought, with a little pang of sympathy, a witness to every minute of his life.

The chief slave confirmed this more strongly. There were so many slaves in the household, he explained, that each pair had specific duties, related to a particular person, function or 'domain', and most of the time were in full view of one or other of their fellow pairs. If they were not required, they were stationed in the slaves' ante-room next to the kitchen, where he personally could keep an eye on them. Therefore, unless there was a conspiracy involving most of the household, we could eliminate any of the paired slaves at once.

Marcus was delighted when he saw the force of this.

'Splendid,' he said. 'That will save a lot of time.'

It was a relief to me, too, though for different reasons. The chief slave was worried about his own safety, but strictly the law requires that if a master is killed by one of his slaves, the whole household should be put to death. The penalty is not often invoked these days, but in the case of someone as important as Quintus, Marcus might easily have felt that a firm example was needed.

Now, however, he was saying, 'In that case, we hardly need to question them at all.'

That was no use, either. 'You are quite right, Excellence,' I said, before he could commit the indiscretion of letting them all go. 'Under the circumstances, we need only question them a little. Naturally, you will wish to hear their stories, in case anything out of the ordinary occurred this morning, or one of them happened to see something significant.'

Marcus gave me a sharp look, but I met his eyes blandly, and in the end he smiled. 'Naturally,' he agreed. 'We'll have them in – in pairs.'

In fact, there was not a great deal to be learned. Whatever the slaves had been doing that morning – fetching and carrying, sweeping and cleaning, bringing chairs and serving food, filling lamps and trimming wicks, running errands, dancing attendance or simply waiting interminable hours for someone to call upon them – they had done it in full view of someone else. Until Quintus's death, there had been nothing unusual about the day's routines, apart from the additional tasks occasioned by our own arrival.

Even the pair who had actually been attending Quintus had very little information to offer. It was their duty, they said, to sit outside the door while Ulpius was receiving clientes and await a summons. They very rarely went into the room while business matters were discussed, unless their master called them in specially. From time to time they were called to take messages or plump up cushions, or to fetch wine, or ink and the delicate rolls of thin tree bark which he used for official documents instead of his usual wax tablet and stylus. Mostly, they just waited.

'At which door?' I wanted to know.

It varied, they said. Usually it was the rear door, into the central courtyard, but for the last day or two Quintus had seemed uneasy about something and had insisted that they wait in the ante-room, where they were closer at hand while he received his clientes.

Marcus was instantly all attention. 'So, Quintus did fear something?' he suggested. 'One of his clientes, perhaps?' He sounded grim, and I realised he was thinking again about the possible connection with Pertinax.

The slaves exchanged uncomfortable glances.

'Well?' Marcus demanded.

There was a pause, and then one of the slaves spoke up. 'I suppose he must have done, Excellence,' he said, doubtfully. 'Sollers thought so. He had the visitors give up their knives and leave them in full view. We . . . we were proved wrong, but we thought it was ridiculous. Many of the visitors came here every day. We knew most of them well – and even the citizens Flavius and Lupus are hardly strangers, at least by reputation. They are illustrious men, their names are well known to everyone in Corinium.'

'And how did they behave today?' Marcus wanted to know. 'Did they seem secretive? As if they were planning something?'

Again that awkward pause. 'Impatient, perhaps, at being made to wait,' one of the slaves said at last. 'They spoke very graciously to us.'

Meaning that they were generous with their tips, I

thought. I said, 'Did your master have some unexpected problem that you know of? Difficulty with his affairs? Something which troubled him suddenly?' That was a leading question. Slaves, listening unregarded in a corner, often know their owner's secret business better than he thinks.

One of the slaves shook his head. 'I do not think so, citizen. If he was anxious, it was only because he had been set on in the street. Of course, I could be wrong. We slaves would hardly know his affairs. Naturally, we didn't listen to what he said to his visitors, and in any case, he kept the discussions general when we were there. If he wanted to talk in private he sent us away.'

So Quintus suspected that you listened, I thought, suppressing a smile, and obviously he was right. Otherwise how did you know what he was discussing? Aloud I said, 'So he did not seem especially anxious today?'

The slave smiled. 'No. Twice he sent us off on unnecessary errands. His secretary could tell you more about that – he was usually there if Quintus was discussing business. Though there were times when the master sent everyone away. When Maximilian came, for instance.'

'Yes,' his companion added, 'and again when Julia visited him, and when Sollers came to bleed him earlier. That was not unusual. Our master was always . . . private, in that way.'

I nodded. Men who have been accustomed from birth to a houseful of slaves simply ignore their presence, treating them as no more than pieces of furniture, and conducting all their affairs – even the amorous ones – as though the watching slave had no more eyes and tongue than a table. Marcus did so himself. Quintus, coming to high position at a later age, clearly preferred more discretion in his private life. All the same, I thought, if a man is frightened for his safety, he does not surround himself with servants and then dismiss them at critical moments.

'So where were you,' Marcus asked, 'when Quintus was attacked?'

'We were in the slaves' room, next to the kitchen, waiting to be summoned back. The chief slave can vouch for that. We were attending our master when Maximilian came in from the front courtyard, stormed past Sollers and ordered us out of the back door. We were to get out till we were sent for, he said, and not to loiter listening in the courtyard.'

'You took orders from Maximilian?' Marcus sounded surprised.

The young man answered with surprising dignity. 'Excellence, we are slaves. We do as we are told. Maximilian is the son of the house and our master did not countermand the order. On the contrary, he dismissed the secretary himself. So we went. The next thing we knew, there was Sollers coming to find us, telling us that Quintus Ulpius was dead, and we were to go out straight away and buy oils for the anointers.'

'If you were in your waiting room,' I said slowly, 'how could you know when Quintus wanted you?'

'He kept a great bronze bowl on the table by his couch,' the lad replied. 'When he wanted us, he struck it with his cane.' He smiled. 'The sound could be heard anywhere in the building.'

Marcus intervened sharply. 'And the secretary? Did he go to the slaves' room too?'

'No. My master sent him somewhere with work to do – I think to this very room – to write some letter on a cliente's account, but I could not swear to it.'

Marcus scowled and turned to the other slave, who trembled at the magisterial attention but could offer nothing to the purpose. 'I regret it deeply, Excellence, but

I did not pay attention. Both my master and his son were in a terrible temper, and to tell the truth we were glad to get into the kitchen, and out of shouting range.'

The boy was right to be alarmed. Marcus was beginning to tap his baton against his hand, a sure sign that he was growing impatient. My patron is sometimes inclined to the good old Roman theory that a sound flogging is beneficial to the memory, and I feared he was about to put the theory to the test again.

I murmured swiftly, 'I am sure, Excellence, that the secretary can tell us that himself. We have learned a good deal already. Perhaps we should now speak to the slaves who discovered the body?'

'Very well. But I shall come to you again,' Marcus said, turning to the boy and terrifying him still further. 'For the moment, you may go.'

But the slaves who found the body seemed to have little of consequence to add. They were the two who had first attended us. They had gone, as Maximilian had instructed, to look for Julia and tell her that Quintus wanted her. They had looked for her: first in her quarters, then, with increasing agitation, in the garden, until it had occurred to one of them that, since she had left us with the intention of seeking an audience for us with her husband, perhaps she had gone to him already. 'We went to our master's room,' the spokesman said. 'The door was shut and there were no slaves on duty. We didn't like to go in – a lack of attendants usually meant that Ulpius wished to be private. But then we heard a noise, a kind of groan, and when we pushed open the door there was Quintus crawling towards us with a dagger in his back. He was moaning for Sollers, but we couldn't find him either, so we came back to you – and the rest you know.'

I asked sharp questions about the time they had spent

looking for Julia. Various people could verify that – Julia's handmaidens, for example, whom they met coming out of her rooms with a pile of garments, and a garden slave who was picking herbs for the kitchen. And they had spoken to the secretary when they looked into the study.

We had him in next. I recognised him at once as the disdainful servant who had looked at me so scornfully in the garden. Now, for the first time, I heard him speak, and I understood something of his arrogance. This was no ordinary slave. He spoke almost perfect Latin, and his vocabulary indicated a certain range of learning. I was fascinated, and longed to hear more about him, but for the moment he was answering Marcus's questions.

He could indeed corroborate the slaves' story and the testimony of Quintus's attendants. Maximilian had come, and demanded a private audience with his father – all the servants had been dismissed, the slaves to the waiting room, and himself to the study where he had been instructed to write a letter. He had remained there until I had seen him myself, crossing the courtyard after the murder.

It was a simple testimony, supported at all points, and Marcus would have dismissed him then and there, but the man interested me. He had an aloof, almost disdainful air, and although he was suitably deferential when speaking to Marcus, there was no mistaking the condescension behind the careful courtesy with which he answered my questions. Mutuus the scribe, for so he styled himself, was an unusual sort of household clerk.

'Who exactly are you?' I said, on an impulse.

'Citizen?' He sounded surprised, as well he might. Even Marcus was looking startled. It is not the kind of question one normally asks a slave.

'Have you been with your master long?' I persisted, and

saw Marcus relax. That kind of questioning he could understand. If Mutuus had worked at one time for an enemy of Pertinax, he might well be a paid informant. Every important household had its share of spies. You could almost see Marcus working it out.

'For Ulpius? A little less than a year. I came to him last Janus Feast.'

I waited for him to say more, but he didn't, and I had to prompt him. 'And before that?'

'Before that I was in another household. Here, in Corinium.'

He was telling us nothing. Marcus tapped his baton impatiently. 'Which household?' he demanded.

There was a perceptible pause. The answer, when it came, astonished me. 'The household of Paulus Avidius Lupus.'

'Great Mercury! Of Lupus! The old man who came here this morning? There was a conspiracy, I knew it. Why did he come here, slave? Why did he send you here to spy?'

Mutuus raised his head defiantly. 'I am no slave. I am simply a bondsman to Quintus, or was while he lived.'

I glanced at Marcus. That was no idle distinction. A man in civil bondage is not a mere living chattel, like a horse or a slave, to be disposed of or used at will. His labour, not his person, belongs to his master. And, as the young man suggested, bondage is often to a named individual. Such a bondsman is free on his master's death.

'*Mancipium*?' I said, giving civil bondage its legal name, and mentally rehearsing the possible reasons why a man might find himself subjected to it. Debtors, gladiators, estate workers and ransomed prisoners of war were the usual categories. Mutuus did not seem to fit any of these. Perhaps he was one of those rare clientes – a poor free man, who had pleaded the ancient customs of republican

Rome and thrown himself entirely on the mercy of his patron, binding himself in the process. But in that case, how had he come from Lupus's household? There was one way to find out. I asked him.

He looked at me with new respect. 'I am a distant kinsman of Lupus. My father, too, had money once, and gave me an education before he died and left me his debts. I repudiated the estate. I became a free-man scribe, and won a little reputation in the market place for the writing of letters and rendering accounts. Then Lupus heard of it. He needed a secretary. He took me into his household, and offered to adopt me as his heir, in return for my skills. I considered the offer for some months, but finally I acquiesced.'

I understood that. A good secretary is a rare prize, and Lupus must have been delighted with his bargain. Mutuus, for his part, would inherit the estate in a few years. What puzzled me was something else. 'He hated Quintus. Why did he send you here?'

Mutuus almost smiled. 'He did not send me here. Quintus demanded me, as legal recompense. He claimed I killed his servant in a street brawl.'

I hardly dared to breathe. 'You attacked him in the street?'

'And stabbed him? No. This was a year ago. I have wondered since whether Ulpius himself arranged it. Lupus had just adopted me formally; he had no direct heirs of his own, and we had to go before the magistrates to legalise the succession. We had just done so when Ulpius went by with his retinue. Naturally he had heard about it. He has long sought to destroy our family, as you may have heard, over an ancient grudge, and when he learned that Lupus now had a formal heir he was furious. I think he hoped there would be no clear line of inheritance, and then there would have been a hearing before the local curia and most of the estate would have ended up in the imperial coffers. No doubt Quintus, as a senior magistrate, would have got his share. There was a struggle.'

'Quintus attacked you?' Marcus was incredulous.

'No. That would have been beneath his dignity. But his servants began hurling insults and then stones, and a scuffle broke out. One bumptious young scoundrel jeered threateningly at me, and I stepped forward and knocked him down. I did not mean to kill him, but according to Quintus, he died an hour later. I was taken before the tribunal. Lupus would have paid compensation, but Ulpius claimed that the slave was Greek and highly educated, and put such a high price upon him and his services that Lupus simply could not afford to pay. He was obliged to give me in noxal surrender, in recompense for the "debt" I owed. Ulpius made me his secretary and forced me to write his letters and witness his accounts. A compliment to my learning, he insisted, but in fact it was a way of parading me before his business cronies and humiliating Lupus.'

'But he trusted you with his affairs?' I was surprised. In Quintus's position, I would have done nothing of the kind.

Mutuus shook his head. 'Having got me, he trusted me with nothing important. He made it clear that he doubted my honour. He checked every word I wrote, and sent me away if there was anything really important to discuss. It was foolish really, he could have afforded any secretary he chose – but he could not bear that Lupus had a finer one. I think that is why he insisted on the noxal surrender.'

'Noxal surrender!' Marcus said. 'Legal surrender into bondage in compensation for a wrong. I knew it was legally enforceable, of course, but it is years since I heard of the penalty being exacted. Noxal surrender of a slave, yes, or a horse. That's common enough. But never of a son. Even an adopted one.'

'If one has enough wealth,' Mutuus said, 'all sorts of ancient laws can be invoked. Especially if one is a senior officer of the curia. And it amused Ulpius to have me here.'

'Just as it amused him to give you your bond name?' I suggested. 'Mutuus, the borrowed one.' From what I was learning of Quintus, he would have found that humorous.

'Exactly,' Mutuus agreed. 'Although, of course, I am his bondsman no longer. His death releases me. Lupus will have his desire.'

'That is what he came for? To ask for your release?'

'Or to bargain for it, I think. I cannot be sure. Ulpius did not permit written communication between us. In any case, Lupus did not write well. That is why he needed a secretary.'

'Because of his stiff hand?' I asked.

Mutuus shook his head. 'I saw, today, that he was favouring his hand. He did not have a problem that I knew of. I only know that he could not write well – nor read for that matter – beyond carved capitals on inscriptions. He could read those. He took me out of town, more than once, to read me the inscriptions on the roadside tombs. I think he was proud of his achievement.'

'But you did not see your adoptive father this morning?'

'I saw him arrive, of course. He was in the ante-room with the other supplicants. I did not speak to him alone.'

'Nor see him do anything suspicious?'

Mutuus smiled wryly. 'Citizen, I was sent to this room. The door was closed and so were the windows. How could I see anything from here? There is glass in the windows.'

I saw Marcus glance at the windows. They were glazed, as Mutuus said, in the latest fashion, with little panes of expensive Roman glass – bluey-green in colour and wonderful for letting in light and keeping out draughts, but impossible to see through. He nodded in understanding.

'I see. Thank you, citizen, you have been most helpful.'

The significance of the title was not lost on Mutuus. For the first time since he had entered the room there was a genuine smile on his lips. 'Thank you, Excellence. Please let me know if I can be of further help.' He bowed deeply and left the room.

'Well,' Marcus said, as soon as he had gone. 'That simplifies matters, doesn't it? Ten *denarii* to an *as* it was Lupus who did it. I thought so when I met him. I've never seen a man look more guilty, but I could not see a motive. Now I understand. Wanted Mutuus back, and chose the quickest route to free him. And he's hated Quintus for years. What do you think, Libertus?'

I was thinking about a number of things, not least the fact that Mutuus had avoided answering my question about speaking to his father.

'I think,' I replied carefully, 'that I should like to take another look around the garden, before it gets too dark to see.'

Chapter Seven

Marcus smiled indulgently but he was adamant. The questioning was merely a formality now, he felt, and the sooner these irksome requirements of justice were over and Lupus was under lock and key, the better for everyone. If this was a mere personal murder and not a political matter, his tone implied, his further interest in it was brisk. Why did I suddenly want to waste time looking around the grounds?

I chose my words carefully. Marcus is a powerful man, and when it comes to the exercise of that power, it is dangerous to thwart him, even if he does call you 'friend'. Sometimes especially if he calls you friend.

'Excellence,' I said, 'I am a humble maker of mosaics. It troubles me to cut a piece which will not fit the pattern. Yet sometimes, seen from another angle, the solution is obvious. The tile which would not match the centrepiece finds a place in the border.'

He looked at me wryly. 'And which are the pieces of tile, to use your quaint analogy, which do not fit the pattern here? Everything points to Lupus. He had a pressing motive. He had the opportunity – he was in the front courtyard when the murder happened. He knew where the weapon was: the dagger was in full view when he was waiting in the ante-room earlier, and when he saw Mutuus leave the building he knew the coast was clear. Perhaps Mutuus even told him so – when you asked if he had spoken to Lupus this morning, he carefully avoided the question.' He leaned forward from his chair and patted me on the shoulder. 'You look surprised, old friend. Did you not notice that?'

In fact, my surprise was occasioned by the fact that Marcus had noticed it himself, but I had more wit than to say so. 'You are perceptive, Excellence.'

He beamed. 'Yes, I believe I am. There may be other suspects, Libertus, but one thing I am certain of: I know guilt when I see it. That old man had the smell of fear about him. Flavius may swear they were together in the garden, but I'll wager there were times he turned his back. And they were at the chariot races, too.' I must have looked dubious, because he waved his hand loftily. 'Of course, I know you will argue that in that case Flavius might have committed the crime himself and that he hated Quintus too – but that old man Lupus has something to hide, or I'm a Druid.'

'I am sure that you are right, Excellence,' I said meekly. I did not mention the conversation I had overheard in the garden, or no doubt Lupus would have been clapped in irons then and there. In any case, I meant what I said. I, too, had the impression that Lupus knew more about this matter than he admitted, but I doubted that the solution was quite as clear-cut as Marcus supposed. It occurred to me, for instance, that an equal opportunity would have existed for Mutuus himself.

Besides, Marcus's reasoning was faulty, in at least one respect.

I put it as delicately as I could. 'Excellence,' I said, 'when Maximilian left his father, he didn't, as far as we know, go into either courtyard garden. He came to us through the interior of the house. One reason I want to examine the grounds is to discover whether Lupus, or anyone else, could possibly have detected that. Otherwise, how could he know that Quintus was alone?'

There was a moment while Marcus digested the implications of this, and then he said rather sourly, 'Perhaps you are right. But don't be long about it. I shall carry on the questioning while you are gone. I shall have Flavius in and ask him about that alibi. Otherwise we shall still be here at dawn.'

This was not at all what I would have chosen, but I could not argue with Marcus, and it was too late to change my mind. I was regretting my decision by the time I reached the door, and when I saw that Maximilian was waiting impatiently on the veranda outside, I regretted it still more. He wore a dignified funeral wreath on his head and a ritual stole of rough sackcloth around his neck to signify sombre grief, but the impression he gave was one of barely concealed truculence.

'At last, citizen!' he exclaimed, as soon as he saw me. 'I suppose this is what a man may expect, in his own house? To be summoned like a common servant and then left on the veranda, to be stared at by every passing menial sniggering behind their hands? My father would not even have used his meanest clients so.'

There were indeed 'menials' about, though they had little time for sniggering. The house and courtyard were abuzz with activity. The door of the ante-room opposite was open now, and through it I could see a press of people – red-faced anointing women packing up their wicker baskets of oils on the table, and pallid funeral musicians tuning their pipes. Four perfectly matched slaves (how Quintus would have enjoyed that) were manoeuvring a heavy gilded bier on a litter from the courtyard in the direction of the reception room, from the invisible recesses of which a plume of pungent smoke was already rising – presumably the first of the herbs and candles were being lighted around the corpse. All this seemed to be taking place under the direction of Sollers, who was supervising operations from the interior of the ante-room. He looked up and saw me, and raised a hand in salute before the litter made its way inside and the outer door was closed again.

'You see?' Maximilian demanded. 'I shall be wanted any minute. It is I who should be there with my father's corpse, not Sollers. My father did not want me living – he has resented me since my childhood – but I should at least be beside him in his death. It is my place to put the coin in his mouth for his ferry fare over the Styx . . .'

'And to start the lament,' I finished. 'I know. I am sure Marcus will not keep you long.'

'There is nothing further I can tell him in any case. I came here to see my father, to do my filial duty, that is all.'

'Except to ask for money,' I reminded him.

He scowled. 'Well, yes. That too. But it was a trivial amount, no more than five hundred sesterces.'

Five hundred sestertces would keep me in comfort for weeks, but I said nothing.

'Anyway, he wouldn't give it to me. Ranted about my extravagance and then sent me off to look for Julia. That's all.'

I was about to tell him to explain it to Marcus, when a thought struck me. 'And did you do it?' I said.

'Do what?'

'Look for Julia? Did you go anywhere else before you came to us?'

He coloured. 'I . . . I don't know. I can't remember. What if I did? I was on my father's errand.'

'Maximilian,' I said patiently, 'think. You came here to borrow money. He refused you, even threatened to cut you out of his will. You were alone with him, and you knew there was a dagger on a table in the adjoining room. Shortly afterwards your father is found crawling about with that same knife in his back and your financial troubles are magically over. One does not need to be a Greek philosopher to draw a logical conclusion.'

He gaped at me, all irritation gone. 'You think . . .?' – I saw the panic in his eyes – 'You really think I killed him?'

'I confess, citizen, that I find the circumstances just a little suspicious. Of course, if you are able to recall where you went when you left – whether you came straight to us, for example – that may assist you. Could anyone have seen you leave your father's room, for instance?'

He seemed to consider this, and hesitated, but he said nothing.

'Well,' I said, 'Marcus is waiting for you. Tell him your story, citizen, and try to sharpen your memory before he finds ways of doing it for you.'

Maximilian gave me a scowl as though I were the personal cause of all his miseries, and slammed past me into the study. Shortly afterwards I heard the murmur of voices.

In fact, simply by coming out here, I had answered one of my own questions. From here, between the screen of trees, I could see the front gate and most of the colonnaded walk: there was a clear view into the ante-room opposite, as I had just demonstrated, and Mutuus had been standing here earlier when he witnessed me eavesdropping by the hedge. Anyone leaving the study, or simply standing behind the open door, could take in most of the garden at a glance, apart from the deliberately secluded arbours. No other spot in the house commanded such a wide vista. Perhaps Quintus had designed it like that, on purpose, so that he could survey the fountains and greenery from the comfort of his study.

I walked thoughtfully down the veranda of the study wing, and past the doorway which led into the atrium and so to the main rooms of the house. Through it I caught sight of pairs of slaves, still hurrying to and fro with platters and wine, and the sound of a lute and a plaintive song wafted from the triclinium. Lupus and Flavius, although unwilling guests, were evidently still enjoying the 'light meal' which Sollers had organised, presumably in Julia's company. I shook myself impatiently. I had come to Corinium, at least in part, in the hope of continuing my search for Gwellia. Why should it matter to me where Julia was?

I walked through the atrium and out into the rear courtyard again.

It, too, was alive with industry. There were slaves everywhere: some scurrying past with serving dishes and lamps for the living, others clearly already preparing the memorial feast of the dead. Kitchen slaves were cutting sprigs of rosemary from the border, others were fetching water in wooden buckets from the fountain, or dried fruit and barley flour in brimming bowls from the stores. A brawny cook appeared, a brace of fat hens fluttering upside down in either hand, and as I watched, a party of slaves returned from the market stalls bearing between them a great side of bleeding meat, long strings of river fish and a dozen dead thrushes on a pole. The ghost of Quintus would not return vengeful from the afterworld because it had not been fed.

The rear court was smaller than the front, and was divided into quarters by walkways radiating from the pool. Each quarter was planted with its own selection of sweet-scented plants and herbs for the kitchen, with a fruit tree at its centre, and each had a small grotto in the corner nearest the pool, presumably with a seat and a statue of one of the gods set on a plinth. Anyone crossing the courtyard, or using the covered path which skirted it, was clearly visible from all sides, and the slaves collecting herbs were constantly in view, unless they were momentarily screened by the statues and the trees, or simply by bending down among the plants.

One figure, however, caught my eye. It was a female slave, with a cape drawn over her head and a jug in her hand, and her manner, as she came out of the kitchens, could only be described as 'skulking'. She looked nervously to left and right, and then scuttled along one of the paths towards the pool. When she looked up and saw me, she dropped the jug and disappeared into a grotto. I was baffled. It was my presence, clearly, which she wanted to avoid – she had walked openly past the other servants.

I waited for a moment, but she did not reappear. I thought of marching in and confronting her, but the girl had seemed so embarrassed that I decided to finish my stroll around the perimeter walk, and explore the grotto later.

Like the rest of the house, the courtyard was built to impress, with fine mural patterns on the inner walls and a paved walkway linking the rooms under the sloping shelter of a roof. All the guest apartments, including my own, were on this side of the courtyard, and were self-contained. So were the kitchens, slave rooms, store rooms and latrines in the separate block at the back. Maximilian had once had a bedroom in the main block, in a small room near his father's reception suite, reached by a second passage to the rear court. But Quintus, Julia and Sollers had their apartments in the wing opposite me.

I wondered if any of the apartments were interconnecting. Usually rooms in courtyard houses are self-contained, with a blind wall to the outside world and a single doorway opening onto the inner walkway. I stopped a passing slave who was rolling a cask of fattened snails towards the kitchen, and he confirmed my guess. The rooms in the farther block were arranged as two suites. Sollers had a sleeping room with a small adjacent study, and there was an interconnecting door between the apartments of Quintus and his wife. For moments when he hoped to make a son, presumably. Marcus would not find that thought pleasing.

I sent the slave about his business and continued my stroll. I kept glancing towards the central grotto, but wherever I stood, it was largely screened from view. The caped figure was invisible. When I turned my back, however, to glance into the slaves' waiting room, there was a scuttling behind me, and I turned around just in time to see her slip out, retrieve her jug and scurry as fast as possible in the direction of the main block. She disappeared into the far passage and was gone.

The light was fading now, and I was anxious to get back to Marcus before he finished his enquiries without me. Since he had mentally identified Lupus as the killer, I knew that his questions to everyone else were likely to be perfunctory.

All the same, I wanted to examine the grotto. The girl had hidden there. Could a killer have done the same – perhaps even as Marcus and I were hurrying to the murder scene? I walked across and examined the bowers carefully, but there was nothing particular to see. No helpful fragments of cloth caught on the stone seats, no wisps of hair trailing on the branches, no footprints with distinctive hobnail patterns imprinted in the earth. I looked at the statues. They were half as high as a man, and elegantly carved. A predictable foursome: Jupiter, Mercury, Mars and Minerva. Quintus, it seemed, had a particular attachment to Minerva. It was her statue which I had also noted in the front courtyard, though this was a far superior sculpture.

I moved a little closer. Certainly, someone in the household favoured the goddess. There had been recent oblations offered at the shrine. Small fragments of bread and morsels of honey cake had been scattered on the plinth, where the birds were accepting them gratefully, if Minerva had not. Someone had offered a libation too; there was a dark dampness in the fresh earth channel in front of the statue, as if someone had poured out a liberal cupful of red wine. I bent and touched my fingers to the earth.

They came away sticky, and I gazed at them in dismay. A swift sniff confirmed my suspicions. The liquid had been red all right, but it was not wine. Someone had offered Minerva a libation of fresh blood.

The caped girl had not put it there. She had dropped her jug before she went into the grotto, and in any case the libation was too old for that. Of course there was another possible explanation. Animal sacrifice is common at Roman festivals, the blood poured out by the officiant and the flesh eaten afterwards. In wealthy households like this, the monthly festivals were usually marked by a family sacrifice. Yet it was far from the first or last day of the month, and the earth was still moist. Even allowing for the general dampness of the air and soil, this blood had been spilled here not many hours ago. Since we had been at the house, I guessed. But there had been no mention of a memorial sacrifice, no family attendance at the shrine, and there had been none of the squawking and squealing which usually accompany the ritual slaughter of chickens, lambs or pigs.

No: the more I thought of it, the more sure I became.

This libation, if that was what it was, had been made earlier, and secretly. And in that case there was a possibility that the blood was human. Not, of course, that there was any way of finding that out for certain.

It was a macabre thought and I got to my feet, shivering. I must report this to Marcus.

As I turned to go, a sudden sound pierced the air, an unearthly, eerie, ululating wail that shivered the blood. It reached out mournfully to every shadowed corner, and echoed dismally around the empty columns.

Maximilian had begun the lament.

Chapter Eight

I re-entered the house, to return to Marcus. In the atrium, however, I encountered a commotion. Two burly slaves swaggered self-importantly in from the front courtyard, each with a knife in his hand, and between them, prodded at dagger-point, with his head bowed and his arms bound firmly behind him, came Lupus.

He was protesting volubly. 'I can explain, I can explain. Let me talk to His Excellence!'

His captors, however, ignored him. There was a rope around his neck, and he was being dragged along, none too gently. As I watched in amazement he was half-pulled, half-prodded along the passage to the narrow staircase and disappeared, still protesting, towards the attics.

The chief slave had come in behind them, and I confronted him at once. 'What in the name of Mercury . . .?'

The chief slave said, 'His Excellence ordered this arrest, citizen. He has found strong evidence against Lupus.' He smiled. 'I confess it is a relief to me. At least now we can admit the funeral guests tomorrow. His Excellence has lifted his restrictions on the gate. But he will tell you himself. He is awaiting you in the study.'

I needed no second bidding. When I got there, Marcus was looking pleased with himself.

'Ah, there you are, old friend,' he exclaimed heartily as soon as I appeared. 'Back from your explorations? I fear you were wasting your time. You know that I have now settled the matter?'

'I know,' I said carefully, 'that Lupus has been arrested.' I had to speak loudly. Outside in the courtyard, Maximilian was excelling himself in the lament and the wailing pipes struck up to swell the sound.

Marcus beamed. 'Lupus is our man,' he said, over the uproar. 'I knew it all along. I've had him locked up in the attics for the night, and I'll order the town gaol to provide an armed escort tomorrow to take him to Pertinax. As a Roman citizen, the old man will have to go to the imperial courts, so there is no point in getting the gaoler out of bed at this hour.'

'Lupus says he can explain,' I said.

Marcus snorted. 'No doubt he does. I've heard half a dozen versions of the story already. But it will do him no good. The evidence is too strong. I don't know what they will do to him in the end. Not execution, probably; more likely he'll be sentenced to the mines, or – given his age – simply exiled and stripped of everything. Nevertheless, a satisfactory outcome. I am only sorry that you were not here to see it.' He smiled at me triumphantly.

I gulped. 'You are . . . certain of this?' I hesitated. 'I felt that the circumstances surrounding Maximilian, for instance, were interesting to say the least.'

Marcus waved a dismissive hand. 'Maximilian is an oaf. If I had been his father, I would have done more than threaten to disinherit him, I would have reminded him that I officially had the power of life and death over him. That would have wiped the smirk from his beardless face. But he had nothing significant to add. Except that he now says he went to Julia's apartments before he came to us. She wasn't there, he says, so he went to his old rooms to see if there was anything of value he could salvage, in case

Quintus carried out his threat and cut him off without a sestertius.'

'Did he now? I suppose it is possible. There is a door there that leads to the rear courtyard. I noticed that a moment ago. But in that case, why did he not say so before?'

'Who knows? He did it, though. Rollo saw him crossing the back courtyard while he was in the slaves' room. I had him in to check. But it was Flavius who provided the really vital information. As soon as I started questioning him, it was clear that although he and Lupus had been sent out to the front garden to wait together, he spent most of the time pacing about the colonnade alone and actually had no idea where Lupus was, or what he was doing for most of the period. Found the old man a bit of a bore, I suspect, and was actively trying to ignore him. When I pressed him to remember, he said he had a dim impression that the old man had been walking about at one stage, but he couldn't swear to it. He couldn't give me a coherent account of what Lupus did and said, even when they were together.'

I could believe that, I thought. If I had come to this house to sue for Julia – if I had been married to her and lost her and now saw her wedded to someone else – I should scarcely have noticed Lupus if that animated skeleton had torn off his toga and danced naked around the fountain.

'All the same, Excellence . . .' I began, doubtfully, but Marcus prevented me with a smile.

'All the same, you are not sure that Lupus is guilty? You are such a doubter, old friend. Then let me tell you this. Flavius had one piece of testimony which even you cannot quarrel with. During the meal just now, a slave was pouring wine. Lupus forgot what he was doing, and stretched out that "stiff" hand of his – and where he had been clutching

91

his toga, there were bloodstains on his sleeve. Flavius swears that Lupus saw him looking, and turned as green as grass. Obviously he had been holding his right arm like that as a way of concealing the marks, but he forgot that it was supposed to be stiff in his desire for wine. Spent the rest of the meal trying to conceal the marks again, apparently, but it was too late by then.'

'Bloodstains?' I was not expecting that. 'I found a blood libation to Minerva in the rear court,' I said. 'I was coming to tell you about it. You don't think Lupus somehow managed to trail his hems in that?'

Marcus looked at me pityingly. 'How could he? He has not been to the rear courtyard. Besides, if he had any kind of excuse, he'd have given it.'

Lupus *had* been trying to give an excuse, I thought, but no one was listening to him. I dared not say that to Marcus, however. 'You are sure they were bloodstains?'

'I saw them myself. And don't tell me that the man may have picked them up in the market. He came here in a litter, dressed for a formal interview with Quintus. In those circumstances a man ensures that his toga sleeves are clean.'

I could hardly argue with that.

'I sent for Lupus,' Marcus said, 'and asked him to lift his arm. He pretended he couldn't do it at first, but when I threatened to have him flogged he managed it fast enough. Fresh bloodstains. Lupus gurgled and burbled but he could not account for them. I told you the man was hiding something.'

'I see,' I said, slowly. 'Stains on his sleeve. That is certainly suspicious. It is only that . . .'

'What?' Marcus demanded. 'A man with motive, means and opportunity is found, after a murder, with bloodstains on his sleeve. Furthermore, he acknowledges that he was at the chariot races. What more do you want? Testimony from the corpse?' He was mocking, but there was real impatience in it. I knew from the way he was tapping his baton on his hand.

I chose my words with care. 'It is only, Excellence, that Lupus is an old man. Of course, you have evidence now that he can use his arm, but that dagger was driven in with dreadful force. You remember Sollers said it had chipped a bone.'

The baton stopped. 'An interesting point, old friend. But even an old man can sometimes find surprising reserves of strength. Perhaps we should ask the *medicus* what he thinks. In any case, I do not believe that Lupus is quite the invalid he pretends in other respects. He talks of his swollen knees and aching joints, but I saw him move with surprising sprightliness just now, when there was a dagger at his back. He could have hurried to Quintus's room swiftly enough if he chose.'

I had to admit the justice of that. I had come to the same conclusion myself. 'And the message,' I said, slowly. ' "Remember Pertinax". You think he was responsible for that too? Today was the first time he had visited the house, yet that tablet was found at least two days ago.'

Marcus frowned. 'He must have smuggled it into the house somehow. Or perhaps he had Mutuus write it for him.' He brightened. 'Yes, that would account for it. Mutuus is his adopted son, and he would have access to wax tablets if he needed them.' He stopped, and added more thoughtfully, 'Lupus must have heard about that attack on Pertinax. I wonder how? He is not on the *curia* now, and it is not common rumour. Doubtless Lupus had his spies.'

I shrugged politely. 'It is possible, Excellence. Who, in Corinium, might have known the truth?'

Marcus looked grave. 'I do not know. Perhaps Lupus can tell us. I shall have him questioned again tomorrow. If the old man knows anything he will tell us, soon enough.'

I took a deep breath. 'In the meantime, Excellence, have I your permission to continue my own enquiries?' Privately I was still convinced that, whatever Lupus did, he was not acting alone. This killing had the marks of bold decision: someone had seen an opportunity and acted swiftly. What I had seen of Lupus did not accord with that. Although, I reminded myself, he had deceived us about his arm.

He looked at me wryly. 'Still doubting, Libertus?'

I thought quickly. 'I should like to be of some help, Excellence. About that wax tablet, for instance. To prove that you did not bring me here in vain.'

He smiled indulgently. 'Very well. You have my permission to keep your eyes open. I suppose at the least you can do no harm. It must be disappointing to find yourself superfluous. I suppose Quintus will not even require his pavement, now.'

I had not considered that. I should have done; that commission was a matter of pressing financial interest. I said, hopefully, 'Unless he has endowed one in his will. We shall know tomorrow, I suppose, when the testament is opened in the forum.'

He made a grimace. 'Yes, and no doubt as house guests we shall be expected to attend the formalities. It is all very inconvenient – since we were in the house when the death occurred, we shall have to be ritually purified as well – but there is no escape, I suppose. In any case, Libertus, it has been a long day. I should like to retire to my quarters. Go and find a slave to help me. I shall require lamps, of course, and a portable brazier if they have one; the night threatens to be cold. And see if the kitchens can send someone with a tray of something warming – I have not dined sub-stantially today. Although,' he added, gesturing towards the courtyard, where the lamentation still wailed and moaned, 'I doubt that I shall sleep, with that confounded caterwauling in my ears all night.'

I did not have to search for long for a slave. The courtyard was dark, but the chief slave had positioned himself outside the door with a candle, and I had hardly set foot on the veranda when I caught sight of Sollers, now dressed formally in a toga, crossing the courtyard with the turquoise page who was holding a lighted link for him. From other rooms in the house one could detect the flicker of lamplight under doorways and through the clouded windows. Maximilian's lament had dimmed to a sobbing moan.

The doctor stopped when he saw me, and came to join me. I was giving Marcus's orders to the chief slave.

Sollers heard me out and then nodded to him sharply. 'See to it instantly. And arrange braziers and lamps for this good citizen, too. He is also our guest.' He turned to the page. 'And you, Rollo, go to your mistress and tell her that I will come directly. Leave us the taper.' The two slaves hastened off together to do his bidding, and Sollers turned to me. 'I am going to prepare a fortifying draught for her, before she takes her turn at the lament. And I suppose a couch should be prepared in one of the public rooms for Flavius, since His Excellency insists that he should stay here, because of his evidence. I hear Lupus is under lock and key in an attic.'

'Marcus is convinced he is the murderer.'

Sollers looked at me, his face shadowed and quizzical in the candlelight. 'But you are not.'

'Are you?'

Sollers grinned. 'I confess I am surprised. He would not

have been my first suspect.' He looked at me, that remarkable face glimmering in the taper-light. 'But I bow to your judgement. You are no mere pavement-maker, I hear. Julia tells me you are an esteemed solver of mysteries.'

It was my turn to smile. 'And you are a thinker yourself. Whom would you have suspected, citizen? You know the household better than I do.'

He seemed flattered that I had asked his opinion, although he was embarrassed at the question. 'It is hardly my place, citizen,' he said at last, 'but in your position I would have questioned Maximilian. He seems to have had the greatest opportunity. And a motive. You heard that his father threatened to disinherit him? He told him so this very morning, too.'

I nodded. 'My thoughts exactly. Except that in that case, one would have expected Maximilian to disguise the fact. Instead, he told me about it himself. And look how he reacted to the body. Almost as if he wanted to be accused.'

Sollers looked at me in surprise. 'I see your point, pavement-maker. I had not considered that. Although Maximilian is a crass young man. He may not even have seen the danger. Or perhaps his arrogance was all a bluff. Certainly he needed money, and he did not love his father. I should not have put it past him to arrange that attack in the street.' He smiled doubtfully. 'But perhaps I am wrong and His Excellence is right. They tell me Lupus had bloodstains on his clothes.'

News travels swiftly in a household of servants. I nodded. 'As you did yourself, earlier,' I said, and had the satisfaction of seeing him look startled. 'Even before you examined the body.'

There was a moment's shocked silence, and then he threw back his head and laughed. 'Did I, indeed? From when I bled him earlier, no doubt. You are observant, pavement-maker. But I see your reasoning. In your place, I should be suspicious of me. After all, I profit by his will. He leaves me, I think, a small gratuity. Although I promise you, citizen, if I had wanted to murder Quintus, I should have used some subtlety.'

I smiled. 'You misunderstand me, medicus,' I said. 'I meant to argue that a man does not have to be a killer to have blood on his sleeve. Oh, of course it had occurred to me to wonder if you had stabbed him. But why should you do that? All you had to do was introduce a little poison into the wound, or give him a potion, and he would be dead within a week, still thanking you for your loving care of him. You say he had promised you a gratuity, but if he disinherited his son – as you knew he was threatening to do – your portion would soon have been even greater. As you say, you are not unsubtle. Why would you, of all people, choose this moment to plunge a clumsy dagger in his back?'

I was holding the candle and his hand closed warmly around mine for a moment. 'I apologise, citizen. I under-estimated you. I should have seen that a man of your intelligence would appreciate these things at once.'

I was unreasonably flattered by his praise. 'I had an unfair advantage,' I explained. 'I saw you tending Quintus after he was stabbed in the street. I know that without you he would undoubtedly have died that night.'

He was surprised. 'You were there?'

'In a shop nearby. I witnessed it by accident. But you did not look like a would-be murderer to me.'

He laughed. 'I see. I thought you were merely a good judge of men!' His face grew serious. 'Now, I must go to Julia. Maximilian is fading in his lament, and ritual requires that she take his place. Is there anything further that you need from me?'

I would have liked to speak to Julia, but this was not the moment. In the morning, perhaps. I was surprised to find how much I was looking forward to it. After all, I thought suddenly, Julia herself could well have stabbed her husband. She was not in her apartments when Maximilian called.

To Sollers I said, 'One question, citizen. I want your professional opinion. Did Lupus have the strength to deal that blow?'

He thought for a moment. 'Perhaps, if he lunged at Ulpius with all his weight. I should like to say "no", and certainly he would have to be lucky to strike so fatally. But it is possible, yes.'

'Thank you, citizen.' I grinned. 'And if you are making a tonic draught for Julia, perhaps you can offer one to Marcus, too. He is worn out by his exertions and complaining that he will not sleep for Maximilian's wailing.'

Sollers laughed softly. 'I will send a sleeping draught on his tray. And one for you too, if you like. But now, here are the slaves coming with the lamps. Excuse me, I must go to Julia. Are you sure there is nothing else you require?'

I was about to say no when a happy thought struck me. 'Yes,' I said suddenly, 'I would like my own attendant. Have Junio sent to me.'

Chapter Nine

Junio was endearingly pleased to see me. He was not accustomed to endless hours of waiting. Back at the Glevum workshop, he was my only servant. He helped me with everything, and I was additionally teaching him the rudiments of pavement-making. One day, when he gained his freedom, when I was gone or he was old enough to manumit, I intended that he would have a trade to support himself.

Several hours of idleness in the attic had been hard for him to bear, and he threw himself into my service with enthusiasm. A pair of matching slaves had been sent to tend me, but Junio would not allow them near me. He insisted on doing everything himself. He stoked the braziers, trimmed the wicks, fetched water to bathe my hands and feet, combed oils through my hair and beard, plumped up my cushions, extricated me from my outer garments, lighted my way to the latrine and finally tucked me up, cleansed and shining, under the woven blankets on the luxurious Roman bed – wooden frame, webbed base, padded mattress and all. When, after all that, he sat down on the floor beside me and began to fold and brush my toga, I took pity on the waiting pair and sent them away.

Junio, who up until then had been according me unaccustomed respect, and speaking only when spoken to, put down his work as soon as they were gone and grinned at me cheerfully. 'No spiced mead tonight, master.' It was my favourite nightcap, but not one I expected to find in a Roman household. 'How will you ever sleep? And on such an uncomfortable bed, too.'

I found myself grinning back. My bed at home was a humble pile of reeds and rags. 'Doubtless I shall manage. The physician has promised me a sleeping draught.' I explained to Junio the events of the day.

He nodded. 'I heard that Quintus Ulpius was dead, of course. Eventually. We thought something must have happened – Marcus's slave and I – we were promised bread and cheese in the attic, but no one came near us for hours. We did not worry at first: we had a gaming board, and I was beating him at twelve-stones.'

I sighed. It was no use remonstrating with Junio: he had been raised in the sort of Roman household where even the slaves learned to gamble as soon as they could count. Even if the dice were loaded, as they often were, he could calculate odds faster than I could measure a pavement. 'I hope he could afford it?'

'I took four *as* coins from him before he lost interest. Then finally one of the servants brought us word.'

'And your bread and cheese, I hope?'

Junio chuckled. 'No, in fact, when the food did come we ate like kings. Pickled beef and fruit. I don't know who authorised it. The girl who brought it gave us the news, and said that the whole household was in uproar.'

I nodded. 'What else did she tell you? I should like to know the servants' gossip.' A man's slaves often know more about his household than he knows himself. 'Did she have anything to say about Julia, for instance? What do her maidservants think of her?'

Junio made a wry face at me. 'They think she takes an insufficient interest in the household, and devotes herself too much to men's affairs. She is vain about her looks, too.

She surrounds herself with unattractive maidservants on purpose, and is forever taking potions and spending a fortune on powders and perfumes. Though it is doubtful that the male slaves think the same. Julia can charm anything in a toga, and I hear that every man in the household has fallen for it to some degree, from the kitchen boy to the surgeon. The secretary in particular is quite besotted with her.'

I thought of tall, awkward, pedantic Mutuus and laughed. 'And what did Quintus Ulpius think of that?'

'His reaction was very much like yours. More amused than anything, from what I hear. This Mutuus is a citizen by birth, taken in noxal surrender. He apparently has ideas above his station and follows Julia about like a pet lamb. He makes himself quite ridiculous. Thinks she values his learning, since she seems to like clever men, though he is simply a slave to her. Quintus thought it was funny, by all accounts, though he could be obsessively jealous if there was any real rival. He hated Julia's former husband, for instance. Flavius, is that his name?'

I nodded. 'It was quite mutual.' I knew that there was no love lost between Quintus and Flavius. 'So Quintus was fond of his new wife?'

'Devoted to her. He quarrelled violently with his son about it. Maximilian resents Julia – he must be the only male who does. He has never forgiven his father for marrying again. His own mother died last year, drinking bad water from a well, but Ulpius divorced her many years ago. She was a beauty once, apparently, but she had no dowry, and then she caught the pox.'

Poor creature, I thought. It would not be the first time an illness had stripped a woman of both her looks and her husband. 'No wonder Julia is so careful of her health and appearance, if her predecessor caught a disfiguring disease.'

'All this attention to her looks certainly seems to work. Quintus Ulpius is delighted with her – or was. He would have liked another son, they say, and was prepared to work very hard to have one.' He gave me a wicked smile. 'But there was no sign of success, and she was consulting Sollers secretly.' His grin broadened. 'Not so secretly as she thinks, of course. One of the slaves found out, and now they all know. Though they do say that perhaps the fault is not with Julia.'

I frowned at him. 'With Quintus, then? But surely, Maximilian . . .?'

'Is not much like his father, do you not think? But this is merely rumour. Of course, if Quintus could not sire an heir, no doubt Mutuus would have been very glad to help.'

'You are not suggesting . . .' I was horrified.

He grinned. 'Oh, no, I don't think so. Quintus would have had his nose cut off if there was any suggestion of that! No, it is just that Mutuus has dreams. The maidservants think it is hilarious.'

'Who told you this?'

He gave me that impudent look again. 'Don't look so startled, master. You've taught me how to ask questions. I was told by a bald-headed slave girl.'

I gazed at him in surprise. 'Bald-headed?'

'Julia isn't a bad mistress, but she is heartless in some ways. She sometimes does buy good-looking slaves. She won't let them attend her, but she gets them for their hair. She has them forcibly shaved and then sold on again when their locks have grown back a little. The girl who brought us our supper was one of them – she was bought and sheared last week and is still balder than a rat's tail. She is feeling her humiliation deeply – it was not difficult to make her talk about her mistress.'

I nodded. A girl with no hair. This, clearly, was the

explanation of that caped female in the garden. She would have been sent to serve the slaves, because she was useless for public duties. The cape was obviously to cover her head while she went to the kitchens for the food. But she would have been punished severely if anyone knew she'd been seen – I was glad I had not confronted her in the grotto. But I could not resist the enquiry. 'Why did Julia want the hair?'

'She has several elaborate hairpieces, for different occasions.'

This was an unpleasant idea. I thought of my Gwellia and her lovely hair. Had that, too, been brutally shaved off to serve some mistress's vanity? Or, worse still, lovingly dressed and brushed to rouse a master's fancy?

I said sharply, 'I want to see Julia in the morning. There is something about her that I can't get out of my mind.'

Junio seized upon my words at once. 'You have felt her charm too, master? You surprise me. I thought you immune to such things.'

'That is not what I meant,' I said severely. 'There is something I would like her to explain, that's all. You should be able to work out what it is.'

Junio gazed at me thoughtfully. I encouraged him sometimes to follow my reasoning and make deductions, just as I taught him to lay mosaics. It was another skill I hoped to leave him with, by and by. He shook his head.

'When she left us . . .' I prompted, and saw the understanding dawn on his face.

'Of course,' he said eagerly, 'she was going straight to Ulpius. Only she didn't go. Maximilian came from his father on purpose to look for her.'

'Exactly,' I agreed. 'So if she did not go to her husband, why not? Where did she go instead?'

'And if she *did* go to him,' Junio said slowly, 'she must

have been the last to see Ulpius alive. Or . . .' he looked at me with dawning comprehension, 'the first to see him dead. I see! No wonder you want to speak to her. I am sorry, master, to have made a jest of it.'

I was just contemplating a magnanimous reply when there was a timid tap on the apartment door. Junio got up to open it, and I saw the turquoise page standing on the threshold, bearing an enormous carrying tray. He came in and set it carefully on the little locking chest beside the bed.

'I am bidden to bring you this, citizen. His Excellence requested food, and it was thought you would require some too.' He glanced covertly at the poor, faded under-tunic which I had kept on as a nightshirt, and which I was now attempting, not very successfully, to hide under the blankets. 'And Sollers has sent you a sleeping draught. I did not realise you had retired for the night.'

I looked at the dishes set out upon the tray, and recognised, not for the first time, the privilege of rank. The kitchens of this house were straining with the preparations for a funeral banquet, which, given Quintus's position in the town, was clearly to be a sumptuous one. Every slave would already be working most of the night, grinding spices and pounding herbs, skinning beasts and turning spits. Every surface would be crowded with spicy doughs and steeping snails, every pan full of simmering sauces, every salver groaning with gilded meats, every pot of oil that was set in the kitchen floor pillaged twice over to prepare for the feast. Had I requested a hot meal tonight I should have been lucky to receive a bowl of soup from the stockpot and a crust of bread. But Marcus, being Marcus, had only to say the word, and someone had sent him a magnificent light supper of braised pork with fennel, honeyed pheasant with mushrooms and something which looked like pickled quails' eggs and peppers.

The problem, from my point of view, was that all of these delicacies had been liberally doused with that disgusting fish sauce, liquifrumen, without which no self-respecting Roman thinks any meal complete. Personally I loathe the stuff. Why anyone should think that a pickle of half-fermented fish entrails and anchovy should enhance the taste of honest food is something I have never understood, although I have sometimes been known to force it past my lips in the interests of maintaining good relations with the wealthy. However, the prospect of doing so at this hour and on this scale for no especial purpose was more than I could honestly bear. On the other hand, if I refused entirely I risked causing offence to my hosts and embarrassment to Marcus.

I looked hopelessly at Junio. He was rather better at fish pickle than I was, having been fed on Roman table scraps from birth, but even he was looking at me warningly. He had 'dined like a king' in the attic, I remembered. I sighed. Even high-society Roman table manners, which permit a man at a feast to tickle his throat with a feather so that he can make room for more, do not extend that toleration to normal household dining. Vomiting in the courtyard was not an acceptable solution for either of us.

'Rollo,' I said, 'I did hear Sollers call you Rollo, didn't I?'

'Yes, citizen.'

'Well, Rollo, I am not sure that I can manage this. I am a poor man, and not accustomed to rich meals at night.'

He looked at me aghast. Poor men who were guests in his master's house obviously did not enter his picture of the world. 'But citizen, it has been prepared especially for you. My mistress came to the kitchens herself to give the orders for it.' He looked at me and, quite unexpectedly, giggled. 'Your pardon, citizen. But it was amusing, really. First the chief slave came, to demand a meal for Marcus. Then Julia arrived to order special dishes. When she had gone, Maximilian stormed in, fresh from the lament, insisting on tasting everything, and ordering extra seasoning to show he was in command. Then Sollers turned up, muttering about "restorative regimen". He is a great believer in diet to balance the humours, and he countermanded half the orders on medical grounds, and added a few of his own. In the end I think the cook just prepared what he thought was best.'

'Each one trying to outdo the others?' I suggested.

He snorted. 'It was like Hadrian's Wall in there, everyone trying to take control. It was the same with bringing your trays. Sollers told Mutuus to bring yours, and sent me to Marcus, since most of the usual house slaves are busy. Maximilian caught us doing it, and insisted we change places.'

I looked at him sharply. 'For any reason?'

'None that I can think of, except to contradict Sollers. Unless . . .'

'Unless?'

Rollo hesitated. 'I am sorry, citizen. I should not have spoken. I cannot tell you that.'

I leaned back on my pillows and said, conversationally, 'Rollo, your master has been murdered today. I am assisting Marcus to investigate. A man has been arrested, but there are some questions unanswered. If I think that you are withholding information, I shall have to tell His Excellency. That pretty turquoise tunic may get very dirty indeed.' I dislike threats, as a general rule, but this one had the desired effect. Rollo paled and swallowed hard. 'You were saying,' I prompted, 'unless . . .?'

The words came out in a rush. 'Unless Maximilian hoped to keep me from Flavius. He is sleeping in the triclinium on a couch, since you and Marcus have the guest apartments, and Maximilian is occupying his old room again. If I had served Marcus with his supper, I should have passed Flavius's door.'

'Would that matter?'

He gave me a crooked smile. 'Everyone sees me as a messenger, citizen. Maximilian did it. He used to get me to speak to his father for him. Flavius has used me several times to take messages to Julia, and Maximilian knew it. He doesn't trust Julia, and sees conspiracies everywhere. Flavius spoke to me privately in the courtyard tonight. I think Maximilian saw us.'

'And what did Flavius want?'

Again that hesitation, before the page said, 'Maximilian was right. Flavius asked me to attend him later. He has a very important job for me, he says. A secret.'

'What secret is that?' I asked wryly.

Rollo flushed. 'Oh dear, here I am, talking too much again. Truly, citizen, he did not tell me what it was. I thought . . . I gathered the impression . . . that there might be money in it. Naturally, I agreed.'

'Naturally.' Money, I imagined, had changed hands on earlier occasions too. I did not blame Rollo. He was a slave, and if a house guest asked for his services, naturally he must give them. 'You are only doing your duty. If there is money in it, that is your good fortune.'

Rollo, though, must have caught the wryness in my tone, because he looked at me anxiously. 'What should I do, citizen?'

'Attend him, of course. But there is one thing you will do in addition. When he gives you the commission, you will come and tell me what it is.' I was relying on Marcus's authority here: I was, after all, asking Rollo to betray a confidence. But I was hopeful. The page said himself that he 'talked too much', and he had already been gossiping to me about the household as if he had known me for years.

He was looking at me doubtfully now, and I hastened to reassure him. 'It may be nothing important – a message to his household, a wager on the chariot race tomorrow – and if that is so, I shall say nothing, not even to Marcus, and the secret is safe. But remember, a message may seem innocent to you, yet have some meaning which you do not understand. So whatever the errand is, tell me before you do it. It is your duty to your dead master. And to yourself. Is that clear?'

The page gave me an uncertain smile. 'Yes, citizen.'

'Good,' I said heartily. 'Now, what are we to do with this tray? I cannot stomach fish sauce at this time of night.'

'Perhaps Flavius would like it,' Junio suggested. 'Or, if you could take something, the rest could be returned as scraps to the servants. No doubt some of them would appreciate it.'

That was an obvious solution, once he had suggested it, and judging by the hungry way Rollo was eyeing the pork and fennel, an appreciative recipient would not be hard to find. I took a spoon, for form's sake, and moved the food around the plates a little, to disturb the symmetry with which it had been arranged, but without actually eating any. Then I took up the cup which contained the sleeping draught.

'Very well, Rollo,' I said, 'you may deal with this tray and then attend on Flavius. Ensure that the platters do not return to the kitchens too full.'

Rollo seized the tray eagerly.

'And don't forget,' I said, 'that you are to come back

when you have spoken to Flavius.'

'I won't, citizen. I won't.' Rollo gave me a conspiratorial look and fled, as though I had offered him a bribe.

Which perhaps in a sense I had. A plateful of good food is sometimes better than money to a slave. At least a man can hide food in a place where no one else can steal it. It was sobering to realise how much such a gift would once have meant to me – fish-pickle sauce or not.

Junio thought so too. 'I think you have won a devoted friend there, master. At no cost to yourself. Now, since you have asked him to return, do you wish to drink this sleeping potion now, or would you prefer that I should sing for you?'

I had taught him some of the old, haunting Celtic melodies. He had a soft, pleasing voice, and he knew it delighted me to hear him.

'Sing softly, then,' I said. 'We do not wish to disturb the lament.'

Outside, Julia was crooning her lamentations, wistful and heartbreaking. Her lamenting was replaced by Sollers, and then one by one by the voices of slaves. The night darkened, and the dawn had begun to lighten the courtyard before I drank the potion Sollers had sent and drifted finally to sleep.

And still Rollo did not come.

Chapter Ten

Neither was he in evidence next morning, when, aroused by a general commotion in the courtyard, I finally awoke.

Junio was standing beside me with a brimming bowl (I still liked to plunge my face, Celtic-fashion, into cold water on awakening), and an appetising morning meal of fresh milk and hot oatcakes. The Romans can keep their breakfast of fruit, bread and watered wine – this was a feast for a king. I said so to Junio as I made the ritual offering of the first few drops from my cup.

He grinned. 'I bought it for you fresh from the street sellers, master. With Julia's blessing. I said that you would like it above all things – though Maximilian was inclined to be irritated that I had scorned his kitchens. The family, of course, will eat only bread and water today until the funeral banquet, but they cannot expect Marcus to do so, or you and Flavius either, so it was easier to send out for something. In any case, the household kitchens are full to bursting with preparations for the feast.' He tucked into one of the delicious oatcakes which, as usual, I had set aside for him.

'Fit for a king,' I said again, when the last warm, fragrant crumb was gone and we were licking our fingers reluctantly.

Junio's grin broadened. 'Well, if His Majesty has sufficiently feasted, perhaps he would like me to help him with his toga? I imagine you would like us to go and look for

Rollo?' He said 'us', I noticed, as if it were inevitable that he should assist me in any enquiries, but I made no comment. I allowed him to drape me in my toga and we went outside.

It was a damp and drizzling day, made drearier by the moaning rise and fall of the distant lament, but the courtyard was full of bustle. Slaves with buckets, cloths, feather dusters, sponges and ladders scampered everywhere, while a pair of lads were already busy scattering sawdust in the colonnade and sweeping it up again with their twig brooms. Clearly the house was to be as clean as the Emperor's armour before the expected guests arrived.

I led the way into the atrium, but there was no sign of Rollo, and we wandered through the front enclosure towards the gate. Visitors were already arriving. News of the decurion's death had spread quickly overnight, and from the murmur outside it seemed that half Corinium was at the gates.

The gate opened to admit a slave in a fancy tunic, clutching gifts of oil and wine. Representing a member of the civic curia, no doubt, and come to offer lamentations by proxy, though his master would attend in person to grace the burial procession and enjoy the banquet.

Then came one of the clientes, genuinely weeping. No wonder, perhaps, if Quintus had been his only patron – without whose good offices he would now struggle for a livelihood. Perhaps he genuinely loved him, or perhaps he masked an inward glee with this show of public grief: if, for example, he expected to be mentioned in Quintus's will, in recompense for favours done, or found himself unexpectedly relieved of the necessity of naming Quintus as one of his own heirs.

All the curia and clientes would attend, in turn. Add to these the funeral orator, the dancers, singers and musicians, the torch-carriers and litter-bearers, the family, the household slaves, one or two favoured tradesmen and a scattering of the simply curious, and you will see that the decurion's funeral procession promised to be a very impressive one indeed.

But of Rollo there was still no sign. I wandered back into the triclinium (unannounced, to the consternation of the slaves at the door), and found Flavius reclining on one of the couches, eating. Someone had brought him a hot pie from a market stall, and he was stuffing it into his mouth as though greasy pastry and early-morning lumps of gristly meat were his idea of an ambrosial breakfast. A goblet of wine stood on a low table before him.

He looked up as I came in, wiped his fingers on the linen napkin he had been given and hastily rearranged his cushions. I had the distinct impression that he was up to something. He gazed at me with a triumphant air.

I had not been present the night before, when Marcus had interrogated him, and looking at that swarthy, fleshy face with its fleeting but unmistakable expression of cunning, I suddenly determined to repair the omission. Without Marcus, however, Flavius was unlikely to tell me anything. My best chance was to unsettle him.

I gave him a cheerful smile and sat down, uninvited, on a nearby stool.

It was an action of such unprecedented insolence, in the presence of a purple-striper, that he almost choked on his pie. I followed it up with another, speaking to my betters without being spoken to, and without the appropriate apologetic preamble. 'Good morning, citizen.' I sensed, rather than saw, Junio at my elbow, sending up silent prayers for my preservation to all the gods he knew.

I was offering a few unspoken petitions of my own. This

was dangerously disrespectful, and Flavius was frowning angrily. I took a deep breath.

'Well, Flavius,' I said comfortably – worse and worse, no honorific titles and using his name like an equal – 'I hear it was your sharp eyes which discovered Lupus.'

The scowl visibly lightened. I breathed out. Flavius was susceptible to flattery. I poured out a little more of it, hopefully, like a householder making a libation of oil to the pantry gods.

'You have sharper eyes than I have,' I said. 'I did not notice the stains.'

He smirked. 'The old goat concealed them in his sleeve folds, by holding his arm against him as though it were stiff. I noticed he was doing it, but I thought nothing of it.' He leaned forward confidentially, the grease of the pie still glistening moistly on his lips: 'I have known Lupus for years, and he is forever complaining of his aches and pains. Every time one sees him he has some fresh affliction – and one dares not ask, unless one wants a whole recital of his woes. He is famous for it in the town. No one would even have thought it odd that he had developed a new malady, until his greed betrayed him. The slave came by with the wine jug, and Lupus couldn't resist holding out his bony arm for more.'

His right arm, I thought. I did a swift calculation. The dagger blow that killed Quintus had been delivered slightly upwards and to the right. Surely that would be most easily inflicted by a left-handed man? It was hard to be sure. Quintus had presumably been reclining on his couch when the blow was struck, so he could have been attacked from any angle. Besides, few Roman citizens would be left-handed – any such tendency was schooled out of them early. The Roman army did not tolerate 'sinister' infantry-men – they spoiled a formation, and left vulnerable gaps in a phalanx – and a similar prejudice ran through polite society. Soldiers and schoolboys learned very quickly, if not to be right-handed, at least to be ambidextrous.

I looked at Flavius. He was supporting himself on his left arm and unconsciously holding his pie in his right hand, but, as in the case of Lupus and the wine, that told me nothing. It is considered polite in most Roman circles for a man to eat and drink with his right hand, and to reserve his left for more intimate duties.

Flavius was looking at me expectantly. I said quickly, 'You have known Councillor Lupus a long time?'

'He is ex-Councillor Lupus, now,' Flavius reminded me, with a certain relish. 'That is why he hated Quintus Ulpius so much. That and some argument over that secretary of his. He was telling me about it in the garden – though I confess I was scarcely paying attention. You wouldn't have done so either, in my place. Listening to Lupus rehearsing his miseries is a famously tedious business. And that is why it is difficult to answer your question, citizen. I have known him, from a distance, for many years, but I have, shall we say, avoided his acquaintance.'

'You did not need his support in the curia?' I suggested. Most men with large estates would court a magistrate, however tedious, if it would assist them to gain contracts and avoid taxes.

He was unabashed by this. 'Naturally, I sent him tribute if it was expedient,' he said, 'but I had other friends on the council. Quintus Ulpius was one of them, until this business with Julia. You heard about that?'

I was on dangerous ground here. 'I heard that she had been your wife,' I said carefully.

Not carefully enough. 'Had been my wife!' he snorted angrily. 'She should *still* be my wife! By Jupiter, Greatest and Best, she was promised me by her father, Gaius

Honorius, when I lent him money to buy a forest. As soon as she was old enough, he said, and sure enough, the day she was twelve he brought her to my house, and gave her a handsome dowry into the bargain. And now, of course, I've lost that too.'

'A *manus* marriage?' I said. I was surprised. That form of legal wedding was almost obsolete, but if that was the case, Flavius certainly had a claim. Of course his bride was very young – we Celts do not usually marry off our daughters while they are still such children – but twelve is the legal age under Roman law, and it is always fashionable, among the socially aspiring, to do in Britain as they do in Rome. In any case, her youth made no difference. In a manus marriage, the wife legally passed into her husband's power, and so did her property. She might even have been fictitiously 'bought' by her husband, in front of the magistrates, in which case she was undoubtedly his. 'Can you prove that?'

He shook his head. 'There was no legal ceremony. And I cannot prove "usage", either – Julia was too clever for that. She has made a point of sleeping away from home for three successive nights every year – so she has avoided legally passing into my family. She claims ours was a free marriage, and therefore she can leave it when she chooses. Her father would have supported me, but he died of a fever years ago, and her brother became her official protector. He has never liked me. He made no secret of it – he was always encouraging her to run home, and I'd have to send after her and woo her back.' He looked at me mournfully. 'Great Jupiter the Mighty, I'd have sought a divorce myself twenty times over if Julia were not so beautiful.'

Or so rich, I thought uncharitably.

Flavius, though, had not finished his complaint. 'The

things I had to promise! I tell you, citizen, I spoiled that woman. I allowed her to go to the baths every day, during the women's hours, though it costs twice as much for a female: I let her have pets, and visits to friends, and yearly outings to the theatre: I even permitted her to learn an instrument and play at banquets which I gave. What more could a man do? And still she was not satisfied.'

I was trying to imagine what Gwellia would have said if I had confined her to such dubious pleasures, but I managed to smile encouragingly.

'You know, she used to complain of my breath, and I spent a fortune on sweeteners to please her. Liquorice root, ginger, dried fennel – I tried everything. I even used ground dogs' teeth and honey to polish my teeth, but still she grumbled that I smelled of fish pickle and old wine. And then of course she met Quintus. After that she never came home again. I believe he went to a sorcerer and had her charmed away. Well, he needn't think he can get away with it. There are laws against things like that.'

There were. The picture of the soothsayer flitted across my mind. 'And that is what you came here to see him about?'

'Of course it is. Or perhaps I should say "was".'

'I see.' I looked at him for a moment. 'Then what was it you wanted Rollo to do for you?'

I have never seen a man's expression change so quickly. The smile faded, and he turned whiter than my toga. 'Rollo?' he stammered. His distress was so dramatic that I wondered for a moment if it had been caused by the pie. 'How did you know about that?'

I smiled, in what I hoped was an inscrutable fashion. 'A courtyard has ears,' I said. I sounded like a rune-reader evading an answer, but I did not wish to implicate the page. Flavius obviously didn't know that Rollo had spoken to me. 'So,' I went on, 'what have you done with the boy? Where have you sent him?'

I was not expecting an immediate reply. I was prepared for hedging and evasion, but I was not prepared for Flavius's startled look.

'But citizen,' he said, in surprise. 'If you have informants, surely you must know. I asked Rollo to call on me last evening, but he did not come. I wanted him to take a message, it is true, but he never arrived. I supposed that Julia had learned about it, and forbidden him to come.'

'You wanted him to take a message?' I repeated.

'A message, a letter. To Julia. Isn't that what this inquisition is about?'

'You wrote to Julia?' I said. I was surprised. It is not usual for a man to send letters to another man's wife, especially not when he is a guest in the same house. But then, I remembered, Julia had refused to speak to Flavius. I was interested to know what this famous message had said. 'Where is the letter now?'

'It was nothing. It is not important now. I have destroyed it.' He picked up the goblet of watered wine from the table and swallowed the contents at a gulp.

'Destroyed it?' That was unlikely. Writing materials are too precious to destroy.

'Erased it, then,' Flavius conceded sulkily.

So it had been written on a wax tablet, I thought. That was interesting. Probably a small writing block, folded in two halves and fitted with a lock and hinge so that the message was private. Just the sort of tablet on which someone had scratched the words 'Remember Pertinax'. I was suddenly very anxious to see it.

'And was that,' I enquired sweetly, 'what you were hiding under your pillows when I came in?'

Flavius assumed a look of injured innocence. 'But there

is nothing under my pillows, citizen. Have your slave search them, or see for yourself.'

For a moment I was taken aback. The tablet, I thought, must be in the room somewhere. Flavius had intended to give it to Rollo, and he had not left the triclinium. My eye lit on the napkin. Of course! I seized one corner of it and swept it away, revealing what Flavius had hidden under it.

The little writing tablet was an expensive thing: the frame was made of carved ivory, the metal clasp finely worked. Flavius sat up and buried his head in his hands. He looked a defeated man.

'Well?' I demanded, like the governor demanding tribute.

He shrugged. 'See for yourself, citizen.' I was the one being accorded the social courtesy now. 'It is nothing. I was trying to send a letter, but I did not send it, and I have erased it, as you see.' He opened the tablet. It was true: the scratched message, whatever it was, had been obliterated by rubbing the wax with the blunt end of the stylus, which was created for exactly that purpose. 'I don't suppose I shall ever deliver it now.'

I took the tablet from him and handed it to Junio, who had been waiting patiently at my side all the while. 'Put this inside your tunic. I think we should show it to Julia. Perhaps she can throw some light on the matter.'

Junio obeyed. To my surprise, Flavius made no protest, although the frame alone must have been worth many sesterces. Indeed, he seemed almost pleased that I had taken it. His face cleared and he said, with urgency, 'Yes, do. Give it to Julia, citizen. I meant her to have it. I would have sent it to her yesterday, but Rollo didn't come.' He frowned. 'What happened to him, I wonder?'

I didn't know. And suddenly I found that worrying.

I got to my feet. 'I don't know, citizen. Excuse me, I

must go and look for him. It may be urgent. Come, Junio.'

And bowing ourselves out as hastily as respect allowed, we went back to the atrium.

Chapter Eleven

Julia was there, overseeing the selection of dark green herbs and foliage which a maidservant was arranging in a large bronze vase. Another slave girl stood by with a pile of other branches to choose from.

Julia looked up when she saw us, but her greeting was addressed to me alone. 'Good morning, citizen.' She was arrayed this morning with stunning simplicity in a long-sleeved white tunic, unadorned except for a simple girdle under her breasts and a funeral wreath upon her brow. She looked shaken and pale, but she had defied popular convention, and there had been no ritual clawing of her face or tearing at her hair. Instead she was the picture of dignified grief.

I looked at her with approval. 'Greetings, lady.'

She turned to me and gave me one of those smiles of hers. I could see why Marcus preened in her presence: that smile would make any man feel like Hercules. She looked me confidently in the eyes. 'Does this look well enough, do you think? I am no expert on such things, but you have an artist's eye.'

It was blatant flattery. A Roman woman, especially a beautiful one, does not usually initiate idle conversation with a comparative stranger, even in her own house, unless she is setting out to charm. And she could not really want my opinion. I am hardly an expert on floral art.

It was hard to know how to reply. Roman funerary

green is too sombre for my taste, especially when displayed in a heavy vase in a huge bronze bowl on a black shale table. And I was anxious to look for Rollo. But Julia was irresistible.

'It has a pleasing symmetry,' I said, and was rewarded with a look of as much admiration as if I had personally carved the finest statue in Corinium.

The slave girls began to clear away the excess leaves and rub down the table top with juniper oil to give it a sheen and prevent the shale from splitting.

'Now, citizen,' Julia said, looking me fully in the face again with those disturbing eyes, 'you are my guest in these doleful hours. What can I do to serve you?'

'Lady, forgive me for disturbing you, but there is a problem with which I should like your help. You know the page, Rollo?'

She furrowed her lovely brow. 'Rollo? My husband's pet page? The little fellow in the embroidered tunic? I know him, of course.'

She had made a pretence of thinking hard, but the readiness of her answer surprised me. In many a household of this size a woman would not be acquainted with all her slaves by name, especially not the handsome little page. Rollo had told me that normally he served Quintus exclusively, probably in ways of which Julia was modestly unaware. Yet Julia identified him with confidence. 'Have you seen him this morning, lady?'

She looked surprised, and I could see her examining the question. She favoured me with another of her glowing smiles. 'I could not say for certain. I have not noticed him.'

I was oddly disappointed in that reply, although it is hard to see how I could have expected anything different. To Julia, of course, the presence of a slave was no more remarkable than the presence of any other piece of household equipment – a footstool, say, or a cushion. In fact, I thought with an inward smile, I was guilty of something of the sort myself. I was classifying this present meeting as a 'private conversation', though I had Junio with me and she was attended by a pair of her maids.

I looked at the girls, waiting dispiritedly in the corner with the vase. Junio was right; they were remarkably plain. Once again, I had that feeling of disquiet. In a household of this kind, where money could buy the prettiest girls in the whole province, there was something very deliberate in this choice, like placing a fine statue against an ugly arch. Julia, I thought, had no need of such a frame – she would have looked handsome between the prettiest slaves in the Empire.

She was giving me one of those smiles again. 'You wish to find Rollo?' She signalled to one of the girls. 'Fetch me the chief slave. He will know where the boy is. Unless, citizen, one of my handmaidens can serve you . . .?'

Perhaps she did guess at Rollo's functions. I shook my head, and the handmaiden vanished.

'I am sorry, pavement-maker, that you have had such a welcome to our house. Quintus, I know, was so anxious for that mosaic floor in the hot room.' She fluttered her lovely eyes at me. Her lids were touched with saffron and her brows and eyelashes tinted black with some dark powder. 'I hope that you will still consent to design it for us, if Quintus leaves money for the caldarium in his will.'

'I should be highly honoured,' I said, keeping my voice controlled. Inwardly I was dancing votive flings. What fool would refuse such a prestigious commission, offered by such a beautiful woman? Especially when it gives him an opportunity to look for his wife. 'Honoured,' I said again.

'We shall know if there is money when the will is read this afternoon,' Julia said. 'I imagine he will have endowed the baths. And some memorial games. Quintus was very fond of chariot racing and watching the gladiators. He would like to leave something spectacular for the town to remember him by.'

I nodded. The greatest heroes of a *civitas*, at least to its citizens, are those who have provided the biggest shows and the most lavish public banquets to be celebrated on their account. Better men, who bequeathed less roasted horsemeat and fewer fights, were often swiftly forgotten.

'You do not think that Ulpius had altered his will in any way?' I found myself asking. When Julia smiled at you like that, you felt that you could ask her anything. 'I heard he had recently threatened to disinherit his son.'

She laughed in surprise, tipping back her lovely head. 'Did he? He was always threatening to reduce Maximilian's allowance, but I hadn't heard that he meant to disinherit him altogether. He can't have done it. It would mean changing the will, and I would have heard of it, I'm sure.' She stopped and looked at me with sudden seriousness. 'When did you learn of this? My husband did not say this before witnesses, surely?'

She was right to be concerned. If he had spoken in front of seven citizens (slaves and other non-citizens did not count, naturally) the will could be questioned and revoked. If that happened, it would go to the courts, and most of the estate was likely to end up in the imperial coffers, whoever won the case.

'Maximilian told me so himself,' I said. 'His father was threatening him with it yesterday. But Sollers seemed to know too. I thought it was general knowledge in the household.'

She smiled again. 'It was probably just a threat. My husband would have consulted me. Though he might have discussed it with Sollers. He consulted him on everything.

And with reason, too. You know that Sollers saved my husband's sight?'

'He did?' No wonder Quintus admired Sollers. Eye disease is a constant problem throughout the whole of Britannica, and its effects can be dreadful. When the poor go blind, there is nothing for them but begging, and even for the rich it usually means the loss of high office. It is too easy to defraud a man who cannot see. I murmured something sympathetic.

Julia was warming to her story. 'Poor Quintus. He was terrified. It was beginning to be difficult. He could not see to read official scrolls clearly.'

I nodded. One reason, obviously, why Quintus set such a store on his secretary.

'He tried to keep it secret at first, but in the end he consulted every oculist in Corinium. They tried everything. Charms and salves and amulets and ointments – everything from zinc and copper to frankincense, gentian and myrrh, but it did no good. And of course, very quickly the whole town knew.'

I nodded. Corinium was famous for its oculists. I had seen several of them when I came before, working from their little booths in the market place, sitting on their consulting stools behind sacking curtains, each with his little blocks of desiccated medicine, *collyria*, all proudly marked with his distinctive stamp, waiting to be cut up when a patient came and dissolved in water or egg white to make the appropriate salve. Some of these men were highly thought of, but even they could hardly resist boasting of their eminent customer. No wonder gossip spread.

'And then?'

She sighed. 'And then he met Sollers. He had been an army surgeon, of course, but he had served in the field, and could turn his hand to anything – oculist, physician, dental surgeon too. He examined Quintus, and said there was a film growing on both his eyes. He could operate, he said. It would be dangerous, but it had to be done quickly. Quintus agreed. Sollers came to the house and took the film off the next day. Tied Quintus to the chair and scraped the film off with a bronze needle, just like that. One eye with each hand.'

I swallowed. I had heard of operations like this – the patient's hands were strapped together and his body tied to the chair while one slave held his head steady, and another stood by with oil lamps to give a good light. Good surgeons could operate with either hand to ensure the angle was correct. The thought of undergoing such an experience, with my eyes open, made my own flesh crawl.

She nodded. 'A dreadful operation. My husband was no coward, but I heard him moaning with fright. Sollers simply bandaged one eye while he dealt with the other, and operated more quickly than it takes to tell. It was wonderful. Sollers bathed the eyes in egg albumen and bound them with wool for a day or two, but the sight was restored. Quintus invited him to join our household permanently.'

'And he accepted?'

'He did, although of course after that everyone wanted him. He could have commanded any sum he wished. But he chose to stay with us, to advise us on our health and to pursue his studies. He is so loyal he has even made a will, naming myself and Quintus as his legatees. Quintus gave him his own apartments, and arranged for him to have books and writing materials. He brought several medical scrolls of his own with him, and Quintus had a whole new manuscript copied out for him – a huge treatise on herbs and treatments.'

'Who copied it?' I asked, although I had guessed the answer.

'Why, Mutuus, the noxal clerk. It took him ninety days.'

Behind me I heard Junio suppress a snigger. I chose my words carefully. 'Did you know the secretary well?'

She coloured. A faint flush of pink swept up her face and suffused her cheeks, under the careful perfection of her skin. She lowered her eyes a moment, and then raised them again to meet mine, great limpid pools of brown which would have melted a stone gorgon. I have never cared for the Roman fashion of white-lead-and-lupin face powder and lamp-blacked eyes, but on Julia it looked ravishing.

'I will be frank, pavement-maker,' she said softly. 'I know Mutuus perhaps a little better than I should. The truth is, citizen, I think the boy has become fond of me. I did not notice at first, only that I met him so often in the courtyard when his duties were finished, and that he always found the means to speak to me, to ask if I wished to have a letter written or a message sent. I thought him attentive, though of course, I had no need of his services. My father was far-sighted. He had me taught to read and write myself, although I was a girl.'

'And what did your husband think?'

'Of Mutuus? It was he who pointed out that the boy was enamoured of me. I think he was amused, as long as he perceived no threat. Quintus was savagely jealous in some ways, but he was always glad to think that other men admired me – he liked the world to envy what he had.'

That fitted, certainly, with what I had seen of the man. The pairs of slaves, the elaborate gardens, the glittering reception room – even the insistence on removing Mutuus from Lupus and installing him as a bondsman. Quintus enjoyed flaunting what was his. It might well have afforded

him satisfaction to send the secretary on errands to Julia,
knowing the helpless passion he was arousing.

'And you?' I said. 'What did you think of this?'

The colour in her cheeks deepened. 'At first I did not
notice, as I say. And then – I suppose I was flattered. It is
always flattering to enjoy a man's attentions. And Mutuus
is a good-looking boy.'

I frowned. This was not altogether what I had hoped to
hear. Mutuus was a pleasant enough lad – tall, broad-
shouldered, handsome in a supercilious way – but he was
angular, moving with the graceless awkwardness of youth.
I should have expected Julia to prefer someone more
mature.

'And later?' I asked, more sharply than I intended.

'I did, I suppose, begin to enjoy his attentions. I started
to send him on errands, asked him to copy verses for me
and read them to me while I sat in the colonnade. I gave
him wax notebooks for the purpose. Quintus did not object
– I did not thrust it under his attention – and Mutuus liked
to do it. When Quintus had finished with him, naturally.
And recently, while my husband has been ill, it has been a
comfort to me.'

I'll wager it has, I thought. Perhaps it was the mention
of the wax tablets which reminded me of Rollo and the
mission I was engaged upon, but suddenly I had a strong
desire to terminate the conversation. But first I had to ask
her the question that had disturbed me all the previous
day.

'And was it Mutuus you went to see yesterday, lady,
when you went to crave an audience with your husband
for Marcus and I?'

She gave a little gasp and clapped a hand to her lovely
face.

I was inexorable. 'For certainly you didn't go to Ulpius.

Maximilian was with his father at the time, and he came to us looking for you. So, unless you killed your husband, lady, you did not go to his room.'

She paled and bit her lower lip till the colour came. I wondered if she knew the effect of that action on a susceptible male. Then she smiled uncertainly.

'You are perceptive, pavement-maker. Yes, I did leave you to go to my husband. I thought Sollers was still with him, but when I approached the door I heard voices raised. He was arguing with Maximilian. I did not dare disturb him – my husband could be furious when roused. I went into the courtyard to wait.'

'I am sorry to press you, lady, in your grief,' I said. 'But you were not there later. The slaves went to look for you, and could not find you.'

Again she coloured faintly. 'No,' she said, 'you are right again. I went to my quarters, briefly, to repair my looks. He likes – he liked – to see me with a touch of Belgian rouge on my lips. My maids could confirm it, if you doubt me. And then I came into the courtyard and saw Sollers. Maximilian was still with his father, and . . . well, the fact is, citizen, we went to my husband's rooms.'

For a moment I was aghast. It must have been evident from my face, because Julia laughed. 'There was nothing improper, citizen. Sollers has been treating me for . . . for a female condition. But I did not wish my husband to know that, and it is hard to find a private time and place for treatment. One of the slaves almost saw us last time, as it was.'

Had seen them, in fact, I thought. Junio had known that she was consulting Sollers secretly. 'And this seemed to be an opportunity?'

'It seemed that Quintus would be busy for some time. I took the herbs and lay down upon the couch in my husband's apartment. The inner doors were shut and the slaves, of course, would not look for me there – indeed, that was the reason I went there. I was afraid my husband would hear of it, and it is hard to keep a secret among slaves. Though that scarcely matters now. But that is where I was. Ask Sollers – he was with me all the time.'

And what kind of secret treatment, I wondered, had the handsome doctor contrived for the beautiful wife? And what was the 'female condition'? Barrenness was the most likely cause, despite the household gossip. Infertility in a woman is sufficient grounds for divorce. But that was not something I could decently ask outright. Julia spoke of these things with the frankness of all Romans everywhere, but I came from a different tradition.

'With your permission, lady . . .' I began, awkwardly, but I was interrupted by the plain maidservant who came scurrying in with the chief slave at her heels.

'Oh, madam,' she cried, and her eyes were full of tears. 'Come quickly. And the pavement-maker too. We have found Rollo.'

Chapter Twelve

Rollo's body was lying in the drainage channel which ran under the latrine. It was a kind of open culvert containing the outflow of the fast-running stream which had been diverted onto the property. The water was forced through a series of cunningly narrowed iron and pottery pipes to feed first the front fountain and then the rear cascade before flowing out through this stone channel, presumably to join the river behind the property. There was a lot of water running in the culvert under the seats, but it was disturbing to think that the boy might have been lying there unnoticed when I visited the latrine earlier on more personal business.

It would have been easy not to see him. The little room which formed the latrine contained only a stone seat with two holes in it, jutting over the open culvert at the rear, and with a small space at the side of each where a man could dip his sponge-stick down into the running stream to perform the necessary ablutions. It was that, in fact, which had caused the discovery. Mutuus, permitted to use the household latrine when no family members were present, had dipped in his sponge-stick and engaged it upon something unexpectedly soft – the running water in the culvert kept the sewer clean of less sanitary obstructions, and the sides of the drainage channel were faced with stone.

Nor could Rollo have fallen in by some freak accident.

He was wedged awkwardly against the stones, and his body, when a party of slaves had dragged it out with difficulty and laid it dripping on the flagstones, showed clearly the scuffs and abrasions he had suffered in being forced down into that narrow space. The head, indeed, had never been wholly immersed, and there were patches of skin missing from his cheek and forehead, and something which looked suspiciously like vomit still clung to the cheek and hair. The once exquisite tunic was a sorry sight, the turquoise fabric stained and sodden, and the boy had lost one of his embroidered shoes. The other was still upon his foot, the patterns he had been so proud of soaked and spoiled, soiled with who knows what. The effect was oddly touching and pathetic.

Sollers, who came hurrying in at that moment, seemed to think so too. He looked from me to the lifeless form and turned ashen.

'Great Hermes!' he muttered. 'What tragedy is this?'

There was quite a crush around the little room. The chief slave and I were there, and Junio of course, along with Mutuus, who had discovered the body, and the two slaves who had been summoned to pull it from the sewer. Even Julia and her handmaidens, who had been prevented by decorum from entering the latrine itself, stood outside in the courtyard looking in, and a number of passing slaves forgot their urgent errands and clustered around to stare. At the arrival of the doctor, however, everyone – including myself – had stepped back instinctively to make way for him.

Of course, he was the senior man present. He was a citizen, and as a retired army doctor, would have medical rank. I was a mere pavement-maker, Mutuus had been a bondsman until yesterday and Julia was a woman. All the same, the deference was so instant, so instinctive that I was struck again by the sheer power of the man's intellect and personality. There was something about that tall grey-haired figure that commanded respect. Even the slaves who had stopped in the courtyard to goggle seemed to recollect themselves in his presence, and disappeared about their business.

He bent over Rollo's body, his face clouded with concentration, probing with his hands and straining as if to catch the faintest flutter of the heart. Then he stood up and shook his head.

'Dead?' I said, foolishly. He did not need to answer. I tried to redeem myself. 'Before he was pushed into the hole, do you think? I notice there is vomit on him. That might suggest poison.'

Sollers regarded me for a moment, the shrewd eyes thoughtful. 'Indeed,' he said. 'That is a possibility. We must not overlook it. Although my first thought was the damage to the body. The same symptoms might be caused by a severe blow to the stomach.'

I looked at him in surprise. 'You think so?'

'It is possible. There is a mark here too, on the neck. A swift blow there will kill a man almost instantly.'

'If the attacker knows where to strike.'

He nodded thoughtfully. 'Or strikes by accident.'

'You do not think it might be poisoning?' I persisted. 'Some poison which acts swiftly, without causing contortions? Aconite, for example?' I said. I had had dealings with aconite before.

He seemed to consider this a little, and then he shook his head. 'I do not think so. Unless, of course, the boy simply ate some food which was poisonous. A bad fish or a piece of harmful fungus can do it. Even an old egg or a piece of pie. I have known that in the army, a whole tentful of six soldiers dying because of something they ate. But how would Rollo acquire such a thing? He has eaten nothing that other people have not had.'

'Could he have been struck first and poisoned afterwards?'

'That seems a little unlikely, don't you think? Though I suppose we cannot altogether rule it out. There may have been some sort of struggle. There is no way of telling after death. But for myself, I believe it was the blow that killed him. And dealt, I think, by a left-handed man.'

That was a telling observation, if it was true. I said quickly, 'How can you tell?'

He lifted up the pathetic tunic, revealing the linen strap fixed around the loins as an undercloth. 'You see here? There is a dark patch on his stomach and side – it looks like a bruise. That would suggest a cruel blow. But see,' he made a feigned blow at the body with his right hand, 'the angle of it is wrong. But if I strike him so,' he repeated the action with his left, 'the mark would fall exactly where it is.'

I had to admit the justice of his demonstration. 'And who is left-handed in a household of this kind?'

It was Julia who answered. 'Maximilian favoured his left hand as a child,' she said doubtfully. 'My husband told me so. He regarded it as a bad omen for the boy. But he uses his right hand now. I have seen him do so many times.'

'Maximilian was watching Rollo last night,' Mutuus put in. 'He insisted that Rollo and I change places when we were bringing the trays to yourself and His Excellence. Muttered that he thought the boy was up to something, and he wanted to keep him away from Flavius.'

Sollers gave me a significant glance. Julia gave a little gasp.

'Speaking of His Excellency,' I said, 'I think my patron should be informed of this death. He had intended to commit Lupus to the gaol today, but now I think he will want to investigate things further.'

Mutuus stared at me. 'But what has this to do with my adoptive father?'

'Perhaps nothing,' I replied, 'but one thing is certain. If Rollo was killed by a blow, the one person who could not have done it is Lupus. He was under lock and key all night.'

Sollers was following my train of thought. 'If it had been poison, of course, then even Lupus might have arranged it. A man can poison by proxy, even if he is locked in the attics.'

'You think the killer was the same man?' Julia asked. She had scarcely spoken since her arrival, and her face and voice told of her horror and shock.

I found myself smiling at her. 'When there are two killings in one house within a few hours, it seems improbable that they are unconnected.'

Sollers nodded. 'Another argument against poison, don't you think, citizen? Two killings, both caused by violent attack. Murderers are said to favour the same method, I have heard.'

'But this is only a slave,' Julia whispered, in the same strained voice. 'An expensive slave, but a slave all the same. And not even an important one. Why would anyone murder a slave? How could that be connected to Quintus?'

Sollers moved to her side. 'Julia, my dear, of course it might be connected,' he said gently. He took her arm, and she leaned against him gratefully. Sollers gave her arm a squeeze and went on. 'Suppose the slave had heard something, or seen something, which would prove someone's guilt? It is easy to see why he might be killed.'

I nodded. That was true – of Rollo in particular. Most slaves learn to keep discreetly silent, but not the little page

– his artless prattling had been part of his charm. If he had witnessed something, however apparently innocent, there was always a chance that he would have let it slip to someone.

'But that would suggest that Lupus was not the guilty man!' Her voice was full of tears. 'I thought it had been settled. But no, the nightmare is not over yet. Oh, Great Mercury! But what could Rollo have seen or done? Poor, silly little plaything.'

It was not grief for the slave, of course, which moved her, but the fear that a murderer was still among us. The little company fell silent for a moment, listening to the distant lament. The moment was shattered, however, by a strident voice from the other side of the courtyard.

'What is the meaning of this?' It was Maximilian at the entrance to the atrium, his face pale with rage. 'Am I never to be consulted about events that happen in my own household? A page is dead, one of my own slaves, and I am not even to be informed?' He strode across the court to join us.

If this was acting, it was an impressive performance. At the sight of Rollo his whole demeanour changed. His confidence evaporated and he began to babble like a woman.

'Oh, dear Mercury, what a disgusting sight. And in the latrine too. Well, what are we to do with him? We cannot leave him here, there is the burial to be attended to – and now Rollo will need a funeral of his own. Quintus would have wished it. He always paid for his servants to join the funeral guild, to ensure them a decent ritual.'

'Then we must contact the guild and let them attend to it,' Sollers said. 'They can come tonight, after the procession for Ulpius has left. Perhaps in the meantime we should have him taken to the servants' room, and at least get him washed and dressed decently. Since this is your household, as you say, would you care to give the necessary instructions?'

Maximilian glared at him helplessly, the thin, tousled figure confronting the strong, controlled one. Maximilian was the first to flinch. 'Let it be done,' he said at last, as if the words cost him an effort. He had come here asserting his authority, but Sollers had once more wrested it from him.

The two slaves who had rescued Rollo's body stepped forward to pick it up again, but Maximilian intervened. 'Fetch a board,' he said, as if he were relieved to find some sensible command to give. 'Let the poor page enjoy a little dignity. And bring some water here. Let him be rinsed before he is taken to the house.' The slaves scuttled off and Maximilian let out a deep breath.

But Sollers did not let him assume control for long. He released Julia's arm and stepped forward confidently. 'We should buy some bread and wine, too, as grave meats for him. We cannot decently use the food prepared for Quintus's feast, but Rollo will need sustenance for the underworld, too, and he will have to bribe Cerberus with food to let him pass the gates of Hades, just as Ulpius will. Whether we are slaves or decurions, that ravening guard dog requires the same tribute from us all.'

'Well, you cannot expect me to provide it,' Maximilian cried petulantly. 'Until the will is read I have no money at all. That is why I came here in the first place.'

Sollers looked at him for a moment, then with a swift movement he produced a purse from within the toga folds at his waist and tossed it to Maximilian. 'Here then, take this. A few *asses* for the purchases.'

Maximilian caught the purse. It was an instinctive action, but a moment later he seemed to realise the indignity and flung it down again. 'How dare you!' he roared. 'Tossing money to me as if I were a common slave. And you, a paid man in my father's house. Well I shall pay you too, citizen, for this insult. With interest – see if I do not!' He turned to Julia. 'And you too, lady. You two have turned my father's heart against me between you, and I am scorned in the house where I was born.'

He turned his back and walked away, but Sollers had made his point. He looked at me to ensure that I had understood. I had.

Maximilian had reached out to catch the purse with his left hand.

Chapter Thirteen

We were still staring after Maximilian's departing figure when the two servants returned with a pitcher of water and a rough board covered with a cloth, and we turned our attention to the decent removal of the page. As the slave pair lifted the lifeless body onto its makeshift bier, the rest of the group began to disperse uneasily.

Julia had been standing with her hands clasped to her breast, looking more shaken than ever. Suddenly she seemed to take a decision. She spoke, and her voice trembled with shock and anger.

'Flavius is not left-handed, citizens, but I suspect his work in this. Though I cannot imagine how he did it. I posted a pair of slaves outside his door all night, in case he tried to approach me while I slept, and they did not see him leave his room. But somehow this must be his handiwork. He has used Rollo as his messenger to me in the past, but recently I have refused to accept his letters. No doubt he blamed Rollo. Poor little page. He meant no harm. And I have lost a good slave, too.'

She shook her head, and, accepting Mutuus's arm, glided gracefully back in the direction of the atrium with her maids. Sollers, I noticed, was watching them grimly.

The two bearers of the makeshift litter adjusted their burden, and carried the page out to the rear enclosure to be arranged for burial. Junio and I found ourselves alone with Sollers.

'A remarkable woman, medicus,' I said. 'Determined, too, posting guards at the door. But what do you make of that? Do you suspect Flavius?'

He dragged his attention away from the door through which Julia and Mutuus had disappeared, and turned courteously back to us. He shook his head. 'Julia is distraught. Flavius frightens her with his insistence, and she sees his hand in everything. Besides . . .' He did not finish the sentence, but looked at me meaningfully.

Flavius was right-handed, he meant. Neither Julia nor Mutuus, I realised, had noticed the trick with the purse, and Sollers did not mention it now. The little demonstration had been intended for me alone, and I felt oddly flattered at having been singled out as an intellect worthy of the distinction.

'So, citizen,' he said, 'what do you intend to do now?'

'I should like to look at the kitchens, if I could do so without arousing suspicion. I would like to see exactly how the food is prepared.'

He raised his eyebrows at me; his striking face was wry. 'You still think Rollo was poisoned? You may be right. It is impossible to tell after death, and we have no samples of food to test. But why, in that case, were there bruises on his body, and why should Rollo alone have been affected? One would have expected all the slaves to die.'

Perhaps I *should* have paid attention, then, to the significance of those marks. But I was following my own train of thought. I looked at him thoughtfully. 'Because,' I said, 'I know something that you may not. Rollo had something which was not shared with the other slaves. He ate the contents of my supper tray.' I didn't mention the fish sauce to Sollers. He had served it to me himself the night before.

'Then you think there was something rotten in your supper? One of those quails' eggs or a piece of fungus?'

140

I chose my words carefully. 'I did not say that, exactly.' Behind me I felt Junio stiffen with alarm.

Sollers, too, was suddenly all sympathetic alertness. 'Great Jupiter! You think the tray was deliberately poisoned?'

'His Excellence was served from the same dishes. It seems suggestive, don't you think, that he suffered no ill effects?'

Sollers whistled. 'No wonder that you want to visit the kitchens. I will take you there, of course; I have to go there myself to see how preparations are progressing. The grave meats must be offered on the household altars before they are interred with Quintus, and Maximilian will not have thought of it.' He led the way towards the kitchen door where a servant, with a basket of wood for the ovens, stood back to let us pass. 'I hope they have prepared the foods as I instructed. Even in death, Quintus would want to keep his regimen.'

The kitchens were abustle with industry and steam. Pots bubbled on charcoal stoves, breads cooked on a rack, while a great pig was roasting over the open fire under the eye of the little lad turning the spit. A dozen servants ceased their stirring, basting, chopping and grinding and stared at us in surprise.

Sollers took a knife from a slave who was chopping herbs, and strode to the spit. 'Seeing a pig like this always reminds me of Galen. I was privileged to see him do a dissection once.'

'Galen?' I was impressed. The great physician had tended Emperor Marcus Aurelius himself.

'Oh, yes, it was fascinating. He cut the nerves of a live pig here,' he pointed to the throat, 'and proved to everyone that the voice is controlled by the brain, not the heart. I was lucky to have witnessed it. My father did not approve of live dissections, and Galen has given up public demonstrations since.' He plunged the blade into the roasting

141

beast and tasted the juices. 'No problem here,' he said, returning the knife to the startled slave, who continued chopping as though his life depended on it.

The gesture was not lost on me. Sollers was surreptitiously testing the food as we passed it. It was a brave gesture, if there was a poisoner abroad. He saw that I had seen, and caught my eye, signalling me not to comment. I pushed aside a dog at my feet who was scavenging scraps from the kitchen floor. 'Your father was a doctor, too?' I said.

Sollers made a disdainful face. 'He called himself a doctor. He even treated patients, but he had no training at all.' He sampled the liquid from a sauce that was bubbling on the coals and motioned to the slave who was stirring it to offer some to me.

I stepped back, distrusting it.

Sollers noted my action with amusement. 'You still fear we have a poisoner in our midst?'

'Don't you?'

'I still ask myself about those bruises on the body. But in any case I have no fear of these dishes. Even if you are right, our poisoner is not indiscriminate. Only your tray was tampered with. Last night your patron ate the same food, without ill effect. These dishes are for the funeral feast. Poison in them would dispose of half Corinium.'

He was right, of course, and I felt duly chastened. I accepted a sip of the sauce – which was delicious – and said, to cover my chagrin, 'Your father taught himself, you say?'

Sollers smiled. 'What little he knew. He believed in carriage rides to rock the system and cabbage water for everything. He had strict ideas about which amulets and incantations it was proper to use at different phases of the moon, but he refused to accept more modern methods.'

I tried to look intelligent. 'I know little about doctors.

My experience of them is limited to having my slave brand removed from my back with hot irons. The operation did not incline me to further my acquaintance.'

'Ah, cautery! That is painful.' Sollers moved over to the table, where a female slave was skinning a half-cooked joint of beef. He picked up a piece of the bleeding meat and ate it. 'But at least it does not draw blood. Do you know that blood flows in the arteries, as well as in the veins? Galen proved it, but my father wouldn't accept that either.'

'I didn't know,' I said, looking at the piece of meat with unease. This conversation was beginning to make me queasy, and I refused to taste anything further, but Sollers strode on, sampling a stew here and a sweet cake there, talking all the while.

'Rats were different, my father said. Galen's experiments might prove that they had blood in their arteries, but men have divine air in theirs. You cannot argue with a man like that. I left him and apprenticed myself to a Roman with more scientific views, and when he joined the army, I did too. A great surgeon. He taught me all he knew. How mandrake root will dull the pain, and pitch and turpentine will seal a wound.' He used the spoon to taste one of the snails in tamarind sauce which a slave was simmering. 'A little more pepper,' he said to the cook, and then to me, 'He had great skill with arrow wounds. I have seen him push back a man's intestines after a sword thrust; he lubricated the loops in olive oil and sewed the stomach up again. The soldier lived for days. An impressive demonstration.'

I glanced at the *amphorae* of oil stacked under the cooking bench and blanched, but Sollers was oblivious. He poked at a pan of cranes, stewing with their necks out of the water so that the heads could later be pulled off whole. 'I came to Britain to serve at the army hospital. When I had served out my commission I decided to stay here rather than go back to seek a civic appointment in Rome. I could turn my hand to most things by then, and I hoped to . . . well, to make a living here in a wealthy household. I hoped that in working for Ulpius, my reputation would spread. But now I shall have to start again.' His eye lighted on a platter spread with a small selection of meats and breads. 'Ah! Here are the grave meats I was looking for. I will go and offer them at once. And I must see to the provision of hobnails – Quintus will be buried in his finest shoes, but his spirit will need stout boots for the journey.' He led the way back into the courtyard, where Junio was waiting for me.

'Master!' the boy cried, as soon as I appeared. 'You did not . . .?'

'Taste the food? Your concern is touching. But the medicus is right. If there was poison last night, it was on my plate alone.'

'You think that someone tried to murder you?' Sollers sounded horrified. Then he looked at me doubtfully. 'With deference, citizen – I know your skills – but you are a pavement-maker. You did not even know Quintus. Why should someone want to murder you?'

'I asked myself the same question, believe me. Urgently too, until an answer occurred to me.'

Junio looked at me anxiously, and Sollers stood stock-still to ask, hoarsely, 'And that was?'

'According to what Rollo himself told me last night, that tray was not intended for me at all. Until Maximilian countermanded the order, Rollo was taking supper to Marcus.'

It was as well that Marcus was not listening. I distinctly heard Junio mutter, 'Thank Jupiter for that!'

Chapter Fourteen

There was a silence.

'He must be warned,' Sollers said, urgently.

'Of course,' I said. 'I shall see that he employs a food-taster. And I shall do the same myself, and ensure that the whole household knows it. No killer is going to waste his poisons if an anonymous food-taster is likely to be the only victim. If you wish, when I have attended on my patron, I will go with my slave and attend to those errands in the town which Maximilian refused. I did not know Ulpius personally, so my absence will not be disrespectful, and you will need all the hands you can spare to manage matters here and ensure that there are no further attempts at poisoning. I can take the purse you gave to Maximilian and buy the necessary bread and wine – and no doubt find the funeral guild as well.'

Sollers looked at me in surprise, but it was Junio who voiced what he was thinking. 'But that is slaves' work, master.'

It was, of course. Sollers's suggestion to Maximilian had been a deliberate provocation, simply to allow the doctor to demonstrate his point. But I was eager to go to the town, not least because the incessant lament was beginning to be irksome. If I went into the town I could pursue my search for Gwellia, and there were one or two enquiries I wanted to make on other issues too.

Of course, Sollers might think it was improper to allow

a guest to go on such a humble mission. I gave him a rueful smile. 'I have been a slave, physician, and such errands do not disturb me. Besides, I have business of my own to pursue. For instance, it would interest me to know exactly where Maximilian went, when he left us yesterday. And what happened to his toga? It was stained, I remember. I took it to be wine at the time, but I should like to be certain. I do not imagine the fullers have quite bleached it spotless yet.' It had occurred to me, too, that Maximilian had been in the kitchens the night before.

Sollers looked at me with interest. 'In that case, citizen, of course you should go if you wish. Though there is no need to run menial errands. I can spare a slave for that.'

Or the household can, I thought. No wonder Maximilian felt diminished by this man.

'I could send Junio to the funeral guild,' I said. 'If someone will give him directions as to how to find it. But I will purchase the bread and wine, if you will give me the necessary coins. Since I am travelling with my patron I have not brought much money of my own.' I did not add that what little I did have was likely to be dispensed in the town, to lubricate the tongues of the fuller's men, among others.

He took the purse from his belt again, loosened the strings and shook out a few bronze coins – almost all that the purse contained. The medicus, who could have 'commanded any price he wished', had certainly not lined his purse with gold at Quintus's expense.

'A civilian purse,' I said, opening the similar pouch which I wore at my own waist. 'You surprise me. I thought you might have preferred an arm purse, military-style.' Most veterans carry their coinage under their wrist-pads, as they learned to do on the march.

Sollers shot me a sharp look. 'Indeed,' he said, 'I do. But

this was a gift from Quintus. It is similar to the pouch he wore himself.'

That was interesting, I thought, remembering how swiftly Maximilian had dropped it, almost as if he had been stung. I recalled Sollers saying that he would not put it past Maximilian to have staged that robbery. I wanted a word with that young man. But not now.

'Thank you, citizen.' I dropped the coins into my own purse. 'Rollo would be indebted to you. As the whole household is, Julia especially. She has told me about your work. She has nothing but praise for your skill.'

He looked at me sharply. 'Has she, indeed? I am surprised that she should confide so much to you. But yes, I have been treating Julia. I was hopeful, too, that my treatment had worked, but now of course it is no longer important. At least, unless she should choose to marry again. She is still young enough for that.'

So, I thought to myself, he *was* treating her for childlessness. Aloud I said, 'Julia told me that you were treating her, but she did not say why. Her praise was for your operation on her husband's eyes.'

For the first time since I had met him, I saw Sollers look less than composed. 'A thousand pardons, citizen. I thought she must have told you—'

'That you were helping her conceive a child?' I took a calculated risk. 'A pity that such a beautiful woman should have problems in that way. But she must have known about it before – she was married to Flavius for several years.'

Sollers hesitated a moment, and then he said, 'Citizen, you are a clever man, and I think you are an honest one. What I am about to tell you is a confidence between Julia and myself. I trust you not to abuse the knowledge, but I know that if I do not explain, you will try to deduce the matter for yourself, and perhaps come to worse conclusions.' He stopped and looked at me expectantly.

'Unless this has some bearing on the killings,' I said, 'Julia's confidence is safe with me. I give you my word as a citizen and a Celt.'

He smiled, amused at this expression. 'Then I will tell you. You guess correctly. Julia was desperate to have a child and create a new heir. I cannot blame her. Maximilian lacks both judgement and respect, and Julia feared that if her husband died – he was, after all, many years her senior – his fortune would be left at the mercy of his son. Ulpius has made provision for her, of course, and her dowry will revert to her; but she cannot do business or sign contracts without a legal protector. She feared that Maximilian would fritter everything away and leave her penniless in her old age. If she could provide a second heir, she could secure at least half the estate.'

'I have heard it suggested,' I interpolated doubtfully, 'that the infertility might not have been Julia's.'

He looked surprised. 'Julia believed that it was. She was, as you say, married for a long time to Flavius.'

'And did not manage to conceive.'

Sollers looked at me gravely. 'And had no children, citizen. That is not necessarily the same thing. On the contrary. Once, after Flavius had forced himself on her, Julia discovered she was expecting a child. She was appalled. A child would give Flavius an emotional hold over her, and besides she had recently met Quintus and was contemplating leaving her husband. To do so, under the circumstances, was to invite trouble. She . . . shall we say . . . took steps.'

I nodded. It was not unknown. Many women took matters into their own hands if they found themselves carrying an unwanted child. I could see what Julia feared.

The world would say the child was Quintus's, Flavius might even have dragged Quintus through the courts for damages, yet Quintus himself would never have accepted the child – and that would have been the end of marrying Julia. She must have been desperate. All the same, it showed a ruthlessness in her which was not altogether attractive. 'So, she went to a physician?'

'I wish she had. She went to a wise woman, secretly. And since then she has failed to conceive. These forceful internal applications of brimstone remove the child, but they can endanger the woman too, and prevent her from future births. That was what Julia feared. And she still had pain. That is why she came to me. She wanted to take advantage of her husband's illness to let me soothe the inflammation, and perhaps effect a cure. She could not guess, of course, that Ulpius would die before she could test the efficacy of the treatment.'

'I see,' I said. 'You have been very frank. But there is something else I need to ask. It is a delicate matter, but it is important that I know. What form, exactly, did your treatment take?'

Sollers hesitated a moment, but then he answered. 'I gave her herbs to drink, and a soothing douche of olive oil and milk. And, before you ask, it was the latter which I administered yesterday. Quintus was engaged with Maximilian, so we took advantage of the moment. So, if you are suspecting that Julia might have killed her husband, I can tell you otherwise. She needed to lie down to have the treatment, and for a little afterwards, and I was with her all the time. She may be embarrassed to tell you this, but it is the case.' The medicus looked at me soberly. 'Is there anything else, citizen, which you need to know?'

It was my turn, suddenly, to feel embarrassed. I was aware of having intruded upon a very private professional relationship, and of having forced the man into disconcerting candour. 'Not at all,' I said hurriedly, 'you have been most helpful. I apologise for having felt the need to ask. And now, if you'll excuse me, I will go and warn my patron. If I intend to visit the town I should do so before the morning is quite over.'

I turned back into the house and made my way to Marcus, with Junio again at my heels.

Marcus was in the blackest of moods. He had been given the best guest apartments, and had been provided with a pair of braziers, as requested. All the same, he had felt the cold. The house was draughty after his first-floor apartment in Glevum, and clearly the hypocaust was not as effective as the one in his country villa. He had scarcely slept a wink, he said; the couch was lumpy and the room was cold.

'The sleeping draught which Sollers provided for you made no difference, Excellence?' I asked solicitously. 'I didn't drink mine until it was almost light, but afterwards I slept like Morpheus.'

My enquiry did nothing to improve my patron's temper. 'It tasted foul,' he replied testily. I guessed that he had hardly tasted it and that my testimony now added to his discontent. He was irritable with cold and fatigue and the provision of a bought pie for breakfast had not helped matters, despite the exquisite tray and silver platter on which it had been served. Unlike Flavius, Marcus preferred more delicate flavours in the morning.

It was not, perhaps, the most propitious moment for making my announcements, but I could see no help for it.

I took a deep breath. 'Excellence, something has happened that I think you would wish to know.' I outlined everything that had happened since we spoke, beginning with Rollo's visit to me the night before, up to the gruesome discovery in the latrine that morning.

Marcus heard me out in silence. He hadn't been to the latrine himself. A glance beneath the bed told me that he had been given a more personal utensil. A latrine is a sign of status, certainly, but important visitors like Marcus cannot be expected to get up at night and walk all the way across the courtyard in the rain.

'So,' he said, when I had finished my tale, 'you think that I have made an error? I shouldn't have arrested Lupus. That is the gist of what you are telling me?'

It was not altogether the response I had been expecting. 'I mean that since Lupus was locked into the attics, on your orders, Excellence, it is impossible that he could have done this. And it would take a stronger man than Lupus to force Rollo into that latrine.'

He looked at me with more interest. 'So you think our killer is still abroad?' He glanced around the frieze of the chamber as though there might be someone lurking among the painted acanthus leaves.

'I think, Excellence, that you should be careful. There is, for instance, one dreadful possibility that occurs to me. Suppose that the boy was poisoned after all? Sollers agrees that it is possible. There may be something unwholesome in the kitchen. Or, possibly, a poisoner abroad.' I did not wish to alarm him unduly, but to my relief he took the bait at once.

He nodded. 'I'll have my slave down from the attic, to act as a food-taster. You can use Junio. One cannot be too careful.'

'And make sure everyone knows you've done it,' I said. 'By the by, Excellence, you have not, I suppose, received a message of any kind?'

'A message?'

'It occurs to me that since there has been another death,

someone might have received another message. Mentioning Pertinax, perhaps. Sollers was right, in one respect at least. Murderers often do repeat themselves.'

Marcus smiled. 'No, I have received no warning. We can take that, perhaps, as a sign that there was no deliberate attempt to poison you?'

I wished that I could be so certain. The message which Quintus had received was not exactly a warning either, unless you knew how to interpret it. In fact, when I came to think of it, Quintus had not actually 'received the message' at all. It had simply been discovered in the colonnade. The identity of that wax tablet troubled me. Was it the same one that Flavius had shown me, the one which Junio now had hidden in his tunic?

'You did not see that earlier tablet yourself, Excellence? The one which Ulpius spoke of in his letter?' I asked the question without any real hope. After all, Marcus had discussed the matter with me at length.

'Oh, yes,' Marcus said, as if it were the most natural revelation in the world. 'He sent it to me with the messenger. It was rather a distinctive thing. I have it with me somewhere.' He gestured helplessly towards the iron-bound wooden box which had accompanied him from Glevum, and which now stood at the foot of his couch. 'If I hadn't sent those wretched slaves away, I could have shown you.'

He could not be expected to rummage in the box himself, he meant. I could only smile wryly. First, because it was so typical of Marcus that he should tell me the details of the story without ever deigning to show me the evidence; and second, because my own bundle of possessions, wrapped up in a piece of cloth, would not have required a pair of slaves to search it: a strigil, a comb, a clean tunic and a fresh pair of under-breeches was all the baggage I possessed.

'Perhaps,' I suggested helpfully, 'if Junio . . .?'

Marcus assented with a nod. 'Why not?' He produced the ring key from his finger and Junio lifted the heavy chest while he opened the lock. 'You will find it in there, somewhere. It is wrapped in a leather pouch, since it is a delicate thing.'

Junio put the chest down gratefully, and fell to his knees beside it. It was full to bursting. Marcus had equipped himself for a visit to Corinium like an imperial general crossing the Alps: toga, cloak, sandals, underlinen, woollen foot socks, oils, combs, nose tweezers, ear scoops, even a travelling shrine and a box of ointments. And underneath, the leather pouch of which Marcus had spoken.

Junio pulled it out and handed it to Marcus. My patron opened it to reveal a fine wax writing tablet set in a carved ivory frame. Junio had just such another object hidden inside his tunic.

I nodded to him and he pulled that out in his turn.

Marcus looked from one to the other in dismay. 'But these are identical. Where did you get the second one from?'

I told him about my interview with Flavius.

My patron frowned. 'So we are back to Flavius again. I should have guessed that he was involved in this. After all, it was his dagger. You said from the outset that Flavius had a motive for hating Quintus. And yet he was so quick to point out the stains on the old man's toga . . . no doubt to deflect suspicion from himself. And he had arranged that Rollo should visit him last night.' He shook his head ruefully. 'Ah, yes, it all fits. Once again, Libertus, I should have listened to your counsel. I was too hasty in forming my judgements.'

He sounded so despondent that I was moved to say, 'Nevertheless, Excellence, one cannot dismiss Lupus entirely. Those bloodstains require explanation.'

He brightened. 'Yes, they do. Perhaps the two men were conspiring? They arrived at the house together, and they spent a long time alone in the front garden. They were whispering to each other in the arbour when you found them, I recall. Oh, Mercury! Nothing is ever as simple as it seems. What do you advise, old friend?'

I considered for a moment. I was not convinced that Lupus and Flavius were totally innocent, but I did think the matter was much more complex than Marcus seemed to believe. I said carefully, 'I think, Excellence, you might leave matters as they are at present. After all, there is no direct proof against Flavius, and one cannot have the whole household locked in the attics. A pair of stout slaves are already posted at his door, and he cannot leave the house, so he is effectively under guard already. As for Lupus, I should leave him where he is. He still has those bloodstains to explain, and even if you are wrong, the old man cannot be more offended than he already is.'

Marcus eyed me doubtfully. He has the Roman dislike of inaction. He would always prefer to be doing something, even if that something was wrong.

I gave Flavius's writing tablet back to Junio, who put it back in his pouch and returned the other to the travelling chest. 'Excellence, I hope you will excuse me. I wish to leave you. There are some questions I would like to ask in the town. The answers may help us to decide what to do with our prisoners.'

I said 'our prisoners' to ally myself deliberately with Marcus's decision. That swayed him. 'Oh, very well,' he said, 'go into the town if you must. I shall do nothing until you return. But do not be too long about it. And remember, I shall expect results.'

I bowed myself out, taking Junio with me. We crossed

the courtyard, passing Julia and Mutuus in furious conversation in the colonnade, and went to the kitchens, where Junio returned Marcus's breakfast tray and collected a jug for the wine we were to buy.

Even then, I failed to see what had been right in front of my eyes.

Chapter Fifteen

We went out through the back gate to avoid the press of visitors at the front. Even so, as soon as we were outside the walls of the enclosure, we were swept up in the activity and bustle of the town. A press of urchins surrounded us at once, offering to sell me everything from knick-knacks and copper pans to love potions and amulets, or simply volunteering to lead us to the best wineshops and dancing girls in town. One disreputable-looking fellow even approached us with a leer to ask if Maximilian had sent us to him. If this was the sort of company he kept, I thought, it was no wonder Quintus disapproved of his son.

We brushed them all aside and made our way down the side streets towards the centre of the town.

Corinium, it seemed, was in a constant state of rebuilding. Everywhere the old thatched timber shops and apartments were being pulled down, and finer ones were going up in their place, mostly built of limestone and roofed with tiles. The narrow streets were made still narrower by creaking carts laden with laths and plaster, or by the presence of lashed wooden ladders, where builders scuttled up and down with baskets of roof tiles or buckets of lime and mortar, while we picked our way along in constant apprehension of their rickety wooden pulleys swinging stone blocks overhead.

Amid this confusion, other stalls were doing a brisk trade, and all the way to the central square we were constantly hailed by shopkeepers hoping to entice us to buy their wares. Bone dealers vaunted their combs and pins, drapers held out lengths of woollen cloth and a draggled woman begged us to examine her 'best spindles, made from antler horn – cheapest in the Empire'. A shoemaker, straddling his bench, paused in his hammering of hobnails to wave a hopeful hand at shelves of ready-made boots and sandals, and when I declined to purchase, offered to measure me for a new pair on the spot.

I might indeed have been tempted by a new hammer from the blacksmith's, but what I had said to the medicus was true. I was not carrying a lot of money. Not, truth to tell, that I had a great deal of money to carry, at least until I had been paid for one or two commissions in Glevum. So it was no use gazing at buckled belts on the leather stall, or the fine bowls and beakers of the glass and pottery vendors. I limited myself to the necessary purchases with a sigh.

We did not go into the forum proper: not being market day, it would be given over to politicians, peddlers and moneylenders, so we confined our attentions to the arcaded shops on the outside of the square. I sent Junio with a jug to buy a measure of sour wine, while I stopped at a baker's shop and bought a cheap loaf of day-old barley bread. Poor Rollo would hardly need a fresh one, served hot on the long-handled iron bread slice straight from the great domed oven. I turned my face against the temptations of the other food stalls, although Junio, who had by then returned, was looking longingly at the honey cakes, and even the wares of the hot pie sellers smelled appetising now.

'What now, master?' Junio asked, tearing himself away from the sugared cakes reluctantly.

'I want to know exactly what Maximilian did yesterday.

It occurs to me that he arrived back at the house with clean garments after he had attended the baths.'

Junio shot me a look. 'Direct from the fuller's, you think?'

'It seems unlikely, since he came dressed in mourning colours. More likely he sent a slave to fetch some from his apartment, or even to buy him new ones. But I would be interested, all the same, to see the toga Maximilian took off. I noticed it was stained when I saw him – though I had no reason, then, to ask what the stains might be.'

Junio whistled. 'I see! Lupus may not be the only one with tell-tale marks on his sleeves. Then we should hurry, before the clothes are cleaned so much that it is impossible to tell.'

I nodded my approval and we hurried on, past the forum and the basilica (where the repairs which Lupus had resented so bitterly were still in progress), through the bleating, lowing, squealing chaos of the meat market and the accompanying fruit and vegetable carts, and so down to the fuller's shop, next door to the baths.

I wanted to visit the baths, too, as part of my enquiries, but it was still too early: at this hour only women were admitted. That visit would have to wait until we had been to the laundry shop. I thrust back the entrance curtain and strode in.

The owner was out when we arrived, and the work floor was manned by three scrawny, underfed individuals in tattered tunics and bare feet, trampling garments in the cleaning tanks.

I went over to them and they stopped at my approach. Supporting one's weight on a pair of stout handles while one treads wet clothes into fuller's clay for hours is a back-breaking business, and they were obviously glad of a moment to rest their weary arms and legs. They looked at me curiously, their pale faces damp with sweat and their overdeveloped thighs glistening with moisture.

'You had a customer, yesterday,' I began. 'From the house of Quintus Ulpius?'

They looked at each other nervously. I took out a purse and began fingering a five-*as* coin in an ostentatious manner.

One of the treaders gave me a grim, knowing smile. 'Two customers,' he began, but he was interrupted by the appearance of a languid youth in an elegant coloured robe. The owner's son, clearly.

'Can I assist you, citizen?'

Mentally I consigned him to Pluto. Any information was likely to cost me a great deal more than a few *asses* now. Unless I could somehow persuade him of my importance.

I put on my best formal manner. 'I am a guest in the house of Quintus Ulpius the decurion,' I said. 'I believe there were some clothes left here for cleaning yesterday.' He was looking at me suspiciously, so I invented an excuse for my visit. 'I suppose they are not ready for collection yet?'

It seemed to work. The youth flushed with consternation. 'I regret, citizen, they are far from ready. It takes days, you know, to get these things done properly. The young man's toga is still bleaching on the frames, and the other garments have not yet been laundered at all.'

'How far have they progressed?' I said, imitating Marcus's peremptory manner as best I could. 'Where are they?'

'Why, here, citizen, I will lead the way,' he said, his manner all abject apology. He could not, however, quite disguise his alarm and impatience. He turned to the treaders. 'Well, what are you waiting for? The return of Hadrian? Get on with your work.'

I felt a twinge of regret. My enquiry was unreasonable –

no one could fuller garments in a day – but the poor fellows would feel the lash of his tongue when I had gone, if not a lashing of a more tangible kind. However, I followed him into the adjoining cell where the wicker bleaching frames stood. A number of garments were already set out to whiten in the lime fumes.

Maximilian's toga was indeed among them – instantly recognisable among the spotless white of its neighbours. However, the treatment was already having its effect on the stained cloth. There were the traces of one or two dark marks visible upon it, but nothing more.

'You have almost removed the stains?' I said, as casually as I could. 'What were they this time? Wine again, I imagine?'

The youth was already ahead of me. 'I wish I could tell you, citizen, but when the slave brought it in we paid no particular attention. Maximilian is always sending wine-stained togas to be cleaned. We simply washed and bleached it as usual. We did not know then that the decurion was dead. I was shocked when I heard about the stabbing – the household has sent its linen here for years.' He looked at me with ghoulish relish. 'You think the stains might have been blood, citizen?'

'It is possible,' I said. 'Maximilian went in to see his father's body.'

'Ah.' Once the suggestion of scandal was removed, the youth's interest was deader than Quintus. 'If we had noticed that, we would have soaked it in salt to remove the stain. As we are doing with the lady's gown.'

I could not have been more surprised if Jupiter himself had suddenly appeared in a clap of thunder.

'The lady's gown?' That was a false move. If I was supposed to be here officially, I should have known what laundry had been sent.

The youth, however, misinterpreted. 'Do not concern yourself, citizen. Everything is accounted for. There were two garments sent here, naturally: the amethyst-coloured stola and a lilac shift. What I meant to say was that only the stola had blood on it.'

My mind was still reeling from the implications of this – there had been no stains on that stola when Julia greeted us yesterday – and I could think of nothing to say. I must have looked so startled that I was in danger of making the youth suspicious of my authority, but Junio came to my rescue. 'You are soaking it, you say? I thought you said that you had not yet begun to launder the lady's garments?'

I sent up mental thanks to my private gods. Junio had avoided the danger of non-cooperation neatly by diverting the fellow's attention to an inconsistency in his own account of things. I caught my servant's eye and gave him an approving wink.

The fuller's son was tripping over his tunic hems in his desire to propitiate. 'Indeed, citizen,' he said, addressing himself to me alone, 'I did not make myself clear. We have only just begun to soak it, so it has not been put into the tubs. I am sorry, citizen, perhaps we should have made a start on it before, but we were busy and these were not the . . .' he hesitated, 'the kind of stains we sometimes see on female dress, and which we always deal with at once. There were only small splashes of blood, on the front of the garment, and only on the stola, as I say. There was nothing on the under-tunic at all.'

It is a long time since I was a married man, and even then my Gwellia was discreet. It took me some moments to perceive what he meant. When I did understand, I felt myself colour with confusion. Junio, who must have received a biological education from somewhere, had turned the colour of carmine, but the youth himself looked comparatively unembarrassed. Presumably such considerations are commonplace if one works in a fuller's shop.

'Come and see for yourself, citizen.' He led the way back into the main workshop. One of the workers, I noticed, was now taking garments from the rinsing tubs and hanging them on wooden slats to dry, while the other two struggled with the screws on the heavy flattening press, to drive out creases from the previously dried items from the rack. The exhortation to work faster had obviously been taken to heart.

The youth stopped before a pottery basin containing a thick salty solution. The top part of a garment was half submerged in it. 'Here is the over-gown I spoke of,' he said, lifting it out, dripping, with a pair of wooden tongs.

I recognised it, without surprise, as the stola which Julia had been wearing the day before. It had been rubbed with salt to remove the stains, but the tell-tale splash marks were still evident. One, indeed, on the underside of the wide sleeve had so far escaped the fuller's attentions. There was no doubt about it: it was blood.

I caught Junio's eye, and he gave me a significant look. I knew what he was thinking. Lupus had been detained in the attics for less. And there had been no stains on this stola when Julia met us yesterday.

The young man saw the stain that I was looking at and immediately began to apologise again. That mark would be dealt with presently, he protested; with such fine cloth it was better to soak a little at a time. I noticed the poisonous look which he aimed at his assistants, however. Free-men labourers or slaves, I wondered? The former, probably: they wore no brands or fetters, and no slave tags round their necks. Whatever they were, they must have hated me. I was heartily glad I was not one of them.

'And the lilac shift?' I demanded, with a return to my peremptory manner.

The youth nodded. 'That, citizen, was hardly dirty; it cannot have been worn more than a dozen times. I wonder the lady thought to have it laundered at all, and did not merely have her maids sponge it with vinegar and milk and lay it on the grass. But I suppose she felt the need to clean it thoroughly, since I presume she was wearing it when she first saw her husband dead. I have known such things happen before, as if we could wash away memories.' He favoured me with an understanding smile.

I nodded grimly. The youth, in fact, spoke more truly than he knew. If that was Quintus's blood on her bodice, and I believed it was, Julia would have wanted the shift sent to the fuller's at all costs. For when, exactly, had she managed to get herself spattered so?

I might have pressed him further, but our conversation was interrupted by the arrival of a fat, florid man in a spotless tunic and a bad temper. It was the owner, clearly, and judging by the way he was scowling suspiciously at us, he was more likely to demand answers than offer them.

'Well,' I said, 'if there is nothing to be gained by staying here, we have other business in the town. I will bid you good day.'

'But citizen,' the youth said plaintively. 'The household account! Quintus Ulpius has not paid us since the Ides, and his son has had several garments cleaned since then.' He gestured to a space on the wall where various accounts had been roughly scratched in chalk. Maximilian, I noted, had run up a sizeable sum in Quintus's name.

And now I was expected to pay it, and I had no money in my purse. I thought quickly, and found a solution. 'The testament will be read this afternoon in the forum. Present yourself among his debtors then.'

The young man nodded, and even the older man's scowl lifted. 'Ah yes, of course! And even if we get no payment then, no doubt Maximilian will be able to meet his own bills in future. Thank you for having the courtesy to call and tell us, citizen.' The fuller looked at my toga thoughtfully. 'And if you should ever require our services yourself, you will find our rates as cheap as anyone's. We could bring that toga up nicely, with a little care.'

I went out of the shop feeling peculiarly humbled.

Chapter Sixteen

'Well, master,' Junio said, as soon as we were in the street again, 'that was an interesting visit. What, if anything, do you deduce from that?'

We were dodging between the wheels of ox carts and I stood aside, under the portico of the baths, to answer his question.

'What do you think I deduce?' I said wryly. 'Julia has been lying to us, obviously. Marcus will take that badly.' In fact, I was ashamed to find how badly I was taking it myself. Julia was a beautiful and wealthy lady, and however much I admired her independent spirit – and her more obvious charms – it was not up to me to be swayed by that and decide that she was automatically innocent. Those bloodstains were certainly suspicious. 'Pluto take her, and the whole affair!' I said savagely. I must have sounded harsher than I meant. Junio looked dismayed, and a passing bather, going into the building with his slaves, looked at me in surprise. I regretted my outburst instantly. 'So, what do you deduce yourself?'

Junio gave me a doubtful look, but he answered the question soberly. It was the game we sometimes played, having him predict my conclusions, but it had a purpose: it not only taught him to reason clearly, but it often helped me to see things in a new light. 'Certainly the lady did not get those stains from putting powder on her cheeks. Could they be from Sollers's treatment, do you think? Did he bleed her, for instance?'

I shook my head dubiously. 'I do not think so. The treatment he described to me did not involve bleeding the patient, and I think he would have mentioned it if it had. In any case, he is practised in the art. If he did bleed her, he would not have splashed her over-tunic in that way. And it cannot be accidental bleeding. Sollers favours gentle methods. My owner's first wife was treated for childlessness, and during her treatment her cries used to petrify the household. They gave her fearsome fumigation, till she sobbed with inner scalding from the vapours, but even then I do not recall hearing that the treatment drew blood.'

'Of course,' Junio said suddenly, 'Julia may not have been wearing the stola when she went to see Sollers. We know she went to her room to beautify herself. Perhaps she changed there into the Grecian coat you tell me she was wearing later. It might have made the treatment easier.'

It was an obvious possibility once he had suggested it, and I rewarded him with a smile. 'Well reasoned, Junio.' I refused to admit, even to myself, how much my pleasure was due to the fact that I could now find an explanation which left Julia innocent. I also refused to contemplate what I already knew – that she had been in the kitchens the night before, and could easily have tampered with the food. Julia would never have tried to poison me, I reasoned. If anything, she seemed to be drawn to intellect, and to find me flatteringly attractive.

(Foolish, I told myself. However warm and intimate her smiles, Julia would never have time for a humble pavement-maker – she belonged to men of substance and standing. And to Mutuus, some inner voice prompted hopefully – but I quelled it at once.)

All the same, Junio had a point. If Julia had taken off her robe, and left it unattended while she went to consult

Sollers, then anyone could have taken it from her room. It was unlikely, but possible all the same. Maximilian, for example, had visited her room by his own admission. Perhaps he tried to implicate her by staining the stola with blood.

I was so pleased with this hypothetical solution that I felt positively benign. 'I must find a moment to ask Sollers what she was wearing at the consultation,' I said. 'In the meantime, I see the baths are opening for male customers. I think I can afford a *quadrans* to go in.'

Junio gave me an impudent grin. 'Going to indulge yourself, then, master? Do you wish me to go and fetch a towel and strigil for you, so that you can bathe?'

I thought about that for a moment. Allowing Junio to leave me unattended would cost me an extra *as* or two. Without him I should have to pay one of the attendants to oil my back, and another to watch my garments in the changing room. There is a merry little trick which is often played upon unwary bathers in Glevum: itinerant fraudsters come to the baths in old tunics, and leave wearing someone else's new one. I did not imagine Corinium was any different, and my wardrobe was not so great that I could afford to take the risk.

On the other hand, I wanted to discover, if I could, exactly what Maximilian had been up to the day before. He had come here, I was fairly sure of that, because he had been attended by four of his father's slaves. But the public baths are places for meeting people as much as for performing ablutions. I was particularly interested to know if Maximilian had spoken to anyone, and if so, what he had said about the day's events.

'Towel, strigil and oil, if you can find some,' I said to Junio. 'When you return, look for me on the stone benches outside the warm pool. Tell the attendant you have come for me and then he should not charge you to enter, but here is a quadrans for you, just in case. You can take the wine and bread back to the house for Rollo when you go.'

'And I will inform the funeral guild for slaves,' Junio suggested. 'The chief slave told me where to find the house.'

I nodded. 'And . . . Junio?'

'Master?'

I took out a little money and gave him my purse. 'Look after this for me.' I dropped a coin in his palm. 'And here is the money for a honey cake for yourself. I think that you have earned it this last hour.'

He gave me a huge grin and disappeared into the crowd before I could change my mind. I watched him until he was out of sight, then paid my quadrans and went inside.

I love the public baths. Like underfloor heating, they are one of the best things the Romans ever brought with them. Of course, I am rarely in a position to enjoy them – not because of the entry price; baths rarely cost more than a tenth of an as even in the most expensive towns – but because in the ordinary way I have business to attend to. People like Quintus may attend to their affairs while sitting in the hot room with their friends, but a man who lays pavements cannot do it at a distance. My ablutions normally consist of the kind of minimal rinse and oiling I had received this morning.

It was with some anticipation, then, that I took off my toga and tunic and left them on the stone shelf in one of the little alcoves in the changing room, under the eye of a disreputable-looking attendant, who looked at my as coin with disdain. A man in a toga, his demeanour seemed to say, should be more generous with his tips. I had intended to ask the fellow about Maximilian, but it was clear that any gossip from this source would have to be bought, so I left my precious clothes with him, together with a veiled promise that there would be a further tip if I returned to find them intact.

That brought a sullen smile to his face, and I left him to it and went into the warm pool where I was soon soaking myself luxuriously. The room was disappointingly empty, however, since it was just past noon and few of the male customers had yet arrived. I would have to gain my information, if any, on my way back from the hotter sections. If necessary, I would have to bribe the youth guarding the tunics, although somehow I didn't trust him. Cloakroom attendants are often casual opportunists, like the boys who offer to hold your horses in the street, rather than sober servants of the baths, and I had an uncomfortable feeling that I had seen this one somewhere before. Remembering the problems with missing tunics at Glevum, I even got up and gazed at him through the intervening arch. However, he was sitting on a stone bench looking bored, and my clothes were still clearly visible where I had left them, so I went back to my bathe.

I stayed for a little in the warm steam of the *tepidarium*, and then, as there was still no sign of Junio, paid the attendant for a phial of oil and went – perfumed but still dripping – into the dry heat of the *laconicum*.

It is not, in general, my preferred routine, insofar as I can be said to have a routine at all in a public bathhouse. When I go, I usually prefer the hot steam room, but if Quintus was to bequeath a new *caldarium* to the populace, it followed that the present one was less than satisfactory, so I chose the drier alternative. I sat for a few moments, feeling the heat opening my pores and making the oil run in little rivulets on my skin, but I am no Roman, and I cannot sustain those temperatures for long. I was about to return to conditions where I was less likely to sizzle, when the inner door opened and the man who had passed us on the entrance steps came in. He splashed a little oil on himself, as I have seen cooks baste a chicken, and sat down with care on the marble seat.

He was, from the snow-white toga he had worn when he arrived, a candidate for public office, and would not normally have given me a second glance, but in a bath-house every man is equal, except perhaps the Jews. (Of course there are those, more Roman than the Romans, who affect special little tunics to bathe in, but even they would probably desist if they heard the comments which follow when they leave. Common opinion is that such men have something – or nothing much – to hide.)

He gave me an affable nod.

I decided to endure cooking for a little longer. 'Very quiet in here today.'

He smiled. I noticed that his armpits were red and angry where he had just had them plucked in the inner room. He must have been a braver man than I am – I could never willingly have endured that torment, and I had not heard him so much as scream. 'You should have been here yesterday.'

I gave him my full attention. 'You were here then? Did you see Ulpius Maximilian here? The son of the decurion?'

The look of boiled affability faded. 'You are a friend of his?'

'Not really. I had business connections with his family,' I said. It was stretching a point, since I had not yet officially acquired the contract for the pavement, but it raised my status in my companion's eyes.

'I see,' he murmured sympathetically. 'And now you will be seeking payment from the heir? The death of Quintus Ulpius is a bad business, in more respects than one. That young son of his is a wastrel. He owes money in all the wineshops of Corinium. He was in here yesterday, looking like a bedraggled traveller instead of a future councillor, whispering with that unpleasant creature who guards the clothes and slipping him money.'

It was the news I had been waiting for, and I got gratefully to my feet. 'Then I must go and have a few words with the attendant myself,' I said. 'Good afternoon. Enjoy your bathe.' I smiled at him and left hurriedly.

It felt cool in the tepidarium after the heat of the dry room. A few more minutes in there, I thought, and I could have saved the cooks the necessity of roasting the pig for the funeral feast. They could have stuffed baked plums and herbs into my mouth and served me up instead. To my delight, too, Junio was waiting for me, so I perched on a bench and let him strigil off the sweat, dirt and oil as I told him what I had discovered, and he then stood by with a towel while I plunged gratefully into the tepid pool.

I ignored the attractions of the entertainments – watching the wrestlers or losing my shirt on the fall of a dice – and finished my ablutions with a brief but bracing swim in the large cold pool outside, and went back shivering to claim my clothes. They were untouched, to my relief. I allowed Junio to dress me, and then, taking the attendant into a corner, took back my purse and drew out a few more quadrans for a tip. The attendant scowled at the size of the offering, but reached for it all the same.

I dropped the money into his palm. 'By the way,' I said conversationally, 'what was it that Ulpius Maximilian was talking to you about yesterday?'

I had been prepared, secretly, to pay for the information; in fact, the poorness of the tip was caused, in part, by the need to keep some coins for the purpose. I need not have bothered, as it happened. The attendant looked at me in horror, as though I had offered to feed him to the wolves.

'Well?' I insisted. 'And do not deny it – I have spies who saw you in conversation.' I wondered, inwardly, what my companion of the hot room would think of being elevated to the role of spy, but this was not a time for niceties.

The attendant looked about him wildly as if seeking inspiration. 'It was nothing. An argument about his clothes. He thought I had failed to guard them properly when he came to dress again. Nothing else, citizen, nothing at all.'

It was a more intelligent lie than I had expected. Nine times out of ten he would have been believed, and even a doubter would find it difficult to disprove the story. Now, however, he was unlucky. This was the proverbial tenth time out of ten.

'No,' I said, in the same conversational tone, 'I dare say that you have a dozen such confrontations every day, but it was not what you were discussing with Maximilian. He sent his clothes from here directly to the fuller's, and had his slaves bring fresh ones when he left, because he needed to leave here wearing mourning. He did not *have* garments in your changing room. Besides, he was seen to give you money. He would hardly do that if he was dissatisfied. No, he was paying you for something. And I don't imagine he was trading in second-hand tunics.'

A look of panic crossed the attendant's face. 'Hush, citizen, I beg you, not so loud. It was a private matter. A favour that I did for him. He was paying me for my services.'

This fellow had a strange definition of 'favours', I thought, but the explanation was plausible enough. It was well known that attendants at the baths in any town – if they were not slaves, and sometimes if they were – turned a dishonest *as* or two by acting as pimps for local dancing girls. Sometimes, if they could afford it, they lent money at exorbitant interest to bathers who had lost all their cash at the poolside gambling games. It fitted the picture I had of Quintus's son.

The attendant smiled at me hopefully. It was an unctuous, unwholesome, lopsided smile, and it was unmistakable. As soon as I saw it I realised where I had seen the youth before. This was the same fellow who had accosted us at the gates this morning, asking for Maximilian.

I taxed him with it at once. 'So that was why you came to the house this morning? To ask for more payment? It must have been a significant favour.' It was, I thought, a singularly inopportune moment to choose, when Quintus had just died. 'Were you aware of what had happened to his father? You knew about the stabbing?'

The effect was extraordinary. The attendant turned first white, then pink, as if he had been plunged into his own cold pool, and sweat began to stand out on his forehead. His voice almost failed him as he croaked, 'If you knew about it too, citizen, why didn't you say so to begin with?' He looked suspiciously to right and left as if the statues in their niches might be listening. 'What is it you want, part of the money? There's no need to come to me, citizen. Now that his father is dead, there should be enough for us both.'

Chapter Seventeen

To say that I was thunderstruck by this reply would be an insult to Jove's thunderbolts. Not only was it the last response I was expecting, but I had no idea what it meant. I shot a look at Junio, who was standing behind the attendant, but he simply shrugged his shoulders at me and opened his eyes wide. He was obviously as baffled as I was.

'Money?' I said to the bath boy, 'I did not come here looking for money. I am interested in Maximilian.'

This answer seemed to cause the attendant more anguish than ever. 'Great Mercury! You are not about to arrest him? Don't do that, citizen. It will solve nothing now. Ulpius is dead, and we shall all be the losers. Leave Maximilian to me, citizen. No one else need know our little secret, and I'll make it worth your while.'

A glimmer of possible understanding filtered into my brain. 'Maximilian is paying you for your silence?'

No answer. If my surmise was accurate, I thought, Maximilian was getting value for his money at this moment at least. I remembered my earlier thoughts about Maximilian, and ventured another wild guess.

'Because you have evidence against him? Evidence about who stabbed his father? Maximilian did it?'

The youth looked at me with contempt. 'No, of course he didn't. At least not personally. It would have been far too dangerous to do it himself.'

My carefully constructed conclusions crumbled at his

words like a wattle wall at a battering ram. However, the fellow was only talking because he thought I knew something. I said with a show of great conviction, 'But you know who did.' I did not make it a question.

The attendant blanched. 'I see, citizen. You have come from them.' He shook his head in agitation. 'No, citizen, I swear to you. On all the gods I swear, I did not recognise the men. I did not even see them properly. All I know is that after the stabbing they went to meet Maximilian. They were standing there, in the shadows, when I came out of the baths. I recognised Maximilian, but I couldn't see the men's faces. I promise you that, citizen.'

I was nonplussed. How could anyone arriving at the baths with Maximilian yesterday be hidden in shadow? 'In the shadows, you say?'

He gave me a shifty look. 'It was dark. There was a moon, but I was carrying no torch or candle, and neither were they. The light was poor, and Maximilian was so busy with the men he didn't notice me.'

Suddenly, I began to understand. A dark night, a clouded moon. This was the night of the chariot races. I remembered it only too clearly.

'It was late,' I said. 'The baths were closed. What were you doing here at that hour?'

'I'd come back to collect . . . something I'd left behind.' Whatever the 'something' was, I thought, ten *denarii* to an *as* he had stolen it from a bather. As he had also, presumably, stolen a key to the door of the building. 'I came out and saw them together. Maximilian was furious, because the plan had gone awry. He kept saying over and over that they were simply supposed to threaten Ulpius and take his purse, not stab him in the stomach, but of course the men didn't care a quadrans for that.'

So that was it! I could imagine the scene: the attendant

skulking in the shadows, taking good care not to be noticed; Maximilian talking to the ruffians. The boy had not observed the men's faces, I thought, but even in the feeble light he had seen one thing clearly enough – the opportunity for profit. Doubtless he hoped that Maximilian would pay a high price for silence.

'Maximilian did not want to pay them, but of course he had to do it in the end. He had bribed the soothsayer, an old woman who hangs around the forum so that she would waylay the medicus on his way back from the chariot races, and leave the way open for the attack. And the men knew it.'

The story was making sense. If Maximilian refused to pay the men, she would presumably go to the authorities, for a price, and testify against him – though of course the attackers themselves would take care to be in another part of the country by then. If he was proved to have bribed the soothsayer, there would be a convincing case for attempted parricide. No court would believe that he merely intended robbery.

'So,' I said, 'you waited until the men had gone and then confronted him? Told him that he could have your silence for a price?'

The youth gave that unattractive smile again. 'Maximilian offered first,' he said, primly. 'I stepped out of the shadows and he offered me half the purse if I held my tongue. There was not much money in it. There should have been more. Quintus had won a good sum on the races. I think the men had stolen half of it, and then Maximilian had to pay them as well.' He laughed unkindly. 'The poor fool gave me all he had, in the end. He didn't even have the money to hire a slave to see him home.'

'And, of course, you've asked him for more money since then?'

'Well, he deserved it. Forever coming in here drunken and gambling. And he arranged to have his father robbed at knifepoint. Why should he get away with it? He would have fared worse at the hands of the *aediles* if I had informed on him. Anyway, I needed the money more than he did. I saw a chance to get out of here – to move from that hovel of a top flat over the wineshop and start a little business of my own somewhere. Some town where I have not been a beggar since I could walk.'

'A trade in second-hand clothes, no doubt?' I enquired. He ignored the barb, and I went on. 'But you are still here, I see?'

He scowled. 'One cannot pick olives from a dead tree. Maximilian has no money to give – he has been trying to fob me off with gifts of jewels and plate. What use are they to me? I can hardly sell them, at least not in Corinium. I should get myself crucified as a highway thief if I tried. But it will be different, now that he has inherited his father's estate. Do not arrest him, citizen. As I say, I will make it worth your while.'

'It seems to me,' I said, 'that Maximilian is not the only one who should fear arrest. I came here to build a pavement for the baths, so you can see I have the ear of the town council. I think they will be interested to hear of this. Not only do you conceal your knowledge of a crime, but you come to the baths at night to collect items you have hidden here – stolen, no doubt, from the customers. You also have, by your own admission, jewels and plate in your possession belonging to Ulpius Quintus, since that is of course where Maximilian got them from – I believe he was hunting in his rooms yesterday trying to find something else to pay you with. No doubt the *aediles* would find them in that hovel over the wineshop that you spoke of.'

He looked at me, horrified. 'But you can't . . .' You could

almost see him weighing up the bribe. At last he burst out
with it. 'How much is it you want?'

'Provided, of course,' I went on, ignoring him, 'that you
survive long enough to be arrested. Maximilian, after all,
knows people who are handy with a dagger. If they will
attack a decurion like Ulpius, I do not imagine that a bath
boy will cause them much concern. I am surprised that
Maximilian has not thought of it before.'

It was too much for the youth. He cast a terrified look
in my direction and, stopping to pick up a small urn from
one of the niches, bolted for the door and disappeared.
Junio was ready to run after him, but I called him back.

'Let him go. We have other matters to attend to, and the
baths will be a better place without him.'

Junio nodded reluctantly. 'If you say so, master. After
all, he wasn't a slave.'

That was no idle distinction. Permitting a slave to escape
is a serious offence – although it is even more serious for
the deserter. Runaway slaves are hunted by everyone, from
the authorities downwards, and are likely to be severely
whipped or fed to the beasts when recaptured. Or both.
Those that fail to escape must often wish that they had
perished less painfully in the attempt.

However, we need not fear the justices. Our man was
one of the freeborn poor. That was why I had let him go. I
should have handed him over to the authorities – he was a
blackmailer and a thief – but I couldn't help feeling a
twinge of sympathy for him, abandoned at an early age
into a poky hovel and scratching a living where he could.
After all, I told myself, he had done no great harm. He had
stolen a few trinkets and forced Maximilian to pay a high
price for his foolishness, but there could be no court case
against him for that, because Maximilian had not complained about it at once as the law demanded. No doubt

most of the things could be recovered – the little weasel was too terrified to return to his flat.

There would be no 'little business' for him now, either. Instead, I guessed, he would join the bands of ragged beggars and tricksters who frequent the highways, supported by whatever he had hidden in that urn. All in all, I did not feel that Corinium would suffer his loss.

In the meantime, the baths were short of an attendant and the place was filling up quickly.

'Marcus will be waiting,' I said to Junio, 'and in any case, I think it is time we left. Prospective bathers are already shouting for somebody to watch their clothes. Besides, I want to go to the forum and hear the reading of the will. It will be starting soon.'

The boy shot me a delighted grin and we went out, back into the hubbub of the town. It was well past noon now, and a crowd was beginning to gather and make its way, jostling, under the carved portico and into the forum. We joined them and soon reached the steps of the basilica, where the ceremony would take place.

The basilica was a fine building, despite the works that were being carried out to it – a huge marble-faced edifice with an apse at one end and a flight of imposing stone steps leading up to the entrance. It was fronted by a number of fine statues, and in particular by Jupiter's column, which had a decided cant. I remembered what Lupus had said about the collection of taxes for its repair.

I had plenty of time to admire it, because there was an appreciable wait. I was beginning to consider giving up and going back to find Marcus before we exhausted his patience, when there was a little stir at the entrance and people stood back to let two litters pass, accompanied by a small retinue on foot. Julia and Sollers had arrived, with Mutuus and a pair of slaves in attendance. I was surprised.

It is not usual for a woman to attend, but Julia had defied convention, and although she wore a loose veil over her head, she had not covered her face as most widows do. She walked to the steps of the basilica with a firm tread and her head held high. What a woman she was. I looked for Maximilian, but there was no sign of him. A pity. I had things to say to him.

A group of toga-ed officials appeared from within the building, some with their staffs of office carried before them by *lictors*, while a chair was fetched and the presiding magistrate seated himself importantly upon it. As a decurion, Quintus could expect to have proper ceremony attending the opening of his will. The precious scroll was produced – an impressive legal document on fine parchment, sealed with heavy wax – the seals were broken (ceremonially, with the crowd crying 'ahh!' at each seal) and the reading commenced.

The will was concise, as far as Roman wills ever are. Quintus had eschewed the common practice of using his will as an opportunity to malign his enemies, and apart from a slighting reference to Lupus, 'that vain and grotesque parcel of lascivious bones', there was little in the preamble to delight the crowd. The endowments, too, were simple enough. His debts were first to be paid (cheers from the bystanders, including the fuller and his son whom I had spotted among the audience). Then, a great feast was to be held in the market square (louder cheers), followed by a gladiatorial contest and chariot racing in the arena. (Prolonged cheering, after which many of the audience began to drift away.) A series of substitute legatees was named, in case the prime and secondary heirs refused to inherit, as they sometimes did, and a number of small bequests were made to clientes 'in remembrance of duty owed'. Manumission for the chief slave and a formal ending of Mutuus's bond were also granted, although the remaining crowd was visibly less interested in these provisions.

Then came the real business of the day. There was a generous sum for Sollers, together with a small but adequate pension for life. To Julia, Quintus left his country house (I was not aware that he had one), and one third of the fortune. The town house and the rest of the estate went to Maximilian, who was named as principal heir. And then came the real surprise.

'I appoint my esteemed friend, Marcus Aurelius Septimus, if he will accept the office, to act as legal sponsor to my wife, in all matters of contract and in the courts, on the understanding that he will act only according to her wishes; and she may marry or use her endowment as she will.'

That would please Marcus, I thought. I wondered if he had known of it.

Maximilian had still not put in an appearance. As the crowd began to drift away. I made my way through the remaining bystanders until I reached the basilica steps. Julia saw me and gave me one of her heart-stopping smiles. As I came towards the little party, she reached out a welcoming hand. There were, I noticed, tears glistening in the saffron-lidded eyes.

'It is a mournful business, is it not? But Quintus has dealt generously with us all. Naming Marcus as my protector was a clever move. It will save me from Flavius. I was afraid he would try to claim jurisdiction over me. And there are a good many public endowments.'

I smiled grimly. 'But not, I fear, anything about pavements.'

'Quintus obviously expected to donate that while he lived.' She turned impulsively to Sollers. 'We might, don't you think, commission one all the same? In memory of my husband?'

He looked at her indulgently. 'Julia, my dear. The fortune is yours. Marcus is notionally your sponsor, but you heard the terms of the will. You are no longer in tutelage, either as a daughter or a wife. You must spend your money as you please. However, since you suggest it, such a gesture would be a gracious one.'

She smiled at me again. 'Then, Libertus, the commission is yours.' She seemed to stop and consider. 'A bold design is best, I think. It will in any case be difficult to see the mosaic through the steam. When the funeral is over, I will speak to your patron about keeping you here a while.' Julia, it seemed, had little difficulty making decisions, once the chance was offered.

I thanked her gravely, although, of course, without a nominated price such a promise does not constitute a contract – as I have learned before, to my cost. I wondered if Julia knew that. She raised her hand in dismissal, then turned and made her way towards the waiting litter.

Sollers might have followed her, but I detained him. I was delighted by the kindness of her offer, but I had concerns about it. 'Will there,' I asked him seriously, 'be sufficient funds for such an endowment? I should not like the lady to overreach herself for my benefit.'

He laughed. 'There is no fear of that. Quintus was worth a considerable fortune. Julia was always wealthy, my friend. Now she is very rich indeed.'

'And Maximilian?'

His face clouded. 'Maximilian even more so. He will have, of course, to take his father's place as decurion in due course, but mercifully he cannot seek election until he is twenty-five. Perhaps by then he will have learned some greater discretion.'

'And you, what will you do now?'

He shook his head. 'I do not know as yet. Nothing,

185

perhaps, for a little while. Quintus has been most generous to me. Much more than I expected or deserved. Perhaps I will seek a civic appointment. Or perhaps Julia will have a use for me.'

He sounded so forlorn that I was moved to say, suddenly, 'Have you no idea at all? What was it that the soothsayer foretold?'

He looked at me in surprise.

'That evening,' I said, 'when you were returning from the chariot races. Did she give you no advice?'

He gave me a wry smile. 'Oh, yes, I had forgotten you were there. It was much as you'd expect. The usual mixture of wild promises and dreadful warnings. I paid no attention to her. I fear the gods, and have a proper respect for omens and the established augurs, but I do not pay much credence to the ramblings of warty old beggar-women who claim to see meaning in a flock of birds. And now, excuse me: I must return to the house. There is much still to do. Do you wish to accompany us?'

The thought of trailing along on foot beside the litters with the slaves while he rode in style with Julia was not appealing. However, I had my excuse to hand. 'I have not quite finished my enquiries, medicus. I have learned something interesting in the town. Something of great significance. Please give that message to my patron and tell him I will not be long.'

He looked at me sharply, but I offered no more and finally he said, 'As you wish, citizen. Till later, then.'

He nodded in farewell, and strode to where the litters were waiting. Julia was getting into one of them, assisted by Mutuus, who was helping her into it with assiduous attention, while Julia smiled her thanks.

At that moment, despite his legacy, Sollers did not look a happy man.

Chapter Eighteen

The slaves raised the litters to their shoulders, and, swaying under the weight, moved swiftly out of the forum. I watched them go. It was starting to rain again, and we took shelter under the portico.

Junio looked at me. 'Further business, you said, master? You want to find that soothsayer?'

I grinned at him. 'I want to visit the slave market. I still haven't made any enquiries about Gwellia. But yes, I want to see this soothsayer, before she disappears like the boy from the baths. It appears that she was little better than a beggar. No wonder she was susceptible to Maximilian's bribe.' That had surprised me a little at the time. Amateur soothsayers are sometimes crazy, but they are usually sincere.

Junio nodded. 'No wonder either that Sollers was unimpressed.'

'I only marvel that he stopped to listen to her at all.'

'I wonder what she said to him,' Junio said with a grin. 'I suppose we can guess what the "dire predictions" were like, since Maximilian was paying her to make them. "Beware the house of the decurion", no doubt. Or something more mysterious-sounding than that, but meaning the same thing. You know what soothsayers are like.'

I grinned back at him. 'It seems that you do,' I said jokingly. 'She didn't get around to telling my fortune. I don't often consult soothsayers. And neither does Sollers, seemingly.' A thought struck me and I added, more thoughtfully, 'Though in that case, wasn't it rather dangerous for Maximilian to choose to delay him with a soothsayer? There must have been a chance that he would ignore her and walk on.'

Junio shook his head. 'I don't know. Sollers talked about "the usual things" that soothsayers tell you. That sounds as if he's talked to them before. And you stopped and listened to her, after all.'

That was well argued. 'Yes, you are right. He would have stopped and listened if a fortune-teller sought him out, even if afterwards he dismissed it. Especially if the "promises" were what he wanted to hear.'

'And no doubt Maximilian would have seen to that.' Junio frowned. 'Sollers believes that Maximilian killed his father. You saw that demonstration with the purse?'

I smiled appreciatively. 'I did. And so, apparently, did you.'

Junio ignored the compliment. 'You do not think the medicus is right, master? Maximilian had much to gain. He was the last to leave his father's room yesterday. We even know that he spoke to Rollo last night. And now this robbery. You must suspect him, too. Yet you are not convinced.'

'Not entirely. Or at least, I am not sure that it is all of the picture. Remember, there are those bloodstains on Lupus's sleeve. They must have come from Quintus, don't you think? Marcus is equally convinced that Lupus did it. And Julia blames Flavius for it all. After all, it was his dagger. And neither of them had any love for Ulpius.'

He smiled impudently. 'It is like the curial elections, master. Everyone with a favoured candidate. Though my own vote would still go to Maximilian. Do you not wish to know, for instance, what he arranged with that soothsayer?'

'I do. And look, the rain has stopped. Perhaps, when we

have finished at the slave market, we could hear her version of events. Though Marcus will be getting impatient for our return by now.'

'That bath attendant told us that she came to the forum.' Junio looked around hopelessly. 'I cannot see her anywhere, can you?'

I hadn't seen her, though I'd been keeping my eyes open since we left the house. 'There will be people who can guide us to her, no doubt,' I said. 'She must be a well-known figure in the town. "Warty old beggar-women" are instantly memorable. We will ask on the way to the slave market.'

I knew where the slave market was, at the back of the basilica. 'Market' was a flattering name for it, since it consisted of a small area behind a fountain where half a dozen slaves were shivering in a line, shackled together by chains at neck, hand and foot, and presided over by a surly fellow in a filthy tunic with a brutal whip in one hand. Only the adult slaves were left at this hour: the children and infants who usually make up the bulk of the merchandise (since they can be bought cheap or collected from temples and dumps where they have been abandoned) having presumably found a readier market.

The slave master himself, bronzed and prosperous-looking in a smart cloak and green tunic, was standing on a wooden chest nearby and vaunting the virtues of his remaining wares, while one or two townspeople showed a desultory interest, feeling the muscles of the younger men and looking at their teeth. No one wants a servant with dental problems.

The slave master saw me coming and turned his attention to me. 'Strong slaves for sale, citizen. Nice little slave girl, now? Guaranteed free from diseases. One owner from birth.'

I shook my head. I have always hated slave markets. I have been on the wrong side of one myself.

He smiled a crooked smile at me. Several of his teeth were missing. 'She's young, she's willing. No tendencies to lust, excessive religion or public spectacles.' These latter were those defects in a slave which a trader was bound by law to disclose to any prospective purchaser.

The girl smiled at me hopefully. Perhaps I had a kinder face than many, or perhaps it was simply because Junio looked well fed. I shook my head again and her face fell.

The slave trader did not give up. 'Only for sale because her master died. Come on, citizen.' He named a price. 'I shall be robbing myself.'

One of the muscle pinchers was beguiled by the offer. He went over and tested the girl for plumpness, and then, apparently satisfied, motioned to the slave vendor, who came down from his makeshift platform. I saw silver coins change hands, together with the certificate of ownership. The girl was unshackled from her comrades by the guard, and handed to her purchaser by the chain around her neck. He, I was encouraged to see, ordered the fetters removed before he led her away.

I took advantage of this break in proceedings to approach the slave trader and ask him my questions about Gwellia. Did he know of a slaver called Bethius who had sold a dark-haired Celtic woman in this market a year or so before? It occurred to me as I asked the question how hopeless the search appeared.

It was not the same man as I had spoken to on my previous visit, and I was not hopeful of the result, but he looked at me shrewdly. 'What did she look like, this woman?'

I told him, as best I could. I realised that I could not

even be sure that my wife's hair was not grey, after so many years.

'You want a dark-haired Celt, I can get you one, citizen. I have good contacts in the trade.'

I made it clear that it was this woman in particular that I sought.

He thought about it for a little while, and then his face brightened. 'Of course,' he said, eyeing my purse reflectively, 'I cannot be certain.'

I blessed the gods that I had not been obliged to bribe information from the fuller's men. I slipped him what money I had left and his memory, thus oiled, began to function less rustily.

'Well, citizen, you've come to the right place. I am Bethius, as it chances. But the woman you are looking for . . . I see so many slaves.'

'It is an unusual name,' I pleaded, 'Gwellia. And she was beautiful.' I did not dare to use the present tense.

He shook his head. 'I could not swear to it. There was a slave, about the age you mention. She had a young man for sale with her, as I recall. Sold them together to some wool trader from the north. Near Eboracum, I think. He wanted an attendant for his mother. Or perhaps it was his wife. Or was that the man who bought the slaves from Gaul? I remember he paid me well. No, I think it was the Celt. But of course, it may not be the woman that you seek at all.'

It was, however, more than I had looked for. Gwellia, alive, in Eboracum? It was possible. I thanked the man and turned to move away.

He called after me. 'Any time you want a slave, citizen, you come to me. Best value in the Empire. Gauls, Picts, Greeks, Armenians, Numidians – you name it, I have them all. Or if you want to sell that boy of yours, I can offer you a good price: British slaves are highly prized among the Belgic tribes.'

I walked away more quickly to hide my distaste. The fellow was only trying to be helpful: many people would have been glad of such an offer. I turned to Junio and saw that he was glancing at me nervously.

'Don't preen yourself that you are going to Belgium,' I told him gruffly. 'After all the trouble I have taken to train you to be half useful with mosaics. Besides, who else could make spiced mead the way you do?'

Junio's face split into a joyous grin. 'Do you want me to be useful now, and ask a few questions about this sooth-sayer of yours?' He tried to sound his normal impudent self, but he could not keep the emotion from his voice.

I nodded. 'Be quick about it then. Marcus will be pacing the study for us by now.'

But no one, not the pie sellers or the fishmongers or the tinsmiths or even the street musicians could give us any news of her, although all of them had regular selling pitches nearby. They knew her, of course, or at least they knew of her – forever accosting travellers and offering to read their palms or throw the dice for them. Obviously a woman of many talents.

It was the miller under the awning, leading his wretched horse in melancholy circles around his grinding-stone while his slave poured coarse grain into the vat above, who gave us the only real indication. He knew the woman, he said; she often stopped by the quern at nightfall to gather up the last sweepings of flour from the bottom stone. He let her have them – the leavings were too full of stone grit for ordinary sale.

I could not resist a grin. As it is there are always little particles of stone in market-milled flour, which wear down the teeth and give the baker's bread a strange, crunchy texture. That was one reason why I generally preferred my oatcakes, with the grain ground painstakingly at someone's home, by hand. The miller saw my smile.

'Call me superstitious if you like, citizen, but I would never cross a soothsayer, especially that one. Halfway to sorceress she was, for all that it is forbidden by the law. If I had turned her away she'd have put a curse on my horse, more than likely, or given me the evil eye. Though there were those who came to her, all the same. I have seen purple-stripers talk to her in secret before now.'

'In secret?' I demanded. 'It hardly seems secret if you knew of it.'

He smiled. 'She makes a bed sometimes in the stable where I stall the horse – I told you, I did not like to turn her away. It is not much of a shelter, just an open space under a slanting roof, but there is enough straw and room in there for a bed and the shelter will keep the rain off, if not the wind. I have seen one of them come there.'

'She makes her home in your stable?'

'Not all the time, citizen. Only when there are storms. In finer weather she sleeps in a tumbledown hovel just outside the walls. She can light a fire there and cook her gritty flour, and anything else she manages to beg from the market – spoiled fruit and old meat. She has other "regulars" like me.'

I nodded. Men may scoff at the idea of 'powers', but they will seldom cross the woman who claims to have them. No doubt her fire, too, came from a friendly baker's, or the superstitious owner of a takeaway cooked food stall who let her carry home a few live coals in a container. 'Outside the walls, you say?'

'Some way beyond the Verulamium Gate, citizen, across the bridge. There is a little valley with a dribble of a stream. The guards at the gate will indicate the way. No doubt

193

they saw the woman come in and go out often enough. The place used, I think, to be a tiler's kiln, but it was built in a hurry to serve the town demand, and it was poorly sited. The valley flooded every time it rained, and the tilemakers soon abandoned it.'

I looked at Junio and grimaced. There was no possibility of taking the time to make the expedition now. The Verulamium Gate was on the other side of town, and Marcus would be impatient enough already. 'We shall have to leave our visit to another day,' I said. 'But thank you for your information, miller.' I only wished I had a few *asses* left, so that my thanks could take a more tangible form.

I wished it even more strongly when I heard him say, quite loudly, to his bedraggled slave as we left, 'Well, I'm disappointed. I thought he was a decent sort of fellow, but he turned out to be another typical Celtic upstart. They are all the same. So proud of their new togas and precious Roman citizenship that they cannot spare even the smallest bronze coin for one of their old countrymen, even when he's doing his best to help. That's the last time I ever offer information to anyone, without seeing the colour of his money first.'

I quickened my pace and hurried all the way back to the house. The lament, I noticed as soon as we approached the gates, was going on undiminished.

Chapter Nineteen

Marcus was not as irritated as I had feared. On the contrary, when I presented myself in the atrium, hot and flustered after scampering back from the market with most uncitizenly haste, he was looking singularly pleased with himself. He did not even seem interested in hearing the explanations I had been carefully preparing all the way.

He had been lunching lightly on bread, fruit and cheese, laid out on the same elaborate tray from which he had been served earlier, while his personal slave stood by, obviously acting as taster. The sight of the meal made my mouth water, but at my approach Marcus pushed the tray aside, motioned to the slave to remove it and then turned his attention to me.

I got as far as, 'Serious news, master. Junio and I have discovered . . .' when he waved his hand in airy dismissal.

'I am sure that you have been as diligent as ever, old friend,' he said, with the kind of smile which told me that, whatever news I brought him, I had been wasting my time. 'But since the reading of the will, matters have altered here. You have heard about my appointment as Julia's sponsor, no doubt?'

I murmured something complimentary.

'Quintus mentioned it to me, in his letter. Afraid something would happen to him, and didn't want his wife left to the mercies of Flavius in the courts. He thought of appointing Sollers as her protector, at one time, but a mere citizen, even a Greek one, would find it hard to match a purple-striper if it came to persuading a court.'

I nodded. Flavius would have to be a brave man to cross a woman who had Marcus as her legal protector. 'You will do it splendidly, Excellence.'

'Yes, I will.' There was no false modesty about Marcus. 'And I was right about Lupus as well. New evidence has come to light that puts the matter beyond doubt. Send that slave of yours to fetch Mutuus: he is waiting in the study. I think you should hear this for yourself.'

I turned to speak to Junio, whom I had posted at the door, but I was too late. He had obviously been listening, because he had disappeared before I had time to utter a word.

Marcus was enjoying himself. He refused to be drawn on what this 'new evidence' was. 'Wait and see,' was all he would say. He did, however, consent to listen to my news, which he received with a kind of smug dismay. 'Maximilian, eh? You said that there was something suspicious about him.' He vouchsafed this consolation in the tones of a man offering a bone to a hunting dog who has lost a rabbit. 'Plotting to have his father robbed. We could have had him sentenced for that.'

'Could have had him sentenced? Why the past tense, Marcus?' It was not an idle question. As the governor's representative, he understood the finer points of law better than I did.

He gave me a forgiving smile. 'Unfortunately, with Quintus dead, there is no chance of a civil case. There is no injured party to bring one, and there must be someone to accuse him.'

I said, doubtfully, 'Surely you could bring a criminal case yourself? As Julia's representative?'

'I could, but there is a chance that I would lose on

technicalities, and that would be bad for my authority. Quintus didn't raise a search for his attackers at once, so he clearly didn't intend to sue – and so on. Then, Maximilian would presumably bring this old woman to testify that he did not intend violence, so the punishment would only be a fine. And that, of course, would be a further complication.'

The appointment as Julia's legal spokesman was clearly going to his head. He had adopted his best magisterial manner to deliver this pronouncement. I asked dutifully, 'A complication? Why is that?'

'Maximilian would have to pay damages to his victim's estate. But most of that estate is now Maximilian's own, which he could presumably use to pay with. That anomaly would bring the whole question of the will before the *praetor*, and once that happened, the entire testament could be declared invalid. I'm sure you can deduce what that would mean.'

Anyone could. Once a *querela* was entered against a will, no one was likely to profit except the imperial coffers. Better for the sake of Julia, Sollers, debtors and even pavement-makers to leave matters exactly as they were.

He smiled grimly. 'Of course, I do not intend to let Maximilian escape entirely. I shall make sure he knows that I am aware of his guilt, and might raise a prosecution at any time. That should ensure that he is properly grateful towards me. A loyal ally in Corinium would be a useful tool.'

'You do not feel, Excellence, that he may be dangerous? He might have killed Quintus. A man who hatches one plot against his father might well propose another.'

'I might have thought so myself if it were not for what I heard this afternoon. But here is the man himself.' He gestured towards the door, where Junio had just reappeared, accompanying an elegant figure.

It was Mutuus, although for a moment I hardly recognised him. Gone were the ochre tunic and the thonged sandals. The secretary was dazzling in red leather shoes and a fine woollen robe which put my toga to shame. Of course he had now regained his status. He would resume his full Roman name, too, though I would never think of him as anything but Mutuus.

'So,' I said, when the formalities were over, 'you have resumed your former status?'

'Not precisely my former status, citizen.' The pedantic Latin sounded better coming from a young man who dressed to match it. Mutuus had somehow acquired an air of intellectual distinction. No wonder Julia had found him attractive. Even Marcus was looking at him appreciatively, although my patron's taste, unlike that of many Romans, had always been almost exclusively for females. Like Julia, for instance.

I was so wrapped up in my thoughts that it took me a few moments to recognise the force of what Mutuus said next. 'I have not returned to my father's power. When a man is freed from bondage, he is not obliged to. He is able to operate – make contracts and decisions – on his own responsibility. He becomes legally a man.'

I groaned inwardly. This was obviously my afternoon for having lectures on the legal system.

'I have gone further than that. I have called seven witnesses and repudiated my adoption altogether, just as I once repudiated my natural father's estate. I shall go back to writing letters in the forum and wash my hands of Lupus and his affairs. It is no great loss: all Lupus's estate will be forfeit, if this crime is proved against him. I would inherit nothing but his dishonour.'

'But the crime is not proved,' I said. 'Flavius still has

questions to answer, and there were suspicious stains on Maximilian's clothes – and on other people's too. I saw them at the fuller's.' Somehow, I could not bring myself to mention Julia by name.

Marcus was looking at me indulgently, as if I were a dancing bear at a street market. This visible condescension made me more vehement than ever.

'Lupus could not have struck Rollo,' I went on, 'and it is hard to see how he could have stabbed Quintus either, without someone seeing him go into the reception room.'

'But that is just the point,' Marcus said. 'Someone did see him. Mutuus did.'

I looked at the young man. 'But when you were asked, you said . . .'

He looked calmly back at me, his shrewd gaze untroubled. 'I told you no lies, citizen. I did not deny seeing my father yesterday morning.'

I nodded. I had noticed the evasion at the time. 'I recall that I asked if you had seen your father and you replied that it was impossible to see through the window glass.'

He had the grace to colour. 'And that is true.'

'But,' I said, 'you were not looking through the window glass. What a pity that you are too young to seek office. You could make a fortune as a magistrate. You juggle words like a Greek.' I did not add that without the inheritance from Lupus, he stood little chance of election even if he were twenty-five. There is a property qualification for public office.

He regarded me stonily. 'I was under obligation then to my adoptive father. I did not know what Lupus had said to you. It was possible that he had told you about the events himself, but I did not wish to bring unnecessary trouble on him if he had not done so. He is vain, foolish and a bore, but he has been good to me in his way.'

There was some truth in this, I thought. There was no way in which Mutuus could know how much Lupus had said – I did not know exactly, myself, since I had not been present either. However, I maintained my hostile demeanour. 'So you said nothing to help us, even though your master had been murdered?'

He looked uncomfortable. 'I didn't volunteer unnecessary information. Besides, I did not believe then that Lupus could commit a murder, especially with a knife. Lupus was not a robust man, and he preferred words to weapons. Later, when I heard about the bloodstains, I wondered if he might have struck in self-defence: Quintus appeared to resent Lupus much more than Lupus hated him. Last night I debated with myself, and this morning after Rollo was found I felt I must say something. Especially since I was no longer legally under Lupus's tutelage.'

I said, 'But Lupus could not possibly have attacked Rollo.'

'If it was indeed the blow that killed him. You heard what Sollers said. It might possibly have been poison, and even an enfeebled old man can administer that. And Lupus would have had the opportunity to give Rollo something poisoned, after Quintus was murdered, when the page was ordered to the study to help prepare it for you.'

I nodded. I could follow that. 'Lupus was still in the front garden then. In fact, when I went looking for him and Flavius, I met Rollo coming out of the study.'

'But Rollo was alive long after that,' Marcus interrupted.

Mutuus looked at me, and said nothing. I knew what he meant. A man does not necessarily eat food the minute he receives it, particularly not if he is a slave and is called upon, for instance, to clear a study or to pour out wine.

Marcus had come to the same conclusion. 'Of course! I see. Lupus gave him a treat, perhaps, which Rollo might have saved to eat later. And of course, if he was poisoned he would go to the latrine. That would explain everything. It is possible that no one else was even involved.' My patron looked extremely pleased with himself for that deduction, so I forbore to mention that in that case, Rollo's corpse must have picked itself up and forced itself into the cavity behind the seats.

'It is a possibility at least,' Mutuus said. 'Rollo was in the study when Lupus was in the garden. He must have seen him. That was where I was, when I saw Lupus.' He glanced at Marcus.

'Tell him the story,' Marcus said, 'just as you told it to me earlier.'

Mutuus nodded. 'Well, citizen, I was standing at the study door. I had been in the *librarium* for some time: Sollers sent me away earlier, when he came to bleed Quintus – he always insisted that my master should rest and recover a little after the treatment. Quintus had been hot and flushed all morning, his earlier wound was paining him, and Sollers felt that he needed cupping before seeing Lupus and Flavius. Quintus disliked them both, and Sollers said their presence would make his blood run hotter and increase the fever.'

'Go on,' I said. So far the account accorded with what I knew. 'You went to the study then, and did not return to Quintus afterwards?'

'In fact I did return, but only for a moment. Quintus gave the signal by striking the bowl, and I collected my tablets and writing implements and returned to him. I had no sooner sat down and picked up my stylus at his instruction, ready to recommence, when Maximilian burst in and we were all sent away again. Lupus and Flavius were in the ante-room, and they were ushered back into the front garden, and I returned to the study to kick my heels once more. I had long since written all the letters that Quintus had instructed me to write. I kept walking to the door, attempting to discover if Maximilian had finished with his father, and I could decently go back for further orders. And that was when I saw him.'

'Saw whom?' I said, stupidly. Marcus had already told me the answer.

'Lupus,' he replied, 'going back into the ante-room, when he thought he was unobserved. He went in, and disappeared.'

'You watched him go? And that did not prevent him?'

'He didn't know that I had seen him. He glanced up and down the garden to make sure Flavius wasn't looking, and then he went in. He did not think to look for me. A few minutes later he came furtively out again. At the time I was amused – I thought that he had burst in on the argument between Quintus and his son, and had tried to tiptoe away in embarrassment. That would be like Lupus. Even when I learned that Quintus had been murdered I persuaded myself that Lupus was too weak and frail to be guilty. But when I heard about the bloodstains, I had to recognise the truth. I saw him go into the ante-room with my own eyes. The dagger was there – I noticed it on the table when I came out. And, as I considered the matter this morning, I realised something else. When Lupus came sneaking out again he was not only whiter than a toga but he was pressing his right arm awkwardly to his side. He was not doing that before. That is what compelled me to tell you, citizens. There can be no doubt about it. Lupus killed Quintus. I saw him go in.'

Chapter Twenty

For a moment there was silence, as I digested this news, then Marcus turned to me with a triumphant grin. 'You see?' he said. 'I knew I was right to arrest him. I tell you, I can smell the scent of fear.' He was looking more cheerful than I had seen him since our arrival in Corinium, and I realised how much the last few days had worried him. For all his apparent confidence in arresting Lupus, he had obviously entertained lingering fears that this might still be a political murder. Now, however, the testimony of Mutuus seemed to have removed his doubts. I was glad I had not mentioned the possibility of deliberate poison on his supper tray. 'I have sent for the town guard. They will be here shortly to take him away. Though this will be a matter for the governor's court, of course. I may even hear the case myself.'

I was unwilling to puncture his bubble of confidence, but there were still matters unresolved in my mind. 'And the wax tablet?' I enquired. 'You think now that the message was unrelated to the murder?'

Marcus frowned at me disapprovingly, but Mutuus looked up sharply. 'Wax tablet?' he said, rather as I had hoped. As a secretary, he might be expected to take an interest in the household's writing materials.

Junio was back at his station by the door and I motioned him forward. 'Show him, Junio,' I said, and for the second time that day my servant produced Flavius's carved ivory tablet holder from his pouch. Mutuus looked at it.

I was expecting a reaction, but Mutuus's face showed nothing but a kind of blank bafflement.

'Well?' I demanded, after a moment. 'Have you seen this writing block before?'

'Yes,' he said, 'of course I have. It belongs to Julia Honoria.'

Whatever answer I had been expecting, it certainly was not that. For the second time in as many minutes, Mutuus's words produced a startled pause.

It was Marcus who broke it. 'To Julia? That is impossible. You must be mistaken. Libertus collected this personally from Flavius this morning.' He took the writing frame from Junio and tapped it with his finger. 'Julia has not spoken to her former husband alone since he came to the house – indeed she has avoided doing so. You wish us to believe that she has somehow entertained private messages from him?'

Mutuus had turned a sullen red, but he remained adamant. 'As to that, Excellence, I cannot answer. I only tell you what I know. That writing tablet came from Flavius, certainly, but it was addressed to Julia. And it did not arrive today. It arrived many days ago. I remember it clearly, because it was the morning of the very day that Quintus Ulpius was set on in the street.'

'Did Quintus know that his wife received gifts from Flavius?' Marcus obviously felt that, if Julia had been his wife, such practices would not have been allowed to continue for long.

Mutuus shook his head. 'Julia did not welcome it herself. I have known her many times repudiate his gifts. On this occasion, too, I think, if Julia had known what the packet contained she would not have accepted it. But there was no greeting on the packet, and none from the slave, who merely delivered the parcel and disappeared.'

'Wait a moment,' Marcus said, 'what slave? What packet? And how, if there was no greeting, could you tell who the gift was from? Tell us the story from the beginning. Briefly, if you can.'

It was beyond Mutuus, of course, to tell any story briefly. But, laced about with circumlocutions and couched in the most pedantic terms, this was the gist of his account.

It was the morning before the chariot races. Quintus, in the prime of health, had dealt with the most pressing business, and was now lying in his room with a jug of wine, while Rollo massaged his feet for him. It was a fine day, and Mutuus, since he was not needed by his master, was sitting in one of the arbours in the front garden with Julia.

Marcus interrupted him sharply. 'Doing what?'

The secretary turned scarlet to his ears. 'I was reciting cadences to her. She likes to hear the old poets, and I have many verses by heart.'

'Ovid, I suppose?' Marcus asked, mockingly – then looked as if he wished he hadn't asked. Reading amorous poems to one's lady was a favourite pastime in some Roman circles. If this youth had been reciting erotic verses to Julia under the trees, Marcus might not wish to hear of it.

Mutuus was redder than Samian ware, but he did not deny the charge. 'Only the *Heroides*,' he answered.

Marcus looked furious. Even Ovid's heroic love letters are not the kind of ditties one would expect a bondsman to be reciting to his master's wife. 'Well,' he said, 'so you were "reciting cadences". What happened then?'

They were interrupted, it seemed, by a message from the gatekeeper. An anonymous package had arrived at the gate for Julia, wrapped in fine silk. Julia had no suspicions. In fact, she was delighted. Quintus sometimes sent her trinkets as a surprise, and she had been dropping hints about some new ivory combs for her hair. Mutuus was sent to fetch the parcel.

'When she unwrapped it,' the secretary said, 'it was a writing block. A pretty thing. Julia still thought it was a present from Quintus. But when she opened it, there was a message inscribed inside the tablet, on the wax itself. "To Julia, a love token to bring you back to me." I saw the writing myself.

'Julia was furious. I have never seen her so upset. She scratched out the message with her nails, and flung the tablet on the floor. That put an end to the little recital in the arbour. She'd had enough of poetry, she said, and she made me accompany her inside while she craved an immediate audience with her husband.'

'And did he grant it?' I asked, remembering that he had retired to his quarters with Rollo and that the slave probably had more intimate duties than merely playing the cythera.

Mutuus looked surprised. 'Of course. Quintus was devoted to his lady. She might have interrupted him at the bathhouse itself if she chose.'

'And the writing tablet? You left it in the arbour. What happened to it then?'

He shrugged. 'I cannot tell you that, citizen. Until you showed it to me just now, I had never seen it again.'

'Oh, come!' Marcus said sharply. 'The tablet is a pretty thing, the frame is carved ivory and cunningly made. It would have a value anywhere. You don't expect me to believe that you left it in the garden where it fell?'

Mutuus was doing his imitation of Samian ware again. 'I did not say that, Excellence. It is true that I tried to recover it. When Julia went in to speak to Quintus, I was no longer required – Quintus always dismissed his slaves when Julia sought private audience with him – so I came back to the arbour, hoping to find the writing tablet. I spent a long time searching, but there was no sign of it. Doubtless one of the garden slaves had stolen it.'

He spoke with bitterness. The slaves had 'stolen' it, I noticed. If Mutuus had picked it up, he would not have described the action that way.

'What did you hope to do with it?' I said, hoping to shame him by the question. 'Sell it? Or show it to Quintus?' It occurred to me that the secretary might have been pleased to drive a little splitting wedge between husband and wife.

I had mistaken my man. Mutuus looked at me gravely. 'I would not have sold it, citizen, far less have given it away. It had been Julia's, you understand – for a brief moment, true, but it was hers.'

'You would have taken it as a keepsake?' Marcus was incredulous. He had enjoyed his share of women, but it would never occur to him to be sentimental.

He spoke at the same moment as I said, 'However could you hide such a thing?' in equally disbelieving tones. I knew how little privacy a servant could possess.

Oddly, Mutuus addressed his answer to me. 'I was a secretary, citizen, and a bondsman. I was not obliged to sleep with the common slaves, like a sheep in a barn. I had a small private partition at one end of the room.'

I nodded. 'So you had somewhere to keep your things? A storage chest, at least?' I blamed myself for not deducing that earlier. He had, after all, produced a spotless robe from somewhere.

'What can a secretary have that warrants a storage chest?' Marcus wanted to know, with more than a touch of impatience. It had not escaped him that Mutuus had unthinkingly answered my question first.

Mutuus inclined his head. 'I have, in my sleeping quarters, Excellence, every stylus that her hands have touched. Believe me, when you feel as I do . . .' He trailed off.

I nodded. I remembered a time when I, too, had treasured a lock of hair, a scrap of perfumed plaid. Marcus, who had never married, but who could command any girl in Glevum at the turn of a coin, was looking less convinced.

'Well! So you could not find the writing tablet, you say? And despite your desire to own it, you did not think that it was worth enquiring for?' Marcus was scathing now.

He wanted to, Mutuus explained, but circumstances prevented him. He went to Julia and told her that the writing tablet had disappeared, hoping that she would start a search for it. Instead, she merely laughed and said that it was of no account. Whoever had found it was welcome to it, for her part – and if a slave had taken it, so much the better. That was all Flavius deserved. What was worse, from Mutuus's point of view, was that she said so in the presence of her handmaids.

'If I had attempted to ask questions and get it back, the maidservants would have told Julia. I did not wish her to think badly of me,' Mutuus finished, sadly. He sighed. 'I never did discover who had it.'

He stopped for a moment, wistfully, and then seemed struck by a sudden thought. 'I wonder how Flavius came to have it? Unless, perhaps,' he glanced at us from under his lids, 'Rollo, you know, was talking to Flavius last night, in the courtyard. He told me he had an appointment to wait upon him later. You don't think . . .'

'I don't think,' I said, 'that this is even the same tablet.'

Mutuus looked scornful. 'I could hardly be mistaken. The wax is set in a distinctive frame.'

I looked at Marcus, and raised my eyebrows

questioningly. He nodded, so I signalled to Junio, who opened the travelling chest again and produced the second writing frame with a flourish. I gave him an encouraging wink and took the object from him.

'You are quite sure,' I said to the astonished Mutuus, 'that it could not have been this one that you saw?' I handed it to him for inspection.

He frowned. 'I . . . that is . . . citizen, it is impossible to be certain. The two are much alike. But no, look – the corner of this one is chipped. That must be where Julia flung it to the floor. I saw it hit the corner of the stone seat as it fell. Yes, you are quite right, citizen. This is Julia's writing tablet, not the other. But how did you acquire this? It disappeared in the arbour.'

'It was sent to *me*,' Marcus said, with a certain emphasis. Mutuus had been addressing his answers to me again. Any moment now my patron would start tapping his baton. Mutuus looked to me for amplification, but I simply smiled encouragingly. One of the secrets of my success with Marcus is knowing when to keep silent.

'To me,' Marcus said again, as if Mutuus might have overlooked the implications. 'It was found here in the colonnade, with a threatening message on it, shortly after Quintus Ulpius was stabbed in the street.'

'A threatening message?' Mutuus looked alarmed. 'You do not suppose that I wrote it, Excellence? That I was responsible for that evening's attack?'

I waited for Marcus to deny that, at least, but he did not.

'Who is more likely than a secretary to inscribe on a wax tablet?' Marcus demanded, taking the second tablet from him, 'and who else knew where this one was to be found?'

Marcus is capable of surprising me sometimes. That

was a shrewd deduction, in its way, although it ignored some obvious indications.

I debated for a moment whether to point them out to him, but I was spared the necessity. The screen door opened, so that the room was filled for a moment with the still unceasing wail of the lament, and then Julia herself came in, with her two plain maidservants in attendance.

'Excellence, since you are now my sponsor, will you speak at the . . .' she began, approaching Marcus with a smile of greeting, but then she saw the two writing tablets in his hands.

The smile withered like a dinner snail in salt. She opened her mouth as if to speak, but no words emerged. Julia Honoria was a strong woman, but if Sollers had not appeared behind her to catch her as she swayed, I believe she would have fallen to the floor in a faint.

Chapter Twenty-one

At the sight of Julia's distress, the normal social formalities were forgotten. Mutuus rushed forward, heedless of protocol in his eagerness to help. One of the slave girls cried, 'Water and vinegar!' and disappeared unbidden to fetch it. Most surprisingly of all, Marcus at once put away the writing tablets and offered his stool for her assistance. I have never before seen him give up his seat to any living person.

Sollers, however, seemed characteristically self-possessed. 'Air,' he said, authoritatively. 'The lady needs air. And hydromel will help revive her too. The kitchens know how to prepare it; I ordered it often for her husband, previously. See to it, slave.' He nodded to Junio who bounded away instantly, without reference to me, as if he, too, had been transformed by events.

She was pale and shaking, and Sollers led her to the stool where she sank down gracefully, her head in her hands, and for a moment we watched her in silence. Then she found her voice. 'Pardon me, citizens,' she managed. 'I do not know what weakness overcame me.'

And why should the sight of Flavius's writing tablets bring it on? That was the question I wanted to ask, but I judged the moment was not propitious. Besides, from the look on his face, Marcus would have considered it unfeeling and I would have risked a stinging rebuke. I held my tongue.

'Momentary faintness like this is not unusual,' Sollers was saying, with a professional air. 'Your mind has sustained some dreadful shocks, and this has produced imbalance in your body. You have a surfeit of dry and airy humours. It often happens, in such circumstances.'

The maidservant came hurrying back at this moment with a goblet of watered vinegar, but he waved it away imperiously. 'Water alone might have helped. Coolness and wet will help correct the imbalance. But vinegar will only add bitterness.'

'Honey and water is better?' I was remembering his instruction to bring hydromel.

'It is.' He smiled towards me as he spoke, and again I felt the flattery of his regard. 'Sweetness will help to drive out sorrow, and also increase her strength. Ah! Here is your servant with some now.' He took the cup from a panting Junio and held it to the lady's lips.

Julia swallowed some hydromel and did indeed seem a little revived. She gave Sollers a faint, glowing smile. 'Thank you. I am better already.'

I was ready to ask my question about the writing blocks, but Sollers intervened. 'All the same, lady, I think you should be cupped. That will draw off the dangerous humours physically. It is a strong remedy, stronger than I would normally advise, but there is need for a swift cure. You have a funeral to attend tonight, and your presence will be required at the banquet too.'

'You are going to bleed her?' I asked, doubtfully. Julia had turned white at the prospect, but obviously the little crisis had affected my social judgement. It was not my place to question the doctor's decision.

He took no offence. 'Not bleed her, no. That is for reducing fever in the blood. This is an affliction of the brain, caused by airy humours: dry-cupping will suffice.'

I had heard of it, the application of suction to the skin to draw the offending humours through it. Julia looked greatly relieved at this reduction of sentence, and glanced at me with the most charming conspiratorial smile. Even so, my next question startled everyone, most of all myself. Ever afterwards I wondered how I dared to ask it. 'Can I assist you, Sollers?' I enquired.

Everyone stared at me in astonishment. The medicus was the first to recover.

'Citizen, a pair of hands would certainly be useful, but there are many slaves here who can help me.'

I shook my head. 'They have a funeral to prepare,' I said. I can be stubborn when I choose, and having volunteered myself to this, I was seized by a strong desire to see it through. 'In any case, I should be fascinated to observe your skill.'

He was visibly flattered by that.

I saw him waver, and I pressed my advantage. 'As you, once, were interested to witness Galen's work,' I added.

He gave a slight smile. 'In that case, citizen, if Julia has no objection . . .?'

She indicated that she had none.

'Then by all means watch me if you wish. Though there is little anyone can do to help, and very little to see. We shall require a cupping bowl, that is all, a little lint and a lighted taper. You will find all these things in the consulting room of my apartments. Or better, perhaps we should take Julia Honoria there. I have good lamps, and an upright chair with arms which I use for operating – it helps to steady my hands. Julia may sit in that and support her arm. My box of salves and remedies will be on hand, too, to restore her after the cupping.'

Julia made no demur, so he placed a firm hand under her elbow, and – with the assistance of Junio, who stepped

forward at my signal – helped her across the courtyard to
the room, with her handmaidens in attendance. I followed
them, as suggested, but the rest of the company, after a
little hesitation, dispersed.

If I had been a patient of Sollers, I thought, I should
either have made a miraculous recovery the moment
I walked in through his door or (perhaps more likely)
expired entirely from fright. One's symptoms could
scarcely be more dreadful than the treatments hinted at
here.

The very sight of the implements set out on the
surgeon's table was enough to induce an immediate fever.
There were blades for cutting rotting flesh; saws for bones
and limbs; heating irons for cautery; hand drills for the
skull; a dreadful four-jawed device with ratchets, for some
internal use; and a pair of fearsome pincers for the teeth. I
remembered that army surgeons were trained to ignore
their patients' cries. The very thought made me shudder. I
turned away.

True, on the shelves around there were labelled caskets
of dried herbs to ease distress – I spotted mustard, crocus,
belladonna, linseed, poppy and mallow – and vessels of
oils, salt, turpentine and vinegar to clean the wounds. But
my eyes were instinctively drawn back to the surgeon's
gallery on the table: it looked like a torturer's armoury.
And, among the rest, as Sollers had said, was a selection of
cupping bowls – some, delicate affairs of horn, with tiny
apertures in the bottom, while others were more robust in
bronze, large hollow bell shapes with a smooth lip at the
edge.

Sollers selected one of the latter, and asked Julia to bare
her arm. She did so herself, waving away the maidservant
who stepped forward to help. I admired her fortitude.
Sollers had lighted a small piece of lint from a taper which

he dropped into the cup, and now, rubbing a little oil around the rim, he was preparing to clamp the bell firmly against the milky skin of the proffered arm.

'Will it not burn her?' I could not restrain the question.

'It will be hot at first, certainly.' Sollers spoke with his customary pride in his own expertise, and I realised that he was enjoying giving this little demonstration. 'But the lint will burn away the natural vapour in the jar, and since nature abhors a vacuum, the excess humours will be sucked out of the arm. They'll fill the space and put the fire out. If we had more leisure, I would have used a bone cupping bowl, and sucked the humours out myself, through the hole in the base. But it is getting late, and Julia must be well enough to face the funeral celebrations tonight. This method is stronger and brings swifter results.'

Indeed, within a few moments he was withdrawing the cup from her arm, and I could see what he meant about the vacuum. There was no fire in the cup, and no actual burning on the arm, although the skin was reddened and marked where it had been drawn up into the cupping vessel. I had, I remembered, seen a similar bruise on the arm of Quintus Ulpius as he lay dead at my feet. I remembered that he, too, had been cupped shortly before.

I tried to imagine Sollers applying this treatment to the decurion. And then something occurred to me. I had been an idiot not to think of it before.

I turned to Sollers, with what I hoped was a disarming smile. 'You did the same to Quintus yesterday morning?'

'Not quite the same, no.' He was rubbing a perfumed salve gently into Julia's arm and she was smiling at him gratefully. 'Quintus was suffering from a fever, so I wet-cupped him. A similar process, but one cuts the vein. It draws blood, and hence the fiery humours are drawn out.'

I took a deep breath. 'And what, on these occasions, do you do with the blood?'

I heard Julia catch her breath sharply. Sollers's hands visibly trembled as they held the salve pot, but it was only for an instant. A moment later he had regained his self-possession, and was saying evenly, 'In general, citizen, one carries it away and washes the cupping vessel in the stream.'

'In general,' I said. 'But what about yesterday morning? What did you do with it then?'

There was a pause, during which Julia looked at Sollers and everyone else looked at me.

'I should warn you, lady,' I said, 'I have been to the fuller's. Your clothes had not yet been laundered.'

Julia turned so pale I thought Sollers would suggest another cupping. 'Great Minerva, giver of wisdom!' she exclaimed. 'Sollers, you had better tell them everything.'

None of the servants moved. One could almost feel the expectation in the room.

Sollers looked at me steadily. 'What Julia did was no crime, citizen.'

'I did not suggest it was. The blood, after all, was withdrawn already, and you have just explained how that is treatment for a fever. All the same, I would like to hear her account of it. Or yours. A petition, was it, or a thank offering? Because the treatment you were giving her had worked?'

Julia gave a little sob. 'A little of both. It was not the first time I had sacrificed to the goddess – though not usually with blood. But we always sent the servants away when I made an offering, and I know we were not observed this time. We did it so swiftly. How did you discover the truth?'

'I examined the altar, yesterday, and the channel around the shrine was wet with blood. I wondered at the time if someone had used it as a way of disposing of inconvenient evidence. It was foolish of me, but I did not make the connection with cupping, until now.'

Julia opened her mouth to speak, and thought better of it.

'Minerva,' I went on, 'giver of wisdom, as you pointed out – and guardian of women's troubles, too. There are several statues of her in the garden. Of course you would make sacrifice to her. You were being treated by Sollers for just such a problem – he told me so himself.'

She turned to him, white-faced, and he burst out, 'And you, citizen, gave me your word upon your silence.'

'I promised not to betray your confidence to others, and I have not done so. The attendants knew already, since they told my servant about it. I have betrayed you to no one. And I won't, unless the matter bears upon the killing. But I would have been glad to learn about it sooner. Blood close to a stabbing requires explanation, don't you think?'

'Oh, citizen!' Julia raised her lovely eyes to mine. 'You are right. It is my fault. I was too terrified, when Quintus was killed, and too embarrassed to explain. I made Sollers promise to keep silent too. After I left you yesterday I went into my quarters, as I said, and put a little rouge upon my lips. I knew that Quintus would be bad-tempered when I saw him, after his argument with his son, and I wanted to humour him as much as possible – partly so that he should greet you with civility. Then, as I came out of my room, I met Sollers in the court. He had bled my husband earlier, and since Quintus was still arguing with Maximilian, was taking the opportunity to carry away his equipment. I needed to wait for Quintus, so . . .' she hesitated.

Sollers finished for her. 'We decided that there was time to make an oblation – and for Julia to have her final treatment, too. It takes only a short time, but it is hard to find a moment when it is discreet. This seemed an ideal opportunity. There was no one in the court, Quintus was busy, you would not look for her, and it was easy for Julia to dismiss her attendants. And once we were in her husband's apartments we were safe.'

'You weren't afraid you would be seen at the shrine?'

'It was a risk, of course, but not a great one. The grotto is hidden from the colonnade.'

That was true, I thought, remembering the bald-headed serving maid. 'This was the final treatment?' I enquired.

He nodded. 'That was the reason for the thank offering. The inflammation was already eased. When Quintus was recovered, Julia could go to him again with every expectation of a child.'

I glanced at Julia, surprised at this disconcerting candour in front of a woman, but Roman wives are more forthright about sexual matters than Celtic ones. Or Celtic husbands, for that matter. She said, with only the faintest flush, 'I had vowed a special sacrifice to Minerva when I was cured, and this seemed a splendid opportunity. What better offering could I make to the goddess than a libation of my husband's blood, freely given? In gratitude and in petition for a son.'

'You poured it from the cupping bowl?' It seemed unlikely as a sacrificial urn.

She smiled. 'No. Sollers was carrying his equipment in a bowl – a large bronze bowl which Quintus kept beside him. It is a fine thing – suitable for making a sacrifice.'

I looked at Sollers questioningly, and he gave an ironic bow. 'It was not, I grant you, the most elegant of solutions. But I had just finished bleeding Quintus when Maximilian barged in. Knife, salve pots, bandages and a cupping vessel full of blood – it was more than a man could carry at one time. So when Quintus ordered me to leave the room, I put it all into the bowl, and carried it that way. When Julia wanted to make a libation it seemed an obvious vessel.' He put away his salve and knelt down beside Julia to place a pad of cotton on her arm and bind it tenderly into place.

'I see!' I said, struck by a moment of illumination. 'That answers a puzzle which has worried me. I wondered why Quintus had not summoned his slaves to his aid when he was attacked. I should have noticed that the bowl was missing from his room. Where is it now? You have not returned it to Quintus?'

'You saw it yourself,' Julia said, 'supporting a vase of funeral foliage in the atrium.'

Where I had overlooked it, I thought. Sollers might compliment me on my perception, but I was not proud of what I had failed to see. 'So you made the sacrifice? Together?'

Julia shook her head. 'Not together, citizen. It was a woman's sacrifice. There was not much time. I made the blood libation while Sollers rinsed the other equipment in the pool and then went to his room to get the treatment for me. He hurried back to help me complete the sacrifice, and then – as you know – we went to my husband's usual room where we could be undisturbed.'

And where, I thought, she could lie down while he administered the treatment. 'And that was when you discovered that you had splashed your stola with blood?'

'I had, a little,' she confessed. 'The bowl was heavy, and I poured it badly. It was too heavy for me to lift it up to the focus on the altar. I had to pour it around the channel in the base. Sollers brought the water from the cascade for us to wash the bowl, as ritual demands. I could not carry it so far.'

'And the clothes?'

'I went back and took them off, as soon as the treatment was finished, but I had scarcely had time to change them

219

before a slave came to my rooms with the dreadful news of Quintus. And there was I with blood on my clothes. Oh, citizen, I could not even grieve. I was too terrified!' She shook her head as if the memory haunted her.

Sollers finished his ministrations and rose to his feet.

'I thought that someone would see the bloodstains and blame me for the murder,' Julia went on. 'Once Quintus was dead, who would believe that we acquired his blood innocently? That it had been let to cure him, not to kill him? I made a parcel of my dirty garments, and as soon as my maidservants had helped me dress I sent them to the fuller's straight away. Sollers came to get me, and I made him promise to say nothing about the sacrifice. Of course, I did not expect that you would guess the truth.'

I turned to Sollers. 'And you encouraged her in this deception?'

He inclined his head. 'I did, although deception is not perhaps the word. I was simply frugal with the truth. After all, it was an innocent event. But we chose a dreadful time to do it – although we could not know that at the time. Maximilian does not love Julia – or me, and as a future decurion he has influence. If he had heard about the blood, he would have raised a case against us and then we would have been lucky to escape with our lives.'

I had to admit the justice of that. 'The timing was certainly unfortunate,' I said.

'And more unfortunate,' Sollers said, 'that we had dismissed the servants from the court. It was not necessary. But Julia had insisted all along that her treatment, and everything connected with it, should be kept as secret as possible. There is too much gossip in a household of slaves.'

There was, I thought. Despite all their care the rumours had still reached me.

'So,' Julia said, 'now you know everything.'

I smiled. 'Not quite everything.' She was looking calmer now, and I felt that the moment had come. 'What was it about Flavius's writing blocks which could disturb you so?'

Chapter 15

Chapter Twenty-two

Perhaps I had still spoken too soon. The colour died from Julia's cheeks and she looked helplessly at Sollers. He turned away and began to busy himself with his cupping vessel, brushing out the ashes from the bell and rinsing it carefully with vinegar from a stoppered jar. At last he spoke.

'This citizen deserves his reputation, Julia. He sees to the core of things, as Quintus told us that he would. I think you should explain your fears to him.'

'Your fears, lady?'

She looked at me, as beautiful as ever, and took a deep breath. 'Fears, yes. Of Flavius. Of course I will have protection now, with Marcus as my legal sponsor, but I did fear my former husband after Quintus died. He would have tried anything to get me back: the courts, bribery, abduction even. He did that when I was at my brother's house, and he would have done it again. Even when Quintus was alive, Flavius never gave up. He had even turned to sorcery. He always claimed that Quintus used spells to lure me away – as though his own clammy hands, his drunkenness and his disgusting breath were not enough to drive any woman away – and he tried to use the same methods to win me back.'

I nodded. I recalled overhearing Flavius in the garden the first time I heard him speak. He seemed to think then that his own natural charms were so irresistible that

Quintus Ulpius must have used supernatural ones. 'There are laws against things like that,' I said, as he himself had said at the time.

She gave me a wry look. 'Indeed there are, but Flavius did not trust the law. In this town, he said, the law was in the hands of the decurions. The courts would find for Quintus every time, and Flavius would have to pay a fine. He was right, of course – they would have decided that, but not for the reasons Flavius believed.' She held out her bruised arm to her maidservants, who folded down her sleeve again as she spoke.

'And so?'

'And so he turned to sorcery himself. He kept sending me "tokens", as he called them, to bring me back to him. Most of them were paltry things. He must have thought they had magic qualities; he cannot have supposed that they would induce me to return otherwise. He used to get Rollo to bring them to me – he frequented the bathhouse on purpose, when my husband was in the hot room with his friends, and gave them to the page while he was waiting to massage his master. Rings and brooches and oils and perfumes. At first I sent them back, but in the end I simply threw them away, and forbade Rollo to speak to him again.'

'But he did speak to him. Yesterday.'

She was dissatisfied with the drape of the sleeve and she motioned to the slaves to do it again. 'So it appears,' she said. 'Poor boy. Of course he couldn't refuse, once Flavius was a guest in this house. Any more than I could refuse to allow Flavius to stay, once Marcus had commanded it.'

I nodded. I had said much the same thing to Rollo myself. I asked, 'If Rollo had gone to Flavius last night, would he have reported that to you afterwards?'

'Of course he would. His first duty was to this household. In any case, I imagine that Flavius *wanted* him to come to me – to bring me one of his tiresome trinkets. He had tried to send it once before. Yesterday, while I was in my inner room putting colour on my lips, someone came to the outer door asking for me. I told my maids to say I wasn't there. But Flavius wouldn't give up. He had a recent superstition from a sorceress: he was to have two matching items carved from one piece of bone, and give one part to me. When the two pieces were reunited, he believed, we would be reunited too.'

'How do you know this?' If I had been Flavius, I thought, I would never have told her of my supposed spell.

'Rollo warned me about it, some time ago. That was why I would not touch any gift from Flavius. But when I saw you with those two wax tablets, I thought for a terrible moment that he had succeeded.' She smiled. 'I cannot believe that any human power could make me return to Flavius, but I mistrust sorcerers.' She looked at the medicus, who was now putting the last of his salve pots on the shelf. 'Although Sollers has always mocked me for my fears.'

He smiled at her. 'I put my faith in remedies and the gods, not in the foolish spells and charms of warty old women who think themselves diviners.'

It was my turn to pale. ' "Warty old women"?' I repeated. 'Are you saying that Flavius went to that old soothsayer in the market? How do you know that?'

'She told me so herself, when she waylaid me that night. She seemed to feel that it was a sort of advertisement, and it would make me listen to her. "An advisor to the wealthy", she called herself. "They all come to me, citizen", she told me. "Rich men like Flavius and decurions' sons." She was very proud of it.'

'She told you this the night of the chariot races?' I asked. 'The evening that Quintus was set upon and stabbed?'

'She did . . .' Sollers began, but Julia interrupted him.

She had jumped to her feet. 'You think Flavius arranged that too? He arranged that the woman should take Sollers aside so that my poor husband could be attacked?'

I shook my head. 'I know that he did not. But someone did. And I know who. Although he does not yet know that I know it.' They were staring at me, turned to stone as if they had come face to face with Medusa herself.

Sollers mastered himself. 'Then who . . .?'

I debated for a moment before I answered him. Then I made a decision. 'It was Maximilian,' I said at last. There was a stir of astonishment among the maidservants, who instantly suppressed it.

Sollers stepped forward urgently, his face alert. 'I thought as much. I told you so before. I have always suspected that young man. He needed money. Quintus was threatening to disinherit him. He was left-handed, too. Perhaps you should search his quarters, citizen. Who knows . . .'

I nodded. 'An interesting suggestion, medicus. I may do that, later. But there has been a new development. Lupus has been arrested. We knew already that Lupus had bloodstains on his sleeve, and now it appears Mutuus saw the old man go into Quintus's room yesterday after Maximilian left.'

'He did?' Julia was wide-eyed, and Sollers looked genuinely shocked.

'He did. The case seems definite. Marcus has already called the guard.'

'But you do not believe it?' Sollers said. 'That Lupus killed him?'

'I could believe that Lupus did it, given the evidence, but I do not understand why he would take such an appalling risk. Why now, of all times? What is so different now that he should suddenly make such an attack?'

'Perhaps it has something to do with Mutuus,' Julia said. 'Lupus was very attached to him. He never forgave Quintus for wresting him away. He has been heard to say it in the council, I understand – that Quintus had a handsome son already, and did not need to steal someone else's.'

'Handsome?' I echoed with a smile. I thought of Maximilian – the tousled hair, the tall figure, the close-set eyes, the petulant young face. I suppose to an old skeleton like Lupus he might seem good-looking. Not much like his father, Junio had said. Like his mother, perhaps? The dowerless woman who had lost her looks and been put aside when the child was small?

And suddenly I made a connection. The piece that did not fit the pattern fitted unexpectedly into the border.

'Julia,' I said urgently, 'tell me quickly. How old was Maximilian when his mother was divorced?'

She gazed at me as though my wits were addled.

'Believe me,' I said, 'this is important. I would not ask you otherwise. Try to remember, did Quintus ever speak of it?'

She was still looking bewildered. 'I believe,' she said, 'that Maximilian was quite a child. Four years old, or five. No more. Quintus had the woman put away, and then she caught the pox. She died a year or two ago.'

'She died?' I said. 'You are sure of that?'

'So Quintus said. Maximilian was distraught. He felt that Quintus had betrayed his mother. They quarrelled bitterly about it.'

'He put her away,' I repeated, 'and then she caught the pox. In that order.' I turned to Junio. 'Come, Junio, there is something we must do. And quickly, before it is too late. I want to go back to the market and find this soothsayer. I think she may hold the key to everything.'

'But citizen,' Julia murmured. 'The funeral . . .!'

'At what time does the procession start?' I asked the question of Sollers. 'As soon as it is dark, as usual?' I have had occasion previously to deplore the Roman preference for interring their dead by torchlight, but tonight the arrangement had advantages. There was still an hour of daylight left, at least, enough for me to make my enquiries and still return in time for the procession.

'But master,' Junio said urgently, 'you should eat something first. The evening will be long before the banquet, and you have eaten nothing since this morning. I at least have had a honey cake.'

Julia was in instant consternation. 'Citizen, a thousand apologies. I have not considered food. The household, of course, is fasting for the day until the funeral banquet. Allow me to send one of my slaves to get something for you.' She gave me one of her beautiful smiles. 'A little fruit, perhaps, and wine? I am sure we could find some quickly. And since Marcus has eaten already, you shall have the finest tray.' She lowered her lids. 'It is a very handsome one. My husband had it brought especially from Rome.'

And then at last I understood, and a trickle of cold fear ran down my back, so physical that I feared my toga would be dampened. Of course. Twice I had seen that 'handsome' tray, and twice Marcus had been served upon it. Naturally it would have been given to him last night as well. It had not come to me.

In exchanging Rollo for Mutuus to bring my supper, Maximilian had not exchanged the trays. Those had still gone to their original destinations.

I had been wrong in my self-satisfied deductions. If Rollo had been poisoned by the food he ate, that poison had not been intended for Marcus. It was intended for me.

Someone was trying to kill me.

Chapter Twenty-three

I tried to hide my consternation, but Junio was too quick for me. He had read my face and knew that something had alarmed me.

'Master?' he said anxiously.

I shook my head. 'I will buy some food in the market place,' I said. 'Hurry, there is little time to lose. Go to my rooms and fetch my warmest cloak.' Junio gave me a worried look and hurried away. I turned to Julia. 'This woman has a hovel outside of the town. It may be getting dusk when I return, and though I have no intention of being shut outside the town gates when they close, I shall be forced to leave the protection of the walls. It is not prudent to venture out there alone in failing light. I shall need torches and an escort.'

Julia looked at Sollers uncertainly. 'But the procession . . .' She had lost her composure now, and her lovely face was crumpled in despair. 'I must have slaves and lights for the procession. I have served Quintus so badly as it is. There has scarcely been time to show him proper reverence. This should have been a time of ritual private mourning, the household all united in its grief, taking turns to watch with the body – myself and Maximilian most of all. But slaves are wailing the lament, and I have had to leave my husband to the hired mourners.' She was almost weeping now.

'Julia, my dear.' Sollers's voice was gentle. 'You have

done all that it is proper to do. The body has been properly anointed and set upon its bier, the vault has been prepared, the candles and herbs are lit in the chamber and there has been unceasing music and lamentation while the household fasts. Quintus's spirit cannot feel unmourned. There have been dignitaries from the civitas coming all day long, and you have arranged that they were met and greeted and that their offerings were accepted, too. You could do no more.'

'It has become a kind of circus spectacle,' Julia burst out. 'The house is full of guests – two of them men my husband hated – and half Corinium has besieged the gates. I have spent my day worrying: deciding on grave goods, arranging for the funeral and feast, and all the time knowing that a murderer is among us. First Quintus, and then Rollo. I pray the gods it does prove to be Lupus. I am half afraid that there will be a dagger in my own back next.'

I was feeling uncomfortable at having occasioned this outburst. 'Lady,' I said, 'do not distress yourself. I will take my own slave, I can hire torches, and no doubt Marcus can arrange a proper escort for me. The guard is coming shortly to take Lupus away. They would take the time to accompany me, if he directed it, and in any case my mission should not take long. This woman knows the whole truth about Maximilian, and about Flavius. Her testimony is vital. Marcus must hear it. I hope to bring her back for questioning, and still be present at the funeral myself.'

Julia looked up, her eyes red-rimmed from weeping. She had controlled herself again. 'I am sorry, citizen. Of course I will help in any way I can. I am sorry for that outburst. I am upset.'

'Julia, my dear,' Sollers said firmly. 'I think you should lie down for a little while and rest. I will arrange some more hydromel for you. In the meantime, leave the citizen to me.'

She nodded speechlessly and left the room, accompanied by her handmaidens. I was alone with the medicus. There was a moment's silence, broken as Junio appeared at the door with my cloak.

It was Sollers who spoke. 'I apologise for that, citizen. Julia is overwrought. I am sure the household can accommodate your needs. Let us not trouble Marcus and the guard. I will find a pair of slaves and some torches and accompany you myself. Do you know where to find the woman?'

'I hear she lives beyond the bridge outside the Verulamium Gate. She has made a home in an abandoned kiln, so I am told.'

Sollers made a doubtful face. 'That is a large and marshy area. How do you think to find the place?'

'I hoped that Flavius might lead me to it.'

'Flavius? But Marcus has him guarded.'

'Why not, since he would still be under escort? No doubt he knows where this woman can be found if he consulted her often. Or better still, Maximilian could take us, if his absence from the house will not distress Julia. He had private dealings with the soothsayer, too, and he did not make those arrangements in the public forum! He can tell us where this hovel is. I don't suppose he will wish to, but in the circumstances I think Marcus will force him to assist us. But if we are to go, we must go quickly. It will get dark and we are already losing time. Besides, I will have to persuade my patron of all this. He is convinced that Lupus alone is his man.'

Sollers nodded. 'I will arrange for torches to be prepared, then fetch my cape and see you at the rear gate. Do you have a weapon, citizen? I will take one. There may be animals, or thieves, in lonely places outside of the town gates.'

'I will see that the escort is armed,' I said, and taking my cloak from Junio, I went out to Marcus.

I found him in the atrium, chafing with impatience. He was not accustomed to spending his days in idleness, especially in someone else's household, without entertainment, business or company. The imported wine and figs with which he had been provided, although he had clearly availed himself handsomely of both, were no substitute for the deferential attention with which he was usually surrounded. Marcus was very obviously bored.

He was also slightly drunk, a state of affairs which often made him belligerent. It was not, taken all in all, a good moment to be asking favours. The baton was tapping impatiently as soon as I appeared.

'Greetings, Excellence,' I beamed, with the heartiest good humour I could muster. 'I bring good news. We are making progress in this matter at last.'

He regarded me sourly. 'When you say "we", in that peculiar manner, I assume you are referring to yourself? Personally, I have made excellent progress already. I regard the whole event as closed. The guard will be here shortly to take Lupus away. No doubt there will be appeals to the Imperial Court, and Pertinax will end up sending him to Rome. But I have done my part.' That was not like Marcus. Usually he was confident of his own ability to sway the governor. He sighed. 'I can't think why the guard is taking so long.' He eyed my cloak gloomily. 'I see that you are dressed for the night air. Is this funeral about to start? I would be glad to see it over, so that I could decently return home – though even then I suppose there will be days of purification ritual to endure, since we were here when the death happened. Why did I ever bring us here?'

He gestured to his slave, who stepped forward to refill the goblet.

'Excellence, I wanted to speak to you about the guard. Could you, most graciously, consent to grant a boon?' When Marcus was in this churlish mood, my only hope was in grovelling supplication. 'I am in need of an escort.' I outlined briefly what I hoped to do.

Marcus took up his cup. 'I do not see that it is necessary,' he said. 'We have our culprit. Lupus went into the room, he knew the dagger was there, he came out with blood on his sleeve and Quintus was dead. We know that he could even have poisoned Rollo. What more information do you need?'

'And the wax tablet?'

Marcus drained his wine at a draught. 'That came from Flavius, as we know.'

'Indeed, and I can even tell you why.' I told him the story of the twin tokens. 'But who scratched "Remember Pertinax" upon the wax, and left it in the colonnade to be found? I am a pattern-maker, Excellence. I do not like a piece that does not fit.'

The mention of Pertinax swayed him, as I hoped. 'Swayed him' was an appropriate phrase. Marcus was unsteady on his feet and pronouncing his words carefully. 'And supposing I agree? What has this to do with Lupus?'

'I am not certain, Excellence.' I was choosing my words with equal care, though for quite different reasons. 'If I am right, then Lupus did Quintus Ulpius a dreadful wrong, even if he did not wield the knife that killed him.'

Marcus regarded me blearily. 'What "dreadful wrong" is this?'

'I think I could persuade him to confess it, Excellence, if you would condescend to have him sent for. But we must make haste; it is important that I find this sorceress quickly. We know she had a part in the stabbing, and she had a part in those wax tablets too. But we must be quick. Someone may have been to see her already, and we shall be too late. She will be gone, like the bath attendant.'

Marcus looked at me doubtfully, but then he said, with all the bravado of the drunken, 'In that case, my old friend, we shall not waste time by having Lupus brought here. We shall be like Hannibal and go to him.' He made a sweeping gesture with his arm to summon the slaves, and led the way through all the rooms of the house, past a startled Flavius in the triclinium, towards the passageway which held the attic stairs.

I followed him, although I was not quite clear as to how we were emulating Hannibal. By climbing up, perhaps, as the Carthaginian had scaled the Alps. Marcus's ascent of the stairs was certainly, if not like Hannibal, at least like one of his elephants. The stairs were not much better than a ladder, steep and uneven and lacking a hand-rope. They had been designed for slaves and storage, not for patrician feet, and Marcus lurched and swayed up them with difficulty.

We found ourselves in a long dark corridor, from which a series of rooms gave off to either side. Most of the rooms were open, sizeable spaces with small, high window spaces in their walls and ranks of straw mattress piles laid in serried rows. Sleeping quarters for the house slaves, clearly, with Mutuus's partition at the end. Others were obviously storage rooms, where extra lamps and platters spoke mutely of their owner's wealth. Nuts and apples lurked in wicker baskets.

The slaves, however, led us to the last room in the row. This had a heavy door, secured with a bolt, and there was a whipping post outside it. Evidently the household place for disobedient slaves. Marcus gave a sign and one of the attendants withdrew the bolt with difficulty and pushed open the door.

Lupus was sitting on the mattress pile. They had given him blankets, in deference to his rank: there was good bread and cheese on a wooden platter nearby and a jug of what looked like watered wine. To many people in Corinium, this would have been luxury, but Lupus evidently did not find it so.

He looked up when he saw us, his face a picture of anger and misery. 'So, you have decided to listen to me at last. Well, I shan't tell you anything, now. I've decided. You may take me to the governor, and I'll tell my story to him. I'll tell him how you refused to listen. I shall appeal to the Emperor. I did not murder Quintus. And don't think you can simply lock me in the town gaol to silence me. I am a Roman citizen, and I am well known in the town. You will not have me to the torturers without a struggle – as if I had not been tortured enough, set to sleep locked in a draughty attic at my age, with no lamp, no brazier, no panes in the windows and nothing but bread and cheese to eat.'

'Lupus,' I said. It was not my place to speak, but if I did not intervene there might very soon be trouble. Marcus with this much alcohol in his veins was likely to lose patience, and have the man whipped on principle. 'Lupus, listen to me. You may still save your foolish balding head, but only if you tell us everything. At once. When you went into Quintus's reception room – and I know you went, you were seen to go – was he dead, or merely dying?'

Lupus looked at me and then his face crumpled and he burst embarrassingly into tears. I was covered in confusion – I have never seen a grown man cry, except under torture – but I was secretly rather glad of this. It distracted Marcus's attention from my question, which might otherwise have led to protracted discussions. As it was, he merely looked disdainful – as if to register that such unmanly exhibitions of emotion are despised in Roman circles.

Lupus mastered himself with difficulty. 'You knew all along?' he gulped.

'I guessed,' I said. 'Answer the question, citizen.'

Lupus shook his head hopelessly. 'He was dead. At least I thought he was. At first I could not see him at all. He had slumped to the floor beside the couch. I thought he had merely collapsed: his eyes were shut, his tunic was pulled sideways and his head was half supported by the stool. I went to him, without thinking, as I might go to any ill man, but when I put my arm behind him to raise him up he fell forward across me and I saw the knife. There was blood on my sleeve. And then . . .' he shuddered, 'and then . . . he moaned. I looked around for some way to summon servants, but I couldn't find one – and next thing, I heard a noise at the courtyard door. If anyone came in, I thought, and found me with him dead, I would be arrested for sure, and blamed for the stabbing. I couldn't prove I didn't do it. I hurried out again and hid in the garden.'

Marcus was looking disbelieving. 'What nonsense is this?'

'It is the truth, Excellence,' I said. 'I think I can prove it to you. Lupus is a fool, and a coward, but I want to hear his story.'

'Coward?' Lupus wailed. 'Why a coward?'

'Only a coward would leave a man there so badly wounded, and think about saving his own skin.'

'I heard someone at the door. I knew they would be with him instantly. I did not wish to be arrested for a killing I had not done.'

'So who did you think *had* killed him?'

'I thought that it was Flavius. He was in the garden with me, but I hadn't been watching him, and he could have crept in, as I did. And it was his dagger – I have seen him with it. Then, of course, I was afraid that he knew that I knew – I didn't want to be the next one with a dagger in my back. And I tried to let him know that I wouldn't betray him.'

'And that you would help him bury the corpse,' I said, 'in your cesspit. I heard you, when you were talking in the arbour. I thought at the time that you sounded like a man who thought *someone else* was guilty of murder.'

Marcus put in impatiently: 'If that is what you think, Libertus, where is this "dreadful wrong" which Lupus did? If this story is the truth – which I am inclined to doubt – Lupus didn't wrong Ulpius, except perhaps by leaving him bleeding on the floor. But that is not a crime.'

'Lupus knows what dreadful wrong he did,' I answered. 'And Quintus suspected it, though he could not prove it absolutely. That is why, for years, he punished Lupus, in every way he knew. How long ago, Lupus, did you guess that Maximilian was your son?'

Lupus said nothing, but he opened and shut his mouth like a fish.

Marcus stared at Lupus, and I could see in his eyes a dawning recognition of the likeness that I had so recently perceived myself. Lupus was stooped and sunken, and time had shorn him of his curls, but once one had seen it, there was no mistaking the similarity of that slack jaw, those distinctive close-set eyes.

'Your son!' Marcus reached forward suddenly and, seizing Lupus by one scrawny arm, pulled him roughly upright. 'What woman, married to wealthy Quintus, could have been drawn to this desiccated skeleton?'

'It was many years ago,' I said. 'Lupus was younger

then. And the woman had no dowry. If she produced no child, she must have feared divorce. So she turned to Lupus. I think Quintus suspected, even then. As soon as the child was four or five years old he quarrelled with his wife and put her away. I assume that was when the likeness became evident. I wondered why, in his testament, he called Lupus a bundle of "lascivious" bones. It seemed an odd adjective to use.'

Lupus was looking embarrassed. 'I wanted her to leave Quintus and marry me, but she wouldn't. He was richer, she said. I hoped she might come to me, when she was divorced, but then she caught the pox. I could not take her then; I should have had the whole town gossiping. But Quintus never forgave me. Nothing was ever said, of course, but he made it clear he hated me. And when I adopted a son of my own, he stole him from me by a legal trick. Deliberately, I believe.'

'Does Maximilian know?' Marcus asked.

Lupus shook his head. 'I am certain he doesn't. And Quintus is legally his father. He took him up from the floor, at birth, to acknowledge fatherhood. He wasn't forced to do that. He could have had the child exposed, or sold into slavery, or even apprenticed to a temple. But once he accepted the boy, he always treated him as his heir. Even when he divorced the mother he kept Maximilian at his side. In fact, he spoiled him – with everything but affection. In any case, with fatherhood, who can possibly be sure? It is only that I have my suspicions, and it seems that Quintus had his.'

'But it might have been true?' Marcus released his arm.

'Oh, indeed, it might have been true. The lady was very beautiful and she wanted a child. I saw her often, when she was supposed to be visiting her sister. Of course, Quintus would have been mocked in the curia if the town had suspected – a decurion who cannot control his wife would be a laughing stock.'

Strangely, now that the truth was out, Lupus seemed to have acquired a kind of dignity – just as Maximilian had grown in stature when the moment demanded. Poor Maximilian, trying so hard to please his supposed father. Quintus always resented me, he had said. I could almost feel sympathy for the young man.

'Speaking of Maximilian,' I said, 'have you had cause to consult a soothsayer about all this? Or a sorceress, I should say?'

Lupus looked surprised. 'That old hag in the forum? Never, though I have heard people talk of her. I have offered a curse tablet once or twice, but only in the temple. These market people are devious. And expensive, too. Quintus ensured that I never had money to spare for that.'

Marcus sighed. 'I suppose in that case we must . . .' He broke off. 'But what is this?'

'This' was the chief slave, who had come panting up the ladder to find us. 'Excellence,' he exclaimed, between gulps for breath, 'you are wanted in the courtyard. The guard has come to take Lupus away. Shall I send them up?'

I looked at Marcus, and he frowned. 'Oh, very well,' he said to me at last, 'you shall have your escort.' He turned to the slaves. 'It seems that Lupus may not be guilty after all. But I will not release him yet. Take him to my room and lock him in. Let him have braziers if he wants them, and a bowl to wash in. As for me, I have a fancy to command a litter and see this sorceress woman for myself.'

I groaned inwardly. The meeting which I had in mind would not be bettered by the presence of the governor's representative, especially a semi-inebriated one. And from the way Marcus was stumbling down the ladder I did not think his company would speed the errand, either.

'With your permission, Excellence,' I said, as soon as we had reached the ground again, 'I should like to go on ahead. Sollers will be already waiting at the gate.'

'Very well,' Marcus said. He was still rather unsteady on his feet. 'I will follow you.' He did not ask for directions, and I did not offer them. Instead he said, 'That business in the attic, old friend. What made you first begin to think of that?'

I winked at Junio, who had been waiting patiently for me at the bottom of the ladder. 'Sometimes,' I said, 'it pays to listen to the gossip of slaves. Quintus wanted a son. The household said the problem was not Julia's. I asked myself whose son Maximilian could be.' I wrapped my cloak around me. 'Your servant, Excellence. Will you command the guard?'

And I went out to the gate to find Sollers and the torches.

Chapter Twenty-four

The medicus was waiting at the gate, wrapped in an impressive coloured cape which put my own to shame. He was accompanied by a pair of household slaves, equipped with torch-sticks, ready dipped in pitch, while a third slave carried burning coals in a metal pot, so he could light them when necessary. Flavius was also there, looking resentful, and flanked by two burly servants with staves.

'This is intolerable,' he grumbled, as soon as he saw me. 'I have business, clients to attend to. Every moment I am kept here is costing me contracts. I am not a peasant to be kept here at your whim.'

'Not my whim, citizen,' I assured him cheerfully. 'You are here at the express command of Marcus Aurelius Septimus, acting in the name of the governor.' That was rather craven of me, since I had encouraged Marcus to send him, and I added, 'Marcus is going to come with us himself. He has already sent us an escort – look, here they come now with Maximilian.'

Maximilian was not under arrest, but he was clearly an unwilling conscript, and the two guards that Marcus had sent me did not look pleased to be there either. It was comic, I thought. The people I had asked to accompany me were reluctant to come, while others, like Marcus and Sollers, had volunteered their presence on the outing.

We went out into the streets. The town was quieter now, although most stalls were still open, and the hot food stalls were already doing a roaring trade among those town dwellers who had no kitchens in their homes. The better ones served up spiced beef for the affluent, while from the less salubrious establishments women draggled by with buckets of hot 'stew'. I didn't envy them their meal. I had tasted that stew before. It is made of remnants from the market and I would have to be very hungry before I had an appetite for half-rotten turnips and floating eyeballs again. Though there were townsfolk, I was aware, who would have sold their souls to Pluto for less.

We turned left at the forum and out towards the Verulamium Gate.

It was as well we were carrying an escort. The watch at the gate were surly and suspicious – a group of Roman citizens, on foot, leaving the town gates just before dusk is calculated to arouse suspicion, even if one of them is a narrow-striper. We were not even going in the direction of the cemetery or the amphitheatre. The sight of the two soldiers, however, allayed their fears and we passed under one of the portals and crossed the fine stone bridge without further hindrance.

Only Maximilian, it seemed, had any clear idea of where exactly we were going. Flavius, as he protested constantly, had only consulted the woman within the gates, and as we left the town behind he was increasingly jumpy. One could not blame him. There was the usual straggle of buildings beyond the bridge, but after that, signs of habitation soon died out and we found ourselves in open countryside.

Not that there was any real danger here. The land around was cultivated, in parts, and there were open spaces where sheep and goats grazed dismally on the winter grass. And there was traffic on the road – men with carts and boys with sledges, peasants dragging home hoes and handcarts, stout women with donkeys, thin ones with firewood, bright-eyed girls carrying water from the stream – and all of them dashing for the verges when a scarlet-cloaked horseman came galloping by, carrying messages for some imperial post.

But we were not on the road for long. Our way led along a marshy track into a valley, hemmed in by bushes on either side. Sollers was looking definitely uneasy, and even Flavius, who had kept up an incessant grumble all the way, ceased his complaining and drew a little closer to his armed companions. I was glad we had brought our escort.

Maximilian, though, was leading the way as if an evening stroll through the wilderness was an everyday event. I waited until the path had widened a little, then went up to walk at his side.

'Marcus told you, I presume, that we know you planned the robbery?'

He scowled at me. 'Why else do you suppose I agreed to come on this miserable errand? If we find the woman, at least she can testify that I didn't intend the stabbing.'

'Marcus may search your apartments while you're out.'

'Let him,' Maximilian said sullenly. 'I don't know what he hopes to find. Anything of any value has been sold long ago, to pay that wretched bath attendant. Not that I ever had much in the first place. If I had, I wouldn't have needed to rob Quintus. I wanted money, that was all, and he refused to give me any.'

I walked beside him for a moment, and then murmured, 'It was you, of course, who wrote "Remember Pertinax" on that tablet?'

His scowl deepened, and he quickened his pace without answering.

'It had to be you,' I said, matching my stride to his. 'You wanted to divert suspicion from yourself, and suggest a different motive for the stabbing. No one else had anything to gain from it. But how did you know about Pertinax? Did Rollo tell you? I know he attended Quintus to the baths, when the council members met. I'm sure he listened to the political gossip, and he was something of a friend of yours.'

'If you know so much, citizen, you hardly need to ask,' Maximilian muttered sourly.

I took that for assent, and we walked for a little way in silence. 'You have consulted this soothsayer often?' I said, at last.

He glared at me truculently. He was showing us the way, his manner said, but he did not have to make conversation as well.

'I am interested to know what she said to you,' I ventured cheerfully. 'She doesn't seem to have been very reliable. Her prophecies for Flavius have proved untrue.' An invitation to complain will often persuade a man to talk when cruder methods fail.

It worked now. Maximilian snorted. 'Untrue! Untrue is an understatement. Everything she told me was a pack of lies. She promised me reconciliation with my father. The shape of some stupid storm clouds predicted it, she said. Well, it didn't happen. Instead, he was threatening to disinherit me.'

I nodded. 'If he had not so conveniently died.'

Maximilian threw me a venomous glance and quickened his pace still further.

'You must have known that she could not be trusted,' I said, picking my way carefully over a muddy patch, and hurrying to catch him up again. 'You bribed her to tell Sollers what you wanted him to hear.'

He tried to walk away from me again, but I trotted after him, and at last he said, reluctantly, 'I only asked her to repeat to him what she had said to me. I thought it would persuade him to go away.'

'What she said to you? She spoke to you about Sollers?'

'About Sollers and Julia. I paid her extra to read the signs for them. They were turning my father against me. I wanted to know what the future held. And when I heard, I was delighted. She was happy to repeat the prophecy to him.'

'Giving you the opportunity to have your father robbed?' He did not answer that.

'And what did she say? What was this prophecy?'

'That Sollers would meet another woman and that she would be his destiny. He would only be happy if he left my father's house and Julia would only bring him doom. It could not have been more direct.'

'It couldn't,' I agreed. It was unusual for diviners to be so unambiguous. Usually they gave the kind of veiled message which Junio had suggested. 'She is no ordinary soothsayer?'

He shook his head. 'No, she isn't. I think she had education once, but life has been hard to her. I wondered sometimes if she told me, not what she saw, but what she wanted me to hear.'

'But you came to her often?'

'Several times. She encouraged me to do so. I do not know why I came. She was ugly, pock-marked, and she smelled. But I suppose I wanted to believe.'

'I see.' I turned to see if we were overheard, but Maximilian's little spurts of speed had left the others far behind. Only Junio was in sight, and he was several yards back down the track. Maximilian, however, was still striding onwards.

I panted after him. 'We have lost the others,' I said.

He shook his head. 'It is not important. The kiln is

straight ahead along this track. If they follow us, they will come to it.' He turned to me, and there was a strange look in his eyes. 'I thought you wished to be alone with me. Is that not why you dragged me from my father's house, an hour before his funeral?'

He was more perceptive than I thought. 'Perhaps,' I said. I looked at him. 'When did you last consult the soothsayer?'

He thought for a moment. 'It was days ago. The last time I lost heavily at dice. I wanted her assurance for the future, but she had nothing to say. She was unwell, she said; she had a headache and she could not read the signs. I had to come away.'

'You lost at dice?' I said. 'Or was it that you had to pay your comrade at the baths?'

He scowled. 'Oh, so you know about that too? A little of both. That is why I had staked so high. With a little luck I could have paid all my debts.'

There was no answer to that, and I tried a different tack. 'And do you know what she promised Flavius?'

He sneered. 'I thought you had heard the tale. Rollo told everyone. Flavius was to make two tokens from a piece of bone and when the two parts were reunited, Julia would be his. It is not an unusual superstition.'

'But it is a superstition,' I said. 'I wonder that you believed her at all.'

He turned away and strode on, and nothing that I said could provoke an answer. In any case, there was no room for speech. The path leading into the valley was narrower now, and wetter, and every step had to be made with care. If the light failed, I thought, we should need more than torches to get us back on the road dry shod. Then, just as I was beginning to despair, we turned a corner and Maximilian cried, 'There it is. That is the place.'

It was indeed an abandoned kiln – more abandoned than I had imagined. It lay at the bottom of the valley, a rectangular chamber half set in the ground, its pierced roof crumbling and its entrance archway cracked. A trickle of water ran along the pathway to the door, flooding the tiled culvert which had been built to contain it. Through the hole in the roof it was possible to see the close-set walls of the over-chamber, where the tiles would have been made, and the arches which supported them over the central flue that ran the length of the kiln. Somebody had thatched over part of the roof, covering the smoke holes, and made a narrow chamber, scarcely the width of a man, between two of these inner walls, while stagnant water lapped under its base and rats scrabbled at the sides. It was the most unlovely dwelling I have ever seen.

I came a little closer and saw that it was even more unlovely than I thought. The woman was there, a pile of old shards and shattered phials beside her. She seemed to be asleep, lying alongside the lower aperture, beside the blackened remnants of a fire.

I looked at Maximilian, and he at me. Then together, we slithered down the slope towards the kiln. But one look at her face told me the dreadful facts. There would be no prophecies today. The soothsayer was dead.

Junio, behind us, had hesitated on the bank, and I called to him. 'Fetch the others. Run!'

Junio set off like a stone from a *ballista*, and we heard him calling faintly down the path. 'Come quickly, come quickly, the woman is dead.'

She had died of a fever, by the look of it, for she was wizened to the bone, her lank hair was plastered to her head, and beneath the warts the death-pale skin was still blotched and red in patches. Maximilian went to move her and I pulled him roughly away. 'Don't touch her. Do you want to be the next? Have you not heard what happened a few years ago in Rome? Thousands died of a fever much like this.'

He drew back, horrified, and I saw the expression on his face.

'You cared for her?'

'I hardly knew her,' he said. 'But there has been so much death. Although,' he went on, his eyes widening in horror, 'I spoke to her some days ago. I hope she did not have the fever then.'

I might have answered him, but there was the sound of feet on the path and Junio and Sollers came running up, with Flavius and the guards not far behind.

'What is it?' Sollers said, clambering swiftly down to join us. 'Dear Hermes, the spotted fever. Do not touch her, either of you. We must get a litter for this body, and have it burned before the fever spreads.' He took a corner of the ragged skirts and pulled it gingerly towards him. The corpse rolled over grotesquely. Junio, who had climbed down after Sollers, drew back in horror.

'How long has she been dead?' I asked.

He shrugged. 'I cannot tell. Not long. A day or two perhaps, no more. The body is cold, although it would not take long to chill it here. But see these reddened marks upon the back – I have seen this before on slaughtered soldiers. The blood seeps down a few hours after death, and where the body lies it makes these bruise-like marks. Yes, poor hag, she has not long been dead.' He got to his feet as Flavius came up, red-faced and flustered, followed by the slaves and soldiers.

Flavius came to where the kiln pit was and peered down. There was a long pause when he saw the body huddled there. His face turned from fiery red to white, and back to red again and then he burst into nervous laughter. 'Where are your spells and omens now, old hag?' he cried. 'Much good they did us, either of us!' He was shaking with emotion.

'I should . . .' Sollers said, and moved towards him, but I motioned to the soldiers.

'Seize him,' I said.

Chapter Twenty-five

Even then, Sollers was too quick for me. Before there was time for anyone to move, he had whipped out his knife and was holding it to Maximilian's throat with one hand while he pinioned the youth's arms with the other.

'If anyone takes another step,' he said, 'the boy dies.'

Flavius stopped laughing. 'What is this?' he demanded, whiter than a toga again. 'Sollers?'

'He killed Quintus,' I said. 'And Rollo too, although I was too stupid to see it. I was not sure of that until a moment since, when he was telling me about the woman here.'

Sollers gave me an unpleasant smile. 'Yes, that was an oversight of mine. I should have realised you would see the implications.' He jerked the knife upwards, making Maximilian flinch. 'Now, I am going to walk away from here. I will take the boy. You will not follow me, unless you want him dead.'

Maximilian was pallid with fright, but he made no sound beyond a sobbing breath. His head was motionless, as if he feared to blink, but his eyes were fixed downwards, watching the hilt of the knife. Sollers began to move away backwards, very slowly, holding the boy in front of him like a living battleshield.

One of the soldiers drew his sword, and Maximilian screamed. 'No!' There was a trickle of blood from his chin where the knife had nicked him. It ran slowly down to drip upon his mourning toga, staining the sober border like a reproach. Sollers was moving again, his eyes flickering suspiciously from me to Flavius, to the soldiers and slaves and back again.

I lifted my hands to show that they were empty, and began to speak. 'What do you hope to gain from this, Sollers? You cannot escape for long. As soon as you have gone we shall alert the watch and they will be searching for you throughout the province.'

Everyone turned to stare. I felt the eyes of them all upon me. That was what I wanted. On the area by the kiln, behind Sollers, Junio was on his knees and, infinitely stealthily, was lifting one of the stones in the culvert. It would leave a jagged hole in the path over the stream. He was skilled at handling stones, and if anyone could do this, it was Junio – but it was essential that no one else should see. The faintest flicker of interest from the soldiers and somebody was dead. I feared it would be Junio.

I was talking for his life. 'Sollers,' I said, 'Marcus is on his way. He has a litter ordered. If he gives the word you will be hunted across the Empire.'

Sollers said nothing, but continued his slow backward progress. He was going to get to Junio too soon.

I took a step forward. And another. We were only inches apart. The knife went up and there were two nicks in Maximilian's chin. Sollers, I knew, would not hesitate to use the knife on me. I thought desperately. 'And Julia,' I said urgently, 'what shall I say to her?'

For a moment, he halted. 'Julia!' he said. 'I thought I was to be the other man – her next husband. The old hag lying there had said as much. I was to make my fortune and Julia would find another man waiting for her. I did not know then that this young fool –' he jerked the knife again '– had bribed the woman and told her what to say.'

'She only told you . . .' Maximilian began, but Sollers gave his arms a savage upward twist and he subsided into silence.

'It does not matter now,' the medicus said. 'I hoped for riches and a lovely wife, but I am content to leave here with my life. I have skills. I can set up somewhere else. And you will not prevent me.' He glanced at the guardsman who was still carrying his sword. 'And do not doubt me, soldier. I will use the knife. I have nothing now to lose.'

The two guards exchanged glances. I could see what they were thinking. Maximilian's life was a reasonable exchange for the capture of Sollers. Maximilian saw it too, because he began to sweat. He was too terrified to cry out, but the moisture stood on his brow and his legs trembled.

Sollers paused again. It was a moment only, but it was enough. Junio had raised the stone and threw it with a thump upon the grass. Sollers turned at the sound.

I lunged forward, seizing with both hands the wrist that held the knife and twisting it with all my force. Sollers turned back to me, striking down at my hands, but he could not fight me one-handed.

Maximilian struggled out of his grasp, and Sollers, with a swift movement, whipped up his other hand and seized the knife. I ducked aside as he brought it down and the blade brushed my cheek. I felt the rush of it, and saw blood on the blade, but there was no pain.

He raised the knife again. The soldiers were now storming down the bank, but I knew with a terrible certainty that they would be too late for me. And there was no hope from Maximilian. He was sitting on the grass, whimpering like a child.

Sollers had seized my toga now, and his grip was like an iron band. I felt, rather than saw, the blade flash down and rip apart the cloth under my arm. Again, if I had not moved in time I would have been a dead man. But I am old, and he was strong. I could not keep this up much longer.

Something small and determined caught him round the legs. Junio has not much weight but his teeth are sharp, and he had the advantage of surprise. Sollers stepped backwards in alarm, and his foot found the hole in the culvert. His leg crumpled under him, and he toppled into the stream with a cry.

By the time the soldiers had marched him back to Corinium his foot was swollen like a pig's bladder.

They locked him in the attics. No blankets or bread and cheese for him. The soldiers had bound his hands and wrists, and they threw him down on the mattress and left him there, while they sent out to find Marcus who was still wandering aimlessly in his litter somewhere, since he had no idea of what direction we had taken.

Myself, I went to Maximilian's apartment. It did not take me long to find what I sought, roughly concealed under the floorboards. A small drawstring pouch of leather, slashed around the neck. I took it up and put it in my toga. I would show it to Marcus when they brought him home.

In fact, he arrived shortly afterwards of his own accord, cold and cross but sober. One of the watch had told him of our return. He arrayed himself for the funeral and sent for me at once in the study.

It was strange, being there again as the lamps were lit, while outside in the courtyard the funeral procession was gathering. We stood at the door and watched the first part of the procession assemble: Quintus, resplendent on his bier, with the torch-bearers each holding his flaming *fax*, and the professional mourners forming up behind.

Marcus looked at me. 'So,' he said, 'are you going to explain this to me? I assume you must be right to accuse

Sollers, or he would not have tried to abduct Maximilian and kill you, but I confess I do not understand it at all. And what is that you have in your hand?'

I put it on the table. 'It is the purse that was stolen from Quintus, Excellence. I found it just now, in Maximilian's room.'

He looked at me coldly. 'Is that important? I suppose Maximilian hid it there, after the robbery.'

'On the contrary, Excellence. Maximilian had no idea it was there. He didn't care who searched his room. I'm convinced that Sollers put it there, and invited me to find it. It is the final piece of evidence against him.'

'Where did Sollers get it from?'

'From the soothsayer, I imagine. Maximilian gave it to her to get rid of it. You should have seen how he blanched when Sollers threw him a similar one, earlier.'

Marcus looked stony. 'Pavement-maker,' he said, 'are you going to explain this to me? And quickly? I am supposed to attend a funeral. In an official capacity. Julia has asked me – as her sponsor – to make an oration. The musicians are already tuning up their instruments.' He sounded both pompous and impatient. My patron was not easy to talk to in this mood. 'So tell me, why should a doctor, who has every chance to kill a man discreetly, suddenly plunge a vulgar dagger into his victim's back? I should have expected Sollers, of all people, to be subtle.'

I said humbly, 'Exactly, Excellence. And that of course is the answer. Sollers relied on anyone of intelligence to think the same. And he could always point it out himself. Because he had such perfect opportunities to kill his patient in other ways, it was absurd that he should stab Quintus so crudely. That was exactly what Sollers intended us to think. It probably was the most subtle way of all.'

'I see.'

'He hoped, of course, that blame would fall on Maximilian. He had discovered that Maximilian arranged the first attack. We were supposed to find the "proof", and if we made enquiries we would learn the truth – Maximilian could hardly disprove that, since it was true. And then, of course, it would seem that Maximilian did the second stabbing too. Sollers did all he could to have Maximilian accused, and he might have succeeded, too, except that foolish Lupus wandered into the reception room and got Quintus's blood on his sleeve.'

We were interrupted by a howling wail. The front gates opened and the pall-bearers took up the litter on their shoulders. The instruments struck up dolefully. The procession had begun.

'You had better go, Excellence.'

'In a moment,' Marcus said. 'They can't start without me. I want to understand. When did you begin to suspect?'

'Sollers suggested the solution himself. Sollers said that perhaps Maximilian's crassness was a bluff. Maximilian did not have the intellect to bluff like that, but Sollers did. Who was more obvious than Sollers, when you consider it? He was in the ante-room. He arranged that the daggers should be placed on the table – where of course he could easily obtain them. Who suggested that the last two clients should be sent away so that Quintus could "rest"? Sollers. Who sent away the servants from the room? Sollers. Who had blood upon his clothes even before he examined the corpse? Sollers. I even mentioned it to him. But he had bled Quintus earlier, so he had an answer.'

'When he bled Quintus, he had him alone in the room. Why didn't he kill him then?'

'Because then it would have been clear who'd done it. But he was preparing for the murder, even then. By bleeding Quintus he drew off a lot of blood, so that there was much less spurting later. It is a well-known medical trick. He described it to us himself. In fact, I think Quintus was being bled when he died.'

'Again?' Marcus was surprised.

'Think. Quintus had his tunic disarranged. His shoulder and his arm were bare and his back exposed. Why would an attacker do that? Yet why would Quintus do it for himself? Then yesterday, when Julia was being cupped, I understood. He had bared his arm to have his doctor cup him. I saw Julia do the same.'

'If Sollers was applying the bleeding-cup, how could he stab Quintus at the same time?'

'With his other hand. We knew the blow was dealt left-handedly. Sollers is perfectly capable of that. He tried to do it to me. Again, I should have seen it earlier. Surgeons are ambidextrous – Julia pointed that out. He used the direction of the thrust to point to Maximilian. I almost fell for it.'

Marcus shook his head. '*When* did he do all this? Sollers started giving Julia her treatment when Maximilian was still with his father. By the time the treatment was over, Quintus was dead. Julia told us that. You do not mean to suggest that she was lying?'

'Oh, yes, she was. And that deflected me, although it was not you and I she set out to deceive. She left us, heard the quarrel and went back to her room, you will remember. Someone – she thought that it was Flavius or his messenger – came to her door and asked if she was there. She told her maids to say that she was not.'

'Yes?' Marcus was impatient.

'But the message was not from Flavius. We know that he was in the front courtyard at the time. It was Maximilian who went to look for Julia – Rollo saw him do it. But her maids informed him that she wasn't there. So Maximilian believed it. He went back to his apartments to search for something else to pay the bath attendant with, and then came to speak to us. While he was doing that, Sollers murdered Quintus Ulpius.'

'But when Julia came out of her room, the quarrel was still in progress.'

'Who said so? Sollers, again. Sollers, who had just come from Quintus's bedchamber carrying a bowl of blood – the same blood he had been letting when Quintus died. He must have been appalled to meet with Julia – he thought that she was safely engaged in receiving us. But he is a clever man. He turned the thing to his advantage. A medicus is the one man who can carry bowls of blood without suspicion. Imagine the cool composure of a man who can persuade a wife to offer as a sacrifice the blood he has just spilled in killing her husband.'

Marcus gulped. 'Great Mercury!'

'Or Great Minerva, in this case,' I said grimly. 'Sollers even persuades Julia to wash the bowl, as part of the ceremony – thus destroying the evidence – and manages to splash her clothes with blood. Of course, once it is known that Quintus is dead, she is terrified that someone will see the stains and make a connection. She actually begs Sollers to keep silence. Even then he is clever. He appears to give her an alibi, by telling us about the treatment – which incidentally gives him an alibi, too.'

Marcus shook his head disbelievingly. 'And then she uses the bowl for funeral decorations?'

'I think that might have been her own idea. Sollers was only concerned to move it from the reception room. He was in too much haste and did not strike quite true. He knew that Quintus was only dying, and was not yet dead, but he dared not stay to strike again. So he took the bowl away. If Quintus found some dying strength – as in fact he did, since he crawled as far as the door – without the bowl he could not summon help. I should have spotted that at once.'

There was a silence while Marcus digested this. In the courtyard the dancers were performing their ritual gyrations, while the mourners, with garlands on their brows, formed up to take their place in the procession. Maximilian was there: I saw him in the torchlight, his toga still stained with his own blood. Julia, in a litter, looking pale. It had been decided not to tell her about Sollers until after the ceremony. Others were appearing in the courtyard. I saw Flavius follow the procession, with Mutuus at his side. Lupus came to join them, but Mutuus turned pointedly away. Poor Lupus.

Marcus was watching them too. He turned to me again. 'When did you know that things had not happened in the order we were told?'

'When I heard about that bowl of blood. Sollers told Julia that he had just finished bleeding Quintus when Maximilian came. Yet Mutuus told us that Quintus had already called his slaves back and was ready to resume work when Maximilian interrupted him. Sollers would hardly have left blood and cupping bells in the room while Quintus was entertaining clientes. That was when I began to wonder if he could have cupped him twice. And then, of course, things fell into place.'

Marcus looked at me approvingly. 'Little escapes you, old friend.'

'In fact, Excellence, I am ashamed to recognise how many things I did miss. Sollers knew that Quintus was threatening to disinherit his son. No one else knew that. He must have been listening, in the ante-room. He was there when Maximilian pushed past him, the slaves told us so. Yet later, there he was in the rear courtyard. How did he get there? He did not pass us in the atrium, and there is no other route from the front garden except through the room where Quintus was. Besides, Quintus himself told us. When he was crawling, dying, to the door, he was not *calling* Sollers, he was naming him. I should have seen that long ago.'

Marcus dropped his head into his hands. 'And Rollo?' was all he said.

'That was an accident,' I said. 'Sollers meant to poison me. I suspected another hand in it, at the time. I reasoned, as Sollers said, that murderers often follow a pattern. But of course, being Sollers, he took good care that no pattern could be seen. His pattern was doing the unexpected.'

'So having stabbed Quintus, he tried to poison you?'

'He chose a subtle route, all the same. He gave me a sleeping draught – but that was not poisoned. That could have been traced to him. Instead, he put the poison in the food, which anyone might have handled. I saw him today, walking around the kitchens tasting and prodding – if that was his habit, it would not be hard for him to introduce poison onto my plate. He slipped it into the fish pickle, is my guess, where it would not be tasted.'

'But you do not care for it.'

'Fortunately for me, Excellence, Sollers did not know that. My dislike of fish pickle saved my life. And poisoned poor Rollo, I'm afraid. I gave him the contents of the tray, and he went to the latrine feeling sick – as you suggested, Excellence – moments after he left me, I should think. Someone found him there and hid him in the drain. Sollers, I believe, but it may have been Flavius – we can discover that when the funeral party returns.'

'I should join it now,' Marcus said, but he did not go. In the courtyard, Lupus joined the procession, forlornly alone, and then members of the curia were carried out in litters, one by one. The front of the cortege, surrounded by lights and laments, had already made its way into the street and had disappeared from sight.

Marcus went to the door, and then turned back. 'And the blow to Rollo's neck and stomach?' he asked.

'There was no blow, Excellence. I understood that tonight, as we stood by that kiln with the body of the soothsayer. Sollers wanted us to concentrate on when she died, not how. He talked about the marking on her body where the weight had been – it looked like bruising, he said. And then I knew for sure. The marks on Rollo's body were similar. We would never have thought of violence if Sollers had not suggested it. Everything suggested poisoning. But because he was a medicus, we accepted his opinion. Of course, he agreed it could be poison. Naturally, since he administered it himself.'

'I still don't understand why he wanted to poison you.'

I smiled. 'You told Julia that I was skilled at solving mysteries, and she told Sollers. He was afraid of my powers of deduction. Sollers and I are in many ways alike. He feared that I had found him out, I think – although at the time, I had no suspicion.'

Again he turned away, and again turned back. 'And the soothsayer? How did you know that she was dead?'

'I fear, Excellence, that I knew no such thing. I thought I could reach her before Sollers did. She would have testified for Maximilian, of course, and then all Sollers's careful calculations would have failed. But I was too late. He had been there already.'

'But she died of a fever, surely?'

'I doubt it, Excellence. She had a fever, certainly – she was too ill to prophesy for Maximilian last time he went to her – but I imagine Sollers helped her on her way. Gave her poison, probably, pretending it was a cure. I saw a broken phial at the kiln. Poor woman, she does not seem to have foreseen her fate. Her predictions were wrong on every count. Flavius was to be reunited with Julia, Julia was to remarry happily, Sollers was to find another woman and Maximilian and Quintus reconcile. Not an impressive catalogue.'

The slaves from the courtyard, and their lights, were swelling the numbers now. We could still hear the front of the procession, the percussion driving away evil spirits, right out to the gates of the town.

Marcus looked at me sharply. 'Who was this soothsayer?'

'Beyond that she was a beggar who lived in a kiln? I don't know.'

'I wondered why Maximilian consulted her. She seems an odd choice for a decurion's son. You do not think there was a reason for it?'

'Because she had lost her looks to warts and to the pox? Her story may have reminded him of his mother. There seems little else to recommend her.'

'You do not think she *was* his mother?'

'He was too old for that. In any case, Quintus kept his ex-wife in fair comfort, even after he put her away. Maximilian seems to have known his mother a little – he and Quintus quarrelled when she died. Besides, don't you think Lupus might have told us that? She was the mother of his son. I do not think he would leave her in a kiln to starve.'

'No.' Marcus looked at his hands. 'Well, if I am to make this funeral oration, I had better go. Julia has arranged a litter for me. It will be waiting. I have made my ritual ablutions already. Are you coming with me?'

I shook my head. 'I have a scratched face and a torn toga. It would be disrespectful now. Besides, I never did know Quintus alive. No, I shall follow Rollo's bier. They will be coming for him shortly. But I have need of money, Excellence. I spent my last *as* buying information this morning.'

'Dear Mercury, why did you not say so earlier?' He fished in his purse and tossed me two silver coins. 'You had better buy yourself a meal, in case the slaves' guild doesn't provide one. You can hardly present yourself at Quintus's feast if you did not attend the burial. Well, I shall see you later.'

I watched him go. Two denarii, that was generous. Enough to have my toga cleaned and mended. Not tonight; the fuller's would be closed. I should have to attend Rollo's funeral as I was.

But Marcus was right about one thing. Junio was being fed at this moment, together with the slaves who were to serve the feast – audible hunger from the servants is frowned on at a celebration. I, on the other hand, had not eaten since this morning. I would go to Rollo's funeral, but first I was going into the town to buy myself a plate of steaming stew – tripes, turnips, antlers, eyeballs and all.

Chapter Twenty-six

Rollo's was a simple funeral. The guild had provided mourners and a drum player, and Julia had given permission for the two slaves who had worked with the page most closely to attend this ritual, instead of joining the procession for Quintus or staying home to prepare the funeral feast. And Junio came with me, so the page was not altogether unlamented.

There were four bodies altogether. In a town the size of Corinium there are always some deaths among the slave population. We were the third house, so by the time we entered the street there must have been a dozen followers altogether. The bodies were carried out on stretchers and placed on wooden biers – clumsily carved and heavy, but more gilded and ornate than Quintus's own. It had come on to drizzle again.

The guild had built a pyre, a long way outside the town – necessarily, since proximity to the gates is a sign of status. The bodies were laid upon it, with decent reverence, and the grave gifts offered to the gods, though I noted that the litters were carefully retained. There was a flowery speech by one of the guild members, about the qualities of a good servant, and then the priest – an old man, inclined to ramble and probably cheap – but a genuine priest all the same – made the offerings and lit the pyre. They had put fat on it to make it burn, and it did so fiercely.

The drummer entertained us while the flames burned

down, and then the remains were sprinkled with wine and water – rather an indecent quantity of water, I thought. The ashes were collected into urns, and buried before they were fairly cool. The neck of each amphora was left above the earth, so that the guild could feed the spirits of the dead.

It would have been difficult, I thought, to work out quite which bit of ash was which, but we made our offering in front of what I thought was mostly Rollo and I went dispiritedly home. The guild had provided a supper, but it appeared that there was to be only one dish, stewed river eels and barley, which I have never liked. Even then it would be accompanied by fish pickle – probably the cheap variety, at that, made from jellyfish instead of anchovies, but tasting just as dreadful. As the only Roman citizen present, I felt I could decently forgo the pleasure, especially since I was already beginning to regret my turnips.

The house was almost empty when we returned; there were only a few servants setting up lamps and couches for the expected feast. I borrowed a taper and, leaving Junio in my room, went up to the attics to see Sollers.

I was glad I had my candle, because he was sitting in the dark. He had managed to take his boot off, despite his bound hands, and his foot – in the flickering light – looked sadly swollen. He looked at me in silence for a moment.

'What brings you here? A desire to mock me?'

'Mock you, no. But I would like to hear, from your own lips, what it was that made you do it. A man with such skill and intellect. You did not need to stoop to this. Surely, it can't have been for money.'

'Oh, but it could, citizen. Of course I had no thought of it at first. But when Quintus was attacked and stabbed, and I began to tend him for his wounds, he started to talk of rewards. A sizeable sum, he said, and a pension. Of course, I was living in comfort, I could have waited for that. But then that wretched Rollo put it all in jeopardy. He found out about my treatment of Julia, and he could never keep his mouth shut. It was only a matter of time before he told his master, and then I risked losing everything. Quintus would have been horrified that we had deceived him.'

'But you did not plan to kill Rollo?'

He shook his head. 'I thought of it at one time, but by then the damage was done. Half the household knew, so if there were enquiries, it was bound to emerge eventually. So when I discovered that Maximilian had arranged that robbery, I saw a different opportunity. I could make it appear that he had murdered his father. I would get my inheritance. I might even have married Julia. I think she would have had me. Money, position and Julia. It was worth gambling for.'

'How did you discover that Maximilian had arranged the robbery?'

'Maximilian is a fool. He has not even the wit to hide his foolishness. I heard him haggling with some scoundrel at the gates about the price of silence on "bribing the soothsayer on the night of the robbery". It did not take me long to work out what that meant.'

'So you found the soothsayer and silenced her? Brought back Quintus's purse and left it in Maximilian's room for me to find?'

He did not bother to deny it. 'I speeded her end, that was all. She was dying anyway. I may have saved her suffering.'

'Yes, I noticed that you touched the corpse, although you forbade any of us to do so. I guessed it was not infection that killed her. Poor woman, she was a fortune-teller, but she didn't foresee that.'

He laughed mirthlessly. 'Perhaps I should have taken her advice, all the same. Left the decurion's house and found another woman. That was supposed to be my destiny.' He looked at me. 'Perhaps it was, in a strange way. I left the decurion's house today, and found her. So now it will be execution for me? Tied bleeding to a post in the arena and left to the dogs? Or at best, a lingering death in the galleys or the mines?'

I did not answer. There was nothing I could say. He knew the penalties as well as I did.

'My foot is swollen, citizen, and it is painful too. I shall pay for what I did, but is it necessary to make me suffer this as well? There is a jar in my room. You will find it on the top shelf behind the table. There is no label. It is a powerful remedy in cases like this. Will you not send it to me?'

I swallowed. I knew what he was asking. For a moment I was tempted. Roman law is savage. I should not see his suffering, but I knew that the image of it would haunt me all my life.

I looked at him. 'Farewell, medicus. I wish that I could help you as you ask. You were a fine surgeon.'

He turned his face away, and I left him.

That was all. I went downstairs with a heavy heart.

The funeral party was just returning. Marcus was in the atrium, and I caught him before he went into the feast. Before we had the time to exchange a word, Julia saw me with him and came forward, giving me one of her glowing smiles. 'Libertus, citizen. You must please join us at the feast. And Sollers too – I am surprised he did not come to the funeral, but Marcus says that he has hurt his leg.' I glanced at Marcus.

My patron nodded.

I took a deep breath. 'I regret, lady, that I have fearful

news. Sollers will not be coming to the feast. We have found your husband's murderer.'

She gazed at me. 'You mean . . .?' She was paler than her tunic. 'And he killed Rollo, too?'

I nodded. Gently, I outlined the whole sorry story.

'Oh, Great Minerva, this is terrible.' She sank down on a stool and buried her head in her hands.

'Not quite so dreadful, lady.' I tried to console her. 'Of course you are upset that Sollers betrayed your trust. But he will do it no longer. At least you can sleep peacefully in your bed, knowing that the killer is under lock and key.'

She shook her head. 'He was good to me. He cured my inflammation, and he kept my secret. He protected me from Flavius, too.'

I looked at her. So beautiful and vulnerable, so hurt and betrayed. Of course, she was vain and flirtatious, and sometimes wilful too – she had deceived both of her husbands. But there was no malice in her. And there was the little question of a dowry, too. She didn't need a legal sponsor, she needed a husband.

I cleared my throat.

'Flavius will not molest you,' Marcus said. 'I give you my word on that. And I will protect your interests in the court. We do not want a *querela* brought against the terms of Quintus's will, just because Sollers cannot inherit. The governor will give me his support in that, especially once I tell him that I have solved this mystery. He was worried about the message on that wax tablet. I shall write him a full explanation when I send Sollers to him with the guards tomorrow.'

About how *he* had solved the mystery, I thought. Such were the advantages of rank. There were others too.

'You are most generous, Excellence.' Julia glowed at him. 'How can I thank you?'

271

He smiled. 'We will find a way.'

I was like Mutuus, I thought. Entertaining thoughts above my station. It was time I stopped dreaming and got back to thinking about Gwellia.

Julia was still gazing at Marcus. 'We must talk about this later, Excellence. In the meantime, may I see Sollers, one last time? I feel I owe him that.'

'But he was a murderer,' Marcus said.

'He was a great surgeon. Without him, Quintus would have been blind, and I . . . well, I would have problems still.' She lowered her eyelids at him. 'I shall not be long. In the meantime, there are guests arriving. Would you, dear Marcus, help Maximilian receive them? There will have to be sacrifices too – Sollers would have seen to it for me.'

Marcus looked flattered. 'I . . . of course I will.'

I smiled. The handmaidens were wrong. Julia did organise her household. Very skilfully indeed.

Julia glowed at him. 'Thank you, dear sponsor. And thank you for finding out the truth. And you too, Libertus. I have not forgotten my promise. I shall commission a pavement from you for the hot room. The design of it, at least. In memory of my husband. Forty denarii, what do you say?'

That was an offer of a real contract, at last. 'A simple design, lady, as you suggested. With blood red, I think, in the border. But I shall have to ask my patron.' Though doubtless, I thought, if I did design a pavement, Marcus would find a way of taking the credit for that too.

'I shall persuade him to spare you.' She smiled at Marcus warmly. 'Perhaps he could be persuaded to stay a little, too? I am sure Maximilian would accommodate you both. Now, excuse me, I will go to Sollers.'

Marcus moved into the atrium and went among the guests. It was some moments before I saw him again. 'Are you joining us, Libertus? We shall be offering the sacrifices shortly. That is, if I can persuade Maximilian to make them. He seems to have become uncommonly intimate with Lupus.'

'Reconciled with his father,' I said. 'Maybe the sooth-sayer read the auguries correctly after all.'

'What are you talking about?' Marcus said, sharply.

'Maximilian was to be reconciled with his father. I was to get my answers when I saw her again. The prophecies seem to have been more devious than most. And when the two bone pieces were reunited . . . If I remember, Excellence, you were holding both the ivory writing tablets when Julia walked in.'

But Marcus wasn't listening. He was looking at Julia. She was walking very upright, and there were two high spots of colour on her cheeks. She looked defiant and her head was held high. 'Julia will bring him doom,' I said, slowly. 'You may find your prisoner never lives to see trial.'

Marcus was gazing at Julia with all the interest of a man who sees a dowry dangled before him by a lovely *vadua*. 'I'm sure you are right, old friend,' he said vaguely. 'You always are. I should listen to you more often. And accept that contract, by all means. I should be pleased to stay in Corinium awhile.' He smiled, and sidled away to join her.

I sighed. I had learned over the years to deal with Marcus. Now, it seemed I might have to learn to deal with Julia too. I looked at her, still composed, smiling at every guest present as if he were the only man in the world. I only hoped that Marcus would learn to deal with her himself. At least, I thought, in future he would be more understanding about my search for Gwellia.

I looked around the room. Marcus was talking to Julia, Lupus to Maximilian. In the far corner, by the Vestal altar, Mutuus was deep in conversation with Flavius. Another

273

wealthy man in need of a good secretary, I thought. Mutuus would not be unemployed for long. And Flavius, also, had no sons.

Ah, well. I fingered the remaining coins in my pocket. Tomorrow I would go into the town with Junio. The toga could wait. Tomorrow I would take him to the baths, not as a slave, but as a customer. It would be a treat for him, and one that I could afford. After all, he had saved my life today.

I went out into the courtyard to tell him the good news. As I walked into the colonnade in the darkness, a figure darted into the grotto. Quickly, but not quickly enough. I knew who it was. It was the bald-headed slave. And there was Junio, leaning against a pillar, whistling as if he had never seen a slave girl in his life.

I was getting old. I left them to it, and taking my candle, I waved aside my slave. I slipped into the bedroom, took off my own toga and went to bed.